Titles by Laurel Osterkamp

Following My Toes
Starring in the Movie of My Life
The Holdout
The Next Breath
The Standout
Just Like the Bronte Sisters
Favorite Daughters
Beautiful Little Furies

Thanks, Sav!
May your next
breath be amazing ♡

J Osterkamp

The Next Breath

LAUREL OSTERKAMP

DRAMA, DRAMA

ISBN: 978-1-933826-86-8

PUBLISHED BY DRAMA, DRAMA,
an imprint of PMI BOOKS. Boulder, CO.

Publisher's Cataloging-in-Publication Data

Names: Osterkamp, Laurel.

Title: The next breath : an angsty and uplifting love story / Laurel Osterkamp.

Description: Boulder, CO : Drama, Drama, 2024. | Summary: Ten years ago, Robin found true love with Jed, but then she lost him. When Nick enters her life, she starts to believe in second chances. As Jed's ghost lingers in her dreams, Robin navigates through heartbreak, loss, and the overwhelming fear of moving on.

Identifiers: ISBN 9781933826868 (paperback)

Subjects: LCSH: Man-woman relationships – Fiction. | Triangles (Interpersonal relations) – Fiction. | People with disabilities – Fiction. | College students – Fiction. | Cystic fibrosis – Fiction. | Grief – Fiction. | BISAC: FICTION / Romance / Contemporary. | FICTION / Romance / General. | FICTION / Disabilities.

Classification: LCC PS3615.S74 2024 | DDC 813 O--dc23

Prologue

My running shoes are soaked. And mud splatters my calves.

The morning was too dark to jog safely. But not too cold. Thirty degrees is my threshold, so I packed my sweats and my sneakers into an old Hoyt College gym bag and drove to my studio. After spending several hours turning an embroidered mother-of-the-bride dress into a sleek, belted cocktail jacket, it was time for a break.

Now, as my rubber soles slap damp pavement, I have a premonition. Things have been too calm, too stable. Dark clouds roll over Des Moines, and I can't shake off this growing unease. It's like that moment right before thunder growls, when the air turns heavy, pregnant with the promise of a storm. The faint yet distinct smell of wet earth snakes up my nostrils, fueling my apprehension, and humid March winds gust against my face. It's a harsh caress, yet not unpleasant. The sun breaks through a cloud, and I'm chased by shadows.

I pick up my pace.

When I arrive back at my studio, Nick waits, holding a takeout bag from Simmer & Slurp. "You went for a run?"

Joy pulses through me—my standard response upon seeing Nick. He's so cute, with his wavy dark hair falling over his mocha eyes. And that roguish grin that weakens my knees.

"My third one this week." I give him a quick peck on the cheek, aware of my salty, sweaty scent.

He wrinkles his nose, amused. "You stink."

I swat his shoulder. "And you're mean. But you brought me soup, so you're also forgiven."

He smiles and takes in my disheveled state as I unlock my door and let us in.

"You're lucky you didn't slip on a patch of ice." Walking into my studio like he owns the place, he unpacks our food from the large brown paper bag. As I clear my worktable, he pulls out a container of soup for us each, plus two freshly baked sourdough rolls.

"There was no ice, only puddles of slush."

"Mmm." Nick gives me a crooked grin. "I can't decide if you're crazy, running in this weather, or if you're a badass."

"Uh huh. Keep wrestling with that while I change out of my sweaty clothes."

Nick shakes his head. "Don't change. I like the sweatsuit. I bet you looked like Rocky Balboa, running through downtown Des Moines. Did you go up any steps?"

I screw up my face. "Huh?"

His mouth drops open. "Rocky Balboa? The famous sports montage from *Rocky*?"

"Starring Sylvester Stallone?"

"That's the one."

I cross my arms over my chest. "You're saying I look like him?"

"Yeah."

When my mouth drops open in horrified shock, he chuckles. "Oh, come on. It's clear that you, in all your leggy-blonde glory, don't actually resemble the Italian Stallion. You're just both determined and scrappy."

"Right." I have no other answer, so I walk off to my bathroom. After closing the door behind me, I peel off my workout gear, splash lukewarm soapy water under my pits, reapply deodorant, and change back into today's outfit: a wide-necked gray sweater that slides off my shoulders, black stretch pants, and pink knee socks.

Then I rejoin Nick in my studio's workspace. "Thanks for bringing me lunch."

Since I no longer smell like car exhaust and perspiration, I give him a proper kiss.

His lips are warm and inviting, tasting faintly of the soup he just sampled. I pull back and smile. "Vegetable minestrone?"

He grins, surprised. "How did you know?"

"I'm a woman of many talents." I grab the container that smells like chicken and roasted tomatoes.

Nick looks me up and down. "Okay. Now that you changed clothes, you're more *Flashdance* than *Rocky.*"

"Oh yeah?" I taste my soup, which makes my mouth water.

"Hey. How come no one talks about the Rocky/Flashdance rivalry?" Nick asks. "It's epic... Philadelphia versus Pittsburgh, boxing versus dancing, men versus women."

"I haven't seen either film, so I can't say."

"What?" His mouth drops open. "That's not right. They're both classics."

"I always meant to watch them. Just never got around to it."

"Well, tonight we'll remedy that." Nick looks at his watch. "I have a showing in twenty minutes, so I should go. Come over around six? Andrea's on her spring break trip, so we'll have the place to ourselves. I've got both movies on DVD. We'll watch them, and you can decide which one's better."

"You're assuming I don't already have plans?"

Nick leans in for a kiss. "That's right. I'm taking you for granted, Rocky."

"Who are you calling Rocky? You just said my look is more *Flashdance.*"

"Uh huh. But your soul is more *Rocky.*"

A laugh bubbles out of me. "And why is that?"

"You'll see." Nick's eyes glint as he puts on his jacket and hums the *Rocky* theme song. "Ba ba BUM, ba ba BUM, ba da ba da BA bum!" He jogs through my studio and out the front door.

All day, the memory of him singing and running makes me laugh.

Later, I arrive at his apartment. "I come bearing cheese steak," I say. "That's what they eat in Philadelphia, right?"

"Come in." Nick pulls me close. His kiss gives me a thrill. "Cheese steak sounds great. But we'll start with watching *Flashdance*. That takes place in Pittsburgh."

"Oh. What do they eat in Pittsburgh?"

Nick shrugs. "Steel, I guess."

I roll my eyes and poke his arm. My finger is met with firm muscle. "Such a comedian."

"Yeah. You love me for it."

My breath catches. Do I love Nick? The answer terrifies me.

Nick leads me into his living room, cozy and warm with the flickering light of his gas fireplace. After he plates our cheesesteaks and uncorks a bottle of wine, we settle in. Jennifer Beals rides her bike under a charcoal sky. Irene Cara sings.

Two hours later, we stretch, take a bathroom break, and move straight to *Rocky*. Everything's great until Nick pauses to make popcorn, and I look at my phone.

Thinking of you. It's the 20th in my time zone. Sending love.

I gasp. How could I forget? How could I be so cozy and oblivious, snuggling up to Nick and watching a double feature of movies about people sweating in cold, industrial cities? The revelation comes right as my earlier premonition makes sense.

It's time to break up with Nick.

We've been together almost three months. My adult relationships never last that long. Besides, I broke my *only-dating-assholes policy* just by dating him.

Nick emerges from the kitchen, holding a bowl of popcorn fresh from its microwave bag.

"Now, I don't want to sway you. But listen hard to the part about champions being contenders who don't give up, okay? Maybe then you'll get why I call you Rocky."

I spin towards him. "What?"

Nick sits back down next to me. "Earlier today? I said your soul is more like Rocky? I'm just saying, listen for that line."

My mouth falls open. I must grow pale. Nick places his hand

on my knee. "Are you okay?"

"I . . . umm, I should go home."

"Now? What about the iconic sports montage? You haven't lived until you've seen Rocky Balboa running up the steps."

"Then why'd we start with *Flashdance?*"

Nick shrugs. "Jennifer Beals is hot."

"You think?" As a fair-skinned blonde, I share few physical traits with Jennifer Beals. Jealousy surges through me. Oh, what does it matter? We're about to break up.

"Sure," Nick says. "But she's nothing compared to you."

Something inside me flips. Part of me believes him and leans into his words and the warmth of his hand on my knee. But another part of me—the damaged part—pulls away.

Nick senses my hesitation and confusion. "Can't you stay over? I'd like you to."

I blink several times, trying to see him for the man he is. "Nick, do you ever get scared?"

Nick's eyes search mine for a moment. His hand has moved from my knee to my fingers and clasps them like puzzle pieces fitting together. "Scared of what?"

"Loss. Heartache. Needing people."

"Yeah, of course. Everyone does."

"Not like me." I look away. "I'm a trainwreck."

"No, you're not."

His gaze is strong, compelling me to meet his eyes. "How do you know?"

"Because," he says, "you're the strongest person I know. You're just bad at asking for help."

My lips part—a silent cue for him to continue.

"You're a contender, a champion. And I"—he takes a deep breath—"I hope it isn't too soon to say this. I love you."

"Nick—"

He cuts me off with a kiss.

"Please stay?" he asks.

I take a deep breath, feeling the weight of his words. My head spins, all my defenses caught off guard by his raw honesty and the sincerity in his eyes. His hand is warm around mine, steady and reassuring.

"Nick." My voice is a whisper against the thick tension wrapping around us.

"It's okay." His thumb rests against my chin. "And whatever's bothering you, you can tell me."

Pressing my foreheads to his, I let the revelation sink in. "I love you too. Nothing's bothering me. And yes, I'll stay."

He pulls me close. Desire swirls inside me as his lips move along mine. His kiss is patient but hungry—a mirror of contradicting emotions that matches my state of mind. I'm relieved and frightened all at once, but I don't pull away. I lean in deeper, surrendering to the sweet promise of his touch.

We pull and tug at each other's clothing until we're skin against skin. His hands travel along my spine, fingers tracing every ridge, every dip, and every scar like he's memorizing me. The air seems to crackle with electricity as his touch sends sparks through my veins. He pulls back only for a moment, just enough to look at me, his eyes dark with longing.

Then, a crooked smile lights up Nick's face. "I can't believe you're mine."

It's a statement, but I hear the uncertainty hidden beneath his words. Nick's hand cradles my face, the heat of his touch making me gasp.

"I am," I whisper, drawing circles on his chest, "all yours."

He kisses me again.

Later, we spoon on the couch. "Should we finish the movie?" Nick asks. "Or go to bed?"

"Don't we have to finish the movie?" I give him a soft jab with my elbow. "Something about not living until I've seen that sports montage?"

He chuckles. "You sure?"

"Yeah. Let me send a text, and then we'll watch the rest of *Rocky,* alright?"

Nick nods, his face guileless. Either he doesn't care who I'm texting, or he's a better actor than I am, with my fancy theater degree.

I'll call tomorrow. Miss you every day. XOXO.

"Everything okay?" Nick asks.

"Yeah."

He throws his arm around my shoulder, and I snuggle against him.

But my mind replays the last thirty minutes, making me oblivious to the film's dialogue or the soft rise and fall of Nick's chest against my side.

Nick loves me. He called me "Rocky."

Would he think I'm a champion if he knew?

ONE

Thursday, June 20, 2013
8:45 p.m.

As secrets go, mine is not earth-shattering. It's not even a secret. It's more like a huge, invisible elephant in the room that Nick hasn't yet noticed. But he's not stupid, and some reference to my past will force me to explain. And if nothing ever comes up, well, I have a time limit. The play opens in a few weeks.

I know it's weak to make a habit out of hiding, but showing my vulnerable side is my danger zone. Nick isn't that way; he lets his guard down with easy confidence. Like right now. A goofy smile lights up his face while he hums the tune he wrote on GarageBand. Nick is an aspiring musician disguised as a real estate agent. That makes him similar to ninety-five percent of all creative people who've ever lived.

We share a bland yet remarkable moment. I'm already nostalgic because life, unlike love, is finite. The sun sets and songs end. I breathe, letting my lungs expand, and my senses revel in my surroundings.

"You okay?" Nick asks, his gravelly voice pulling me from my thoughts.

"Of course," I tell him. "Keep playing your song."

We sit on my grubby living room carpet. I'm wearing shorts, so bits of dust and dirt press into my thighs. Outside, the moon struggles to appear, even though we're approaching 9 p.m. In the fading light of my apartment, we drink beer and stretch our legs.

"Okay, wait. This is my favorite part." Nick plays a riff on his keyboard, which is plugged into his laptop. I start belting out the lyrics to that 90s classic, "Song for the Dumped." But I stop when he stares at me.

"What?" I demand. "Your song sounds a lot like Ben Folds Five."

"True." He scrunches his forehead in surprise. "I always figured your knowledge of music didn't extend past Adele."

Nick is right; there aren't many songs on my iPod that aren't also played on Top 40 radio stations. But I have a sordid history with that particular song. "There are all sorts of things you don't know about me," I joke.

Nick doesn't laugh.

"Like?" He leans in with an intensity that makes the hairs on the back of my neck rise.

It's not a big deal. Now isn't the time to explain. I imagine his expression upon hearing my confession. The wounded eyes, the sputter of bewilderment . . .

I scoot towards Nick and press my lips to his.

"Like, I'm a fool for a guy who can carry a tune."

He grins in his adorable, crooked way, changing the geography of his face. "Stick with me, Rocky." He strokes my bare arm with his fingertips. "And I promise I'll learn to sing."

I laugh and we fall into each other—a slow dance on a mild summer evening. He tries to remove my black gingham blouse, but his thick fingers stumble over the bright pink buttons.

"Be careful. It took me hours to sew those buttons on right."

His grin says I'm worth being high maintenance. "Maybe you should take it off yourself. I don't want to wreck it."

Keeping my eyes locked on him, I take off my blouse as he watches, his arms outstretched in anticipation of holding me again. I pull the fabric over my face, and we reach for each other. Soon we grow so close that there's no distinction between where one of us ends and the other begins. I surrender to a welcome pull of desire.

But somewhere in the back of my mind is the thudding knowledge that pretty soon I'll have to come clean.

Friday, June 21, 2013
6:00 a.m.

I wear a corset. Someone from behind pulls it tight, squeezing my organs and reducing my ability to breathe. Standing in front of a mirror, I'm ready to perform, but how will I say my lines without enough air to speak? He steps out, his reflection next to mine.

My heart drops.

"Jed? What are you doing here?"

Jed offers a ghost of a grin, an imitation of his usual cocksure smile. And goddammit if it doesn't make my heart flutter. "Why wouldn't I be here?" His voice is low and controlled. "It's my play."

"But Georgie doesn't wear a corset."

He ignores me and pulls the strings so tight that my rib bones grind together. "Is it tight enough?"

I try to inhale, but I gasp instead. "Too tight, actually."

Jed shakes his head. "You'll never stay in character if you can breathe."

Several thoughts compete for my attention. Should I tell Jed about Nick? How will I perform when I don't know my lines? And will Jed be offended if I tell him breathing is important to me?

Jed puts his hands on my shoulders and kisses my neck, meeting my eyes in the mirror. "I've missed you, Robin. After the play, we should catch up."

Lucas walks in. "Places, Robin. It's time."

He walks off, all officious, with his stage manager headset and clipboard. Jed fumes.

"That guy has a lot of nerve."

I turn to face him. "What happened with Lucas was forever ago."

"No, it was just last week."

"But . . ."

11

Jed pushes me towards the stage, a few feet from where we stand. "Go. Break a leg. We'll talk later."

I stumble, fighting for air and to extinguish my sizzling nerves. The glare of lights makes me blink, and then I realize the morning sun streams through my window.

I'm awake.

It's no shock I dreamt about Jed; if anything, I'm surprised it hasn't happened sooner. Still, this is the first time he's appeared in my dreams since last March. As always, I can't decide if I want to shake off the images or cling to them.

When I close my eyes again, my brain shouts, *You're not going back to sleep.* I turn and Nick lets out a soft groan. He tightens his groggy arm, pulling me close as we spoon. No wonder I dreamt of corsets.

"I have to get up," I say.

"You're self-employed," Nick murmurs. "You don't *have* to do anything." He kisses my neck, and his muscles are taut against my stomach. I take a moment before resisting, then resting my head against the pillow and enjoying his heat. But soon I sit up, freeing myself from his grasp. Without the covers and the warmth of him, the air-conditioning prickles my skin.

"I can't sleep, so I'm going before it's too hot out."

He opens one eye. "Again?"

"When I can't sleep, I have to get up and get moving."

Nick smiles, closes his eyes, and nestles back under the covers. "I'm glad I'm not you," he mumbles. I push him in response, but he just laughs and starts humming the *Rocky* theme song. "Have a good run, Rocky."

I get out of bed, brush my teeth, and change into my running gear. After securing my shoulder-length blonde hair into a ponytail and lacing up my Nikes, I exit my apartment building into the soft Midwest morning.

I start running through the streets of my neighborhood. There are more hills than you would expect for a place like West Des

Moines, and my lungs squeeze as I try to maintain an eight-minute mile. Right now, my legs are like sandbags. I should have stayed in bed with Nick. I would have stayed in bed with Nick, except I know my pattern of insomnia. Once I wake up, no amount of tossing or turning puts me back to sleep.

So I keep running, even after the stitch in my side squeals to slow down. Sweat soaks my tank top, but I increase my pace. My lungs must work harder. By now, they should know that little trick of moving fresh air in and wasteful gases out.

Then I turn a corner and approach the house, where I always see her.

Flashdance Girl.

Is it serendipity that she showed up in my life? A sign from the universe? Weeks after Nick hosted that double feature, she started making regular appearances on my morning runs.

She's way too young to know the movie. I guess she streams films made a decade before her birth. Anyway, she has the hairdo: dark, curly, and held back by a headband across her forehead. She wears a t-shirt with a ripped collar, which falls off her shoulders, revealing the straps of her sports bra. And, like in the song, she wears the expression of someone who's dancing (or running) for her life. Her doe-like eyes stay wide and her lips stay parted, no matter how fast she goes. The one exception is when she first sees me. Every morning she waits in her yard, and every morning she sneers right before she takes off.

That curled lip is a challenge, and if I wasn't so winded, I would say, *Sure, hit me hard. I'll keep moving forward.* But I didn't pace myself right. I never pace myself right. And when she crosses over to my side of the street just to gain on me, I can't rise to the challenge.

I try to run fast, but my legs refuse to cooperate. The stitch on my side migrates across my entire stomach. Her footsteps get louder behind me, and they gain speed. It's like she's part cheetah. "On your left!" she demands. I move over, let her pass, and resist the urge to trip her.

"Show off!" I yell. But my yell is weak, and she has on

headphones, so I bet she didn't hear me. Anyway, she couldn't be older than sixteen. What am I doing, getting so worked up by someone almost half my age?

Stupid Flashdance Girl.

When I get home, Isobel, my neighbor/bestie since college, sits on her porch. The still-rising sun bounces light off her shiny black hair, and her blue eyes match her T-shirt.

"Hi," I say. "You're up early."

Isobel sips her coffee. "Couldn't sleep. Are you ready for rehearsal tonight? We're blocking your death scene."

Rolling my shoulders back, I stretch out my calves. "Yeah." I keep my eyes on the pavement. "I'm very ready."

"Liar," Isobel retorts. My head snaps up in shock.

"It's going to be emotional, Robin. Don't kid yourself. I hope you'll come prepared."

I stand up straight and nod. "You're right. Guess time doesn't heal *all* wounds, right?"

She takes another sip of coffee, contemplating. "Or old wounds get reopened."

"Yeah."

We're both quiet as the first evidence of rush-hour traffic begins. People pull out of their driveways, and car radios blast from several feet away. I let out a sigh. "Well, I should take a shower and get moving. I'll see you tonight."

"See you tonight," she says.

I go inside, past my still-sleeping boyfriend, and into the shower. My heart rate slows to normal as I let the water's spray bathe my face. I'm more centered and less shaky than I was when I first woke up, like running exorcized all my demons. I grab the shampoo bottle and squeeze some into my hair. But when the soapy run-down stings my eyes, I think of Isobel . . . and why I agreed to do Jed's play in the first place.

• • •

Last October, Isobel and I were both used to being alone. Living next door provided the perks of a roommate without the sacrifice of privacy, leftovers, or deleted shows on the DVR. We often hung out in the evenings, and sometimes we watched *The Holdout*, the reality show I was on. Isobel applauded when I did well in the competitions. And she yelled at the TV if anyone betrayed me.

Isobel was in the middle of her divorce, and we needed each other like a sea anemone riding on the back of a hermit crab. (Isobel, always the more stable one, was the hermit crab.) One evening, after the latest episode of *The Holdout* ended, I grabbed her remote to shut off the TV, and she turned to me with this Nancy-Drew-like glint in her eyes. I expected some projection about the rest of the season.

I was half right.

"You made it to the jury," she said. "That's huge! Robin, you're a celebrity and you have to capitalize on this."

I scraped the bottom of the popcorn bowl for the last edible kernels and shoved them in my mouth. "I'm not a celebrity. People will forget about me in less than a month."

Isobel shook her head with the force of a hurricane. "Don't let them forget about you."

"I'm fine with being forgotten."

She scooted closer to me on her sagging couch. Then she grabbed my knee, both her grip and tone robust. "Do a play with me. It will be like old times, and the PR will be great. 'Robin from *The Holdout*' starring in a Mirror Image Production!"

Mirror Image is Isobel's theater company.

I laughed, trying in vain to get her to laugh too. "Come on, Isobel. I haven't acted in years."

"But you'll be great!" Her enthusiasm was big enough to sit between us and invade my personal bubble. "You sorta sweat charisma. The audience will adore you, and I bet we'd make record box office. We'll do whatever play you want, okay? *A Doll's House* or *Miss Witherspoon*. Just name your dream role!"

I didn't know what my dream role would be, but I did know that after Isobel caught her ex-husband cheating, the look in her eye said 'leave me alone.' Not now. Her theater company was floundering, but she'd found a way to save it, and that made her come alive. How could I refuse?

"I suppose it might be fun," I conceded. "But I'd get the final say on the costumes."

Isobel bounced up and down in her seat and clapped her hands. "Yay!" she cried. "This will be awesome! Which play should we do?"

"I don't know," I laughed. "I'll have to think about it."

Isobel drew her knees up, resting her chin against them. "You know, we *could* do Jed's play."

There was a time that idea would make me break out in a cold, clammy panic-sweat. Instead, my pulse quickened and my chest thumped, both from nerves and excitement.

"Yeah . . ."

Isobel's voice was as indulgent as Merlot. "You said we'd do it someday."

"'Someday' is always supposed to be a ways away."

"Still," Isobel sighed, "it *has* been a long time. You won't be the right age to play Georgie for much longer."

"True." I grabbed a pillow and put it over my lap, like I needed protection.

"Robin . . ." Isobel paused until I looked at her. "I won't pressure you about this. But I don't want you to never do the play and then regret it later, you know? This *would* be the perfect opportunity. We could get other people from Hoyt involved, like Andrew and Miranda." She jabbed a playful finger into my shoulder. "Hey, I heard Lucas is back in town after working at the Guthrie. He could stage-manage."

"Lucas? Really?"

"He's the best around. Don't you want the best?"

I tilted my head, trying to loosen the knots in my neck. With a deep breath, I turned back towards Isobel. "Catherine is studying abroad this year. Could we wait until summer? She'd never forgive me if she couldn't come."

"Of course." Isobel smiled. "Summer is perfect."

• • •

As I finish my shower, it occurs to me that, at the time, summer seemed a comfortable distance away. Of course, that was before I'd even met Nick, before I fell in love for the second time in my life. Now summer is here, and the past keeps nudging up against my present-day emotions. My heart is getting a little claustrophobic.

I rinse the shampoo out, turn the water off, grab a towel, and wrap it around me. I exit the steamy bathroom with half a mind to crawl back into bed with Nick and give him a proper good-morning. But when I get to my bedroom, I find an empty bed.

Nick left without saying goodbye.

4:30 p.m.

Throughout the day, thoughts of rehearsal, Jed, and everything I've pushed aside flit through my mind. I keep the doors to my studio space open, so people walking through the East Village of Des Moines can check out my clothes—dresses made from old coats and men's shirts, blouses made from old dresses, and scarves made from whatever I could find.

It's not that I dislike designer clothes. I appreciate a new outfit as much as your next *Vogue* subscriber. And sure, that thrift store smell often makes me wonder if it's worth the trouble of turning trash into treasure. But when it works, it's magical—desperate threads given a new lease on life, woven into something beautiful and unique. The charm of a beat-up vintage leather jacket or the unexpected beauty of a repurposed cashmere sweater. The hidden stories in each piece are worth the effort. I see my creations as statements—bold declarations that there's always a second chance, one more life to live.

And I love my studio, with the occasional customer wandering in, but most of my sales are made online. So I'm alone, working on a forest green minidress with a removable cape collar, when Nick walks through my door wearing dark pants, a shirt and tie, and black shoes. It's his real estate agent outfit.

"Hi!" I say. "This is a surprise. What brings you here?"

Nick puts on his impish grin. "I'm in the market for an upcycled three-piece suit. Do you have anything in corduroy?"

I raise my eyebrows and smirk. "Corduroy isn't your color."

"Touché." He laughs. "Truth is, I came to apologize."

"For what?"

He fiddles with his watch. "Rushing out this morning while you were in the shower. You should have pushed me out of bed. I was almost late meeting some clients."

"So you're apologizing and blaming me in the same breath?"

"Nah." Nick juts out his chin at a charming angle—an expression he must have learned in third grade. It's dangerous for a grown man to attempt such cuteness without years of experience.

"Was Flashdance Girl out this morning?"

"Yeah, and she almost ran me off the sidewalk."

"What a bully."

"I know."

"I still can't quite believe she exists. Are you sure you're not hallucinating her?"

"I swear, she's as real as you and me." I toss a few buttons onto the dressing table.

"Always out there in those headbands and off-the-shoulder sweatshirts. Besides, why would I create a jogging nemesis for myself?"

"I'm not saying you would. It's just a coincidence. You're Rocky. She's Flashdance Girl . . ." He leans his arm against the door frame. "She sounds like a character from a comic book. Flashdance Girl:

The sidewalk sprinter. Sworn enemy of anyone going in for another round when they don't think they can."

"And that's me? Going in for another round?"

"Yup," he answers, his voice velvety. "We both know how tough you are." The look he gives me squeezes my heart.

"Why are you standing all the way over there?" I ask. "Come closer."

"Okay." He walks up to me and places a light kiss on my mouth. I pull at his loosened tie to steal another smooch. This time, our mouths linger.

"Hey," he mumbles. "How's your day?"

"Getting better," I mumble back. I run my fingers through his short, dark brown hair.

He slides his hands down my torso. "Is this one new? I don't think I've seen it before."

Nick is referring to my red sailor blouse, which I made from a 1990s sundress and this awesome gray figure eight trim that I found at Michaels. "Yeah," I say. "I decided it's too nice to sell."

"A hazard of the profession," Nick replies, kissing my neck. "I like it. You should wear it when we go out sometime."

"Okay." My smile forms at the small of my back. "Not that I'm complaining, but what are you doing here?"

He goes in for a kiss right below my ear. "I was showing a house nearby, and I wanted to talk to you." His dark brown eyes widen, and I'm tempted to lock the door, unbutton his shirt, and change his earnest expression into something a little less appropriate.

"You need to talk to me?" I let go of him. "That's never good. What is it?"

Half of his mouth smiles. "Nothing bad. I need to know when your dad's birthday party is. Also, your play. And anything else that should be on my radar." He whips out his phone from his back pocket. "Can you give me the dates so I can put them on my calendar?"

"Look who's organized!" I go to my desk and turn over pattern books, sketch pads, and fabric remnants before I find my own phone, underneath a piece of lavender oxford cloth. I swipe to display my calendar.

Nick cocks his head to the side. "Well, I have stuff coming up. I need to make sure I don't overbook and miss something important."

"What do you have coming up?"

"You know. Andrea's getting back . . ."

"Andrea doesn't get back until August." Andrea is Nick's little sister, and he's her guardian. But this summer, she's working at a summer camp, so Nick has more freedom than he's had in years. "And even if she was back, she'd be welcome at my play and at my dad's birthday."

"Yeah, no, I know. But I have showings in the evening sometimes and networking events . . ." He slows down after talking too fast. "This isn't a problem, is it? Trying to figure out my schedule in advance?"

"No, of course not."

I shouldn't be surprised that Nick's planning ahead. His mother died of breast cancer soon after he graduated high school. Nick dealt with it by becoming everything to everyone, taking care of details, filling out official forms, and raising his younger sister, Andrea.

"Is that all?" I ask. "You want to figure out your schedule?"

"Of course." He grins and holds his finger poised over his cell phone, ready to type in dates.

"You don't have to go to anything of mine, not if you don't want to."

Nick narrows his eyes. "What? Before, you said they were important."

"Yeah." I use the piece of lavender oxford cloth to wipe the screen of my cell phone, which makes it more smeared. "But I don't *need* you there."

"Rocky . . ." Nick lowers the hand that holds his phone. He steps towards me. "Don't be like that."

I meet his eyes. "I'm serious. You shouldn't feel burdened. It's okay if you have other stuff going on."

He clenches his jaw and juts out his lower lip. Like he's trying to figure out the correct response. Like he can find it on a multiple-choice exam. He reaches for me, brushing a wayward curl from my forehead. "Being there for you isn't a burden. It's what I want."

"I appreciate that, Nick," I say, swallowing down my unease.

"But . . .?" His finger brushes my cheek.

"But I'll tell you the dates." I yank at both ends of the oxford cloth, as if playing tug of war with myself. "That way, you can choose to come or not."

7:00 p.m.

When I get to rehearsal, Isobel is on stage with Miranda, waving her arms in exaggerated gestures. She sees me, her movements halt, and she skips to the edge of the stage. "Oh good, you're here. We just began blocking the death match. I was thinking you could stand stage left and when you start fighting, she could sort of drag you over here." Isobel flails out her arms to demonstrate.

"Watch it!" cries Miranda. She shields her face with her hands to avoid getting smacked by Isobel.

"Sorry!" Isobel's cheeks redden. "I'm just excited for this scene."

"Because you want to kill me?" I joke.

Isobel puts a dramatic hand to her heart. "Never, my dear! You're too precious to the guild!" She bats her eyelashes at me in a theatrical way that makes Miranda and me laugh.

The play, *The Next Breath*, follows a struggling writer plagued by relationship woes. One fateful night, he pours his heart onto the page. The next day, miraculously, his girlfriend acts out the exact scene he wrote. But as the story continues, all he can do is improvise, unable to control the chaotic turns that lead to her unfortunate death. Act One ends with tragedy, but Act Two delves into his desperate attempts to write her back into existence.

21

It's a dark comedy wrapped in loss and heartbreak, reflective of life's unpredictable twists and turns.

"So do you want to skip warm-ups and just go right into blocking the scene?" I ask.

"Oh." Isobel swings the hand that holds her script and uses her other hand to scratch her temple. "Sorry. Of course we should warm up. I wasn't thinking." She calls for the stage manager. "Lucas, do you want to lead warm-ups while I go over my notes?"

Lucas agrees, and Andrew, the other actor, comes over. We stand in a sloppy circle, and Lucas takes us through exercises we all learned in college. Controlled breathing, rolling our heads from side to side, making our mouths wide while reciting tongue twisters, and to get our energy going, The Hokey Pokey. All the while, I look around this dim theater, with garage-sale rehearsal furniture and well-worn audience chairs, and imagine the network of nerves surrounding my brain, heart, and lungs. Is it possible to pinpoint one tiny little nerve, snip it out, and relieve this heaviness inside? I need to be light.

Because in a few minutes, I'll die again. And it's always for Jed.

10:30 p.m.

"How was rehearsal?" Nick asks.

"Weird. Difficult."

"Do you want to talk about it?"

I'm lying flat on my back, talking on my phone, and staring at the bedroom ceiling. I hear ambient bar noises behind the sound of his voice.

"That's okay," I answer. "Where are you?"

"At The Keg Stand, hanging out with Dave." The Keg Stand is a popular bar in our area. Nick met Dave in a college music course years ago, before Nick had to drop out. But they're still music buddies.

"I'm super tired. You should stay and have fun."

"I'll call you tomorrow." Nick's voice is soft enough to cuddle me through the radio frequencies that connect us. "Love you."

"Me too. Bye."

I shut my phone off and let it fall to the pillow by my side. It's been a long day, and fatigue presses into me. Summoning the necessary energy to rise, brush my teeth, and slip into my nightshirt doesn't seem worthwhile.

There's no point in fighting it. I close my eyes and let the memories materialize.

TWO

Saturday, September 2, 2000

My freshman dormitory met my expectations. Everything was a muted shade of orange—the walls, the linoleum, the lounge furniture. New students milled around, and self-important RAs wandered, wearing authorized smiles, saying things like "Hi, I'm Evan! How can I help you settle in?"

My dad helped me find my room. When we unlocked the door, it swung open in a squeaky lurch worthy of a horror movie. We lugged my stuff inside, plopped my bags down, and stared. There were two twin beds that could be stacked on top of each other, matching wood dressers and desks, and one window with its white venetian blind already pulled up.

"Do you want help unpacking?" Standing there, my dad seemed larger, like he had grown in the last couple of minutes, just to make my room seem small. Better to rip the Band-Aid off right away. I shook my head and rushed into his arms.

With a tearful hug, I muttered into his shoulder, "I'll miss you, Dad."

I could feel him quiver. "You're only a few hours away. We'll see each other plenty, unless you get too busy, which would also be great." He let go of me. "You'll have a fantastic time here, Robin. I know you will."

I was more worried about him than me. My dad never remarried after my mom died in a car accident sixteen years ago, and my

24

brothers were already off on their own. Now Dad would be alone. "I won't be too busy, Dad. I'll come home and visit a lot."

He kissed me on the forehead. "We'll see. But I won't turn down a phone call now and then either, okay?"

I nodded and gulped down more tears. "I love you, Dad."

"I love you too." He turned and tilted his head towards the ceiling. His Adam's apple rose and fell, and I knew he was trying not to cry, probably for my sake. I expected he'd let loose in his car.

He turned back with a brave smile. "So I should hit the road, then. I'll call you tomorrow, okay?"

I wiped my face with my sleeve and nodded. "Drive carefully."

And then his tall, lanky form disappeared through my door. I sat on the edge of my bed and allowed myself to cry for no more than ten minutes. Then I got up, blew my nose, and unpacked.

I made my bed with my new cotton Indian-print bedspread. I hung my Playbill *Fosse* poster on the wall next to my desk, and I put my copies of *The Complete Works of Shakespeare, Roget's Thesaurus, Franny and Zoey,* and *A Room with a View* in my bookshelf. (I put my trashier romance novels in a box under my bed.) I set up my CD player and put my CDs on its side. I filled my closet with jeans, leggings, Doc Martins, and the two long, hooded cardigans that I'd saved up to buy because they were the latest thing that fall.

Finally, I put my new laptop on my desk. It was my graduation present from my dad, not just to use for term papers but also so we could email each other.

Just looking at it made me miss him again.

I shook off the melancholy and headed out for a walk to explore campus. Outside, it was hot, and the humidity was so intense I almost needed an umbrella. I was glad to be wearing a black tank top and my favorite pair of khaki drawstring shorts; maybe I wasn't making much of a fashion statement, but today I was more concerned with comfort.

I still thought about my father. I pictured him preparing some frozen meal for dinner and eating in front of the television. Would he fall asleep watching *This Old House?* Who would wake him if he did? Nobody. He'd rise with a sore back and a lonely emptiness that wouldn't go away. But I shouldn't worry so much. He was a grown man who could take care of himself. Still, I resolved to call my brother, Ian, and make him promise to eat dinner with Dad at least once this week.

After arriving at this conclusion, I brushed off my blues and enjoyed exploring. The first buildings I found were the library, the student union, and the theater, where I planned to spend most of my time. On Monday, when classes started, I would go inside. For now, I stood before it with reverence, like visiting a monument.

"Hey, Sunshine."

I turned. A bulky guy wearing a *Property of Hoyt Athletics* T-shirt loomed over me. I'm tall, so most guys don't loom in my presence, but this one managed.

"Got plans tonight?" he asked.

"Um, you must be confusing me with somebody else. I don't know you."

His pervy smile negated his toned biceps' appeal. "Come to our party. We'll get to know each other."

He handed me a flier.

"*Beer Blowout! Live DJ! Free Admission for Hot Girls!*" I looked back at him. "Is this for a frat?"

"Sigma Pi. Best house on campus. Best parties too." He gave me a wolfish grin. "So you get in free, okay? Just tell them you know Ricky."

"Wow. Thank you."

"Sure." He tapped my shoulder, and that brief moment of contact made me wish for a shower. "What's your name?"

"Jezebel," I said quickly.

Ricky spoke in a low, lounge-singer sort of voice. "Pretty name. I'll see you tonight, okay, *Jezebel?*"

"Sure. Bye." I turned around to get away. Then the most piercing set of blue eyes in the entire world accosted me.

They belonged to this skinny guy, who sat on a bench nearby. He must have heard my conversation. His bright, blaring gaze leapt out at me, and his diagonal smile took up at least three parking spots.

Standing there, facing him, with the sun and heat pressing down and newness in the air, I had the weirdest sense of déjà vu. No way did I know this guy, but somehow, I was supposed to know him.

"You should go to the party," the skinny guy said. "Frat boys have fragile egos. You don't want to hurt his feelings."

As I approached, it was more like we were about to resume a conversation than begin one. "Do you know him? Ricky?"

He shook his head. "No."

"So you don't belong to his frat?"

He raised one bushy eyebrow. "I don't belong to any frat. Even if I wanted to, no way could I make it through hazing."

He was almost gaunt, but he had strong-looking biceps. I spied tight abs underneath his gray T-shirt. "Don't sell yourself short. I bet you could drink beer and get paddled with the best of them."

"Maybe," he replied, squinting at me. "Hey, something tells me your name isn't Jezebel."

"Wow, it's like you have a window inside my soul."

He laughed and shielded his gorgeous eyes, blocking out the sun. "What *is* your name?"

"Robin."

"Nice to meet you, Robin." He smiled again, this time with dimples showing. "I'm Jed. Are you new at Hoyt?"

"Yeah. I'm a freshman. What about you?"

Tilting up his gaze, he made no invitation for me to join him on his bench. "This is my second year, but I'm still a freshman because I go part-time."

"Oh."

There was a pause as he looked down at his hands, his fingers tracing the wood grain of the bench. He grunt-laughed. "I expect you hear this a lot, but you're pretty."

I was more amazed at his bluntness than flattered by his words. Jed looked back at me and widened his eyes.

"Thank you," I said.

Then we both ran out of things to say.

I twirled a strand of hair around my finger, unable to take my eyes off of him. Despite his feminine lips and long lashes, thick eyebrows and a hint of stubble made him masculine. The weirdest part? He was at once fascinating and familiar. Like I'd known him in a past life. Like I was rereading my favorite book.

"Why are you sitting outside the theater? Are you a theater major too?" I asked.

He shook his head. "Kind of. My major is creative writing, with an emphasis on playwriting."

"Oh. What sorts of plays do you write?"

"Comedies, I guess. Hey, you should take Professor Johnson's course." He coughed. "All actors should know how to write."

"Oh yeah? Why?"

"So you can create your own parts!" He rolled his eyes. "Achieving your dreams comes by taking fate into your own hands. Don't you think?"

Looking down, I scuffed the rubber toe of my sneaker against the pavement. "You could be right."

"But . . . ?"

"But," I responded, "I just said goodbye to my father. I'm a little sad right now for philosophical conversation."

"You'd rather go drink beer at a frat party?" He sat up straight, energized by this idea. "Hey. What if we have a philosophical conversation *while* drinking beer at a frat party? How would that be?"

"Right." I wrinkled my nose. "Why are you sitting out here? Are you waiting for someone?"

"You ask a lot of questions."

I shrugged.

"I'm waiting for my mom." He held up his arms in a

self-deprecating gesture. "I know. A guy with his mother nearby is a sexy proposition. So what time should I pick you up for Ricky's party?"

Crumpling the flier in my fist, I realized I didn't want to go to the party with Jed. No, I wanted a more intimate setting. I was about to ask if he liked movies when his head snapped towards what had to be his mother's voice.

"Jed!" she shouted. "We have to go. That took longer than I thought."

A middle-aged woman with a small frame, flowing brown hair and square-rimmed glasses walked towards him.

Jed got up. "Sorry. Guess I can't stay. That's my mom." Then he spoke in an exaggerated whisper. "She's head of the Hoyt theater department."

Before I could brazenly ask him out, he followed after his mom and walked away.

Sunday, September 3, 2000

My roommate finally made an appearance at around 6:00 p.m., with her swishy auburn ponytail and a throaty laugh. "I'm April," she said, plopping down her huge suitcase and backpack.

"Nice to meet you," I replied. "Where are you from?"

"Rochester." Rochester is a southern Minnesota town that exists because of the Mayo Clinic. Hoyt is in the northernmost part of Iowa, around forty minutes away.

"Oh, cool." Sitting on my bed, I hugged my knees to my chest. "I hope it's okay I took this side of the room."

She stole a glimpse of herself in the full-length mirror I'd hung on the door. "No problem. In fact, you get this room to yourself most of the time. I'm staying with my boyfriend." She opened her suitcase and started unpacking and making her bed. "But I'll leave some stuff around. If my parents ever stop by, they'll think I live here."

Loneliness squealed inside me, but I silenced it with a casual smile. "Oh."

"Hey, if they do ever show up, can you tell them I'm at the gym or something? Then call me?" She grabbed a Post-it from my desk and wrote her name and phone number in large letters. "Is that cool?"

"Um, sure."

"Wonderful. And hey! You get a room to yourself. That's awesome, right?"

It was and it wasn't. I had dreams of late-night heart-to-hearts, movie marathons, microwave brownies and crying over life's painful blows. But sure, having my own space was also great. I could decorate how I wanted—no compromise. I could leave my books scattered and my clothes draped over furniture. And if I wanted to play songs late into the night while I studied, no one would ever complain.

Monday, September 4, 2000

I was in the dark, windowless classroom of the theater building. My instructor, Elaine, was of the young, tiny, high-energy variety. "Welcome to *Voice and Movement*," she said in a singsong. "We're going to have an incredible semester! And we're not wasting any time! Now take off your shoes and rise to your feet! Let's get in a circle. I'll teach you the vocal warm-up."

I was glad to skip the part where we went around and learned each other's names. And thank heavens, we didn't have to do that trust exercise where I'd stand on a table, fall backwards, and let everyone catch me. I did that once in high school and was dropped.

Instead, Elaine taught us this routine that combined yoga stretches, tongue twisters, and— I'm not kidding—groaning and squealing. She told us we'd start every class with it, and we'd all take turns leading. So we leapt around and used our full vocal registers.

I took a moment to check out the rest of the class.

There were three goth girls, dressed all in black (including their lipstick), and they rolled their eyes when Elaine said perky things, like "Yes! Good! Use those vocal chords to their full potential!"

There were a few shy kids who didn't know why they signed up for a theater class. They wore jeans and cropped T-shirts, exposing their bellies when they stretched, blushing as that happened.

The best-dressed kid in the class introduced himself as Andrew. He wore slim-fitting pants, a gray satiny vest, and a tie. I expected him to be pent-up, but his vest came off with his shoes, and the tie was flung on a chair. He was in his own world, experimenting with multiple octaves and pitches, flinging his limbs around, letting loose.

At the end of class, Elaine told us we needed to regroup, so we sat back down in a circle. "That was an excellent, excellent beginning, you guys! I am so excited for this semester. I can tell we're going to make fantastic progress together!" She coughed a little and patted her chest. "Sorry," she said. "That vocal warm-up can bring up a lot of gunk. I recommend drinking hot tea afterwards. Anyway . . ." She held up a book. It was a small paperback with *Spoon River Anthology* written on the cover. "Homework!" she cried. "You need to buy this book and pick a poem, whichever one you want. Have it memorized for next class. Okay?" She looked around at all of us, wide-eyed, until we nodded. "Excellent!" she sang. "See you Wednesday."

I went straight to the bookstore and picked up *Spoon River Anthology*, along with the other books I'd need: *An Introduction to Theatrical Design and Construction*, *A Beginner's Guide to the Humanities*, and *Health Psychology*.

I went back to my dorm room, put all of my new books on the shelf above my desk, and checked my reflection in the mirror.

I was in my French phase. Wearing a tight pair of guy's Levi's rolled up at the cuffs, red ballet flats, and a navy blue T-shirt with white stripes, I grabbed my red accent scarf from my top dresser drawer. Should I wrap it around my neck or use it as a headband? Neither, I decided, since it was almost ninety degrees outside. Fashion looks ridiculous if it defies comfort or common sense. I tried never to cross that line.

Satisfied with myself, I decided to eat lunch. I couldn't face the cafeteria, so I grabbed my copy of *Spoon River Anthology*, bought a sandwich and a soda, and walked to the theater building, to the same bench where skinny-guy-Jed sat two days before.

While eating my chicken-salad sub, I read *Spoon River Anthology*. Each poem was about someone from this fictional town, Spoon River, and they all spoke from the grave. Some poems were short and funny, others were more serious, and there were ones I had no idea what they were about. I was supposed to pick one to memorize.

"Hey, it's you."

My head snapped up. My plan had worked.

"Oh, hi, Jed." I grinned and wiped the residue chicken salad from the corners of my mouth. "How are you?"

He sat down next to me. His jeans had a rip, and a pale, knobby knee stuck out through the hole. But his T-shirt was cauliflower blue, which made his eyes as bright as a smurf. "I'm good." He grabbed my book and started leafing through it. "*Spoon River Anthology*? Let me guess. You have to memorize a poem for class."

"Yeah. Any suggestions?"

He turned the pages while scowling. "Nah," he grumbled. "That would be wrong. I can't tell you which poem to use."

"I wasn't asking you to choose for me. But if you're familiar with the book—"

"Jed!" It was his mom again. She walked over to our bench. "Don't wander off like that. We're already running late."

He smiled. "Mom, this is Robin. She's in the theater department, and she's auditioning for *As You Like It*." He turned to me. "You are, right? Every actor on campus auditions for my mom's plays."

"Pretty perceptive." I was embarrassed to look at his mother. Keeping my eyes on him, I resorted to sarcasm. "Do you read palms?"

She made a clicking sound with her tongue. "Jed, we need to go."

He stood. "Robin, this is Catherine, my mother. She's very nice when she isn't late for an appointment."

"Nice to meet you," I said to her. She nodded and tugged on Jed's arm.

"Let's go," she pleaded. They started walking, but then he turned back.

"Hey!" he said. "Good luck picking a poem. I'll want to know which one you chose."

He disappeared towards the parking lot, so I kept reading, and when I got to the poem titled "George Gray," I dog-eared the page after reading the final paragraph:

To put meaning in one's life may end in madness,
But life without meaning is the torture
Of restlessness and vague desire—
It is a boat longing for the sea and yet afraid.

Tuesday, September 12, 2000

"No," I said. The phone was pressed against my ear. "My classes aren't that hard. So far, the workload is fine."

"Just don't let it pile up," my dad replied. "If you put things off, it's easy to get overwhelmed."

"Yeah, I know." I primped in front of the mirror while we spoke. After deciding my red lipstick was too bright, I grabbed a tissue and wiped it off. "I'm keeping up. But I need to go. I have an audition."

"Already? For what?"

"*As You Like It.* It's the main-stage production this fall. I prepared a monologue. It will just be me on stage, performing for the director." I took a sharp inhale and tried to quell my twitching stomach butterflies. "I should run. I want plenty of time to pace around the lobby before they call me in."

My dad laughed. "Good luck, honey."

"Thanks." I straightened the neckline of my blouse and wondered if the pattern was too busy. Should I have gone for a solid color? "You're eating dinner with Ian tonight?"

"Yup." I could hear his television blaring in the background, and I hoped he was telling the truth. That Dad wasn't eating dinner with *Law and Order*.

"Say hi for me," I offered.

"I love you, Robin."

"Me too, Dad."

I hung up, put on fresh, subtle pink lipstick, and changed into a black V-neck T-shirt. Tucked into my wide-legged pants, it would look formal enough, like fine china on a cheap placemat. Then I grabbed my bag, left my dorm room, and trekked across campus to the theater.

When I got there, the first person I saw was Andrew, the well-dressed kid from Voice and Movement Class. Today he wore a blue linen dress shirt, black chinos, and a black tie. He pulled on his tie, loosening it like a businessman home from a tough day at the office.

"Hey," I said. "Did you go already?"

"Yeah."

"How was it?"

"Nerve-wracking!" Andrew softly yelled. "Catherine tapped her pencil during my entire monologue. I don't think that's a good sign."

I placed my fingers against his shoulder. "What piece did you do?"

"Shylock from *The Merchant of Venice*. 'The quality of mercy is not strained.'"

"Oh." I tried to keep my voice level, but Andrew caught me raising my eyebrows.

"What?" he demanded. "Too overdone?"

I shrugged with my hands held up. "How would I know? I'm

34

sure it was fine. The important thing is how you performed. I've seen you in class; I bet you were awesome."

Andrew nodded. "What's your piece?"

"It's from *Troilus and Cressida*."

The stage manager emerged from the theater doors and called my name. "Robin Bricker?"

"Yeah, here!" I waved.

"You're up," he said.

"Break a leg," said Andrew.

I smiled my thanks and followed the stage manager inside. Earlier, upperclassmen advised me to walk directly on stage and introduce myself and my monologue. I had to cup my hand over my eyes, but I spotted Catherine sitting at a table in the front row. The stage manager was next to her.

"Hello," I said. "My name is Robin Bricker, and my piece today is Cressida, from *Troilus and Cressida*."

"Great," Catherine said. "Whenever you're ready."

Closing my eyes for a couple of seconds, I imagined I was an entitled girl rendezvousing with her forbidden love. Then I looked up, gazed at the clock on the far wall, and spoke as though the clock was a hot, young Troilus.

"Hard to seem won: but I was won, my lord,
With the first glance that ever—pardon me—
If I confess much, you will play the tyrant."

Someone coughed. Loud, like they were hacking out a lung. Then there was murmuring. Without meaning to, I broke character and looked away.

"I'm very sorry," Catherine said to me. Then, in a fierce whisper, she spoke to the offending cougher. "Jed! What is wrong with you, disrupting her audition? You know better!"

Oh. Jed was here.

"Hey, Robin. Sorry about that." He smiled and waved like he was my next-door neighbor standing on his driveway.

"Do you mind starting over?" Catherine asked.

My throat went dry. "Um, sure. Yeah, okay."

So I began again, hyperaware of Jed and even more nervous than before.

"I love you now; but not, till now, so much
But I might master it: in faith, I lie;
My thoughts were like unbridled children, grown
Too headstrong for their mother. See, we fools!
Why have I blabb'd?"

My body temperature rose by at least five degrees. Somehow I got to the last line—*stop my mouth*. Clamping my hand over my lips, I prayed I hadn't made a fool of myself.

After a second, I reverted to Robin and forced myself to look through the glare of the stage lights. My eyes found Catherine. "Thank you."

"Thank you, Robin," she replied. "The call-back list will be up Thursday."

As I climbed down and walked out, Jed clapped with broad, slow strokes. I had the urge to leap through the aisles and strangle him, but also to wink and give him a thumbs-up. Instead, I pretended his presence was immaterial—that I couldn't be bothered.

On my walk back to the dorms, I consoled myself. My monologue worked well. Cressida is supposed to be nervous as she confesses her love to Troilus. But the moment I was back in my room, I buried my head under the covers and groaned into my pillow.

Friday, September 14, 2000

It was just after midnight, but callbacks had finished at 10 p.m. In between, I went to Perkins with Andrew and other auditionees, killing time by drinking coffee and eating pancakes. Now we were back, sitting in the darkened theater lobby and staring at the light that came from Catherine's office.

That light flickered off, and two shadowy figures moved towards the callboard in the entryway, separated from the lobby by glass walls and a door. Catherine hustled out, toward the exit nearest the parking lot, like fleeing a crime scene. The stage manager, Lucas, lingered, a sheet of paper in one hand and a stapler in the other.

I grabbed Andrew's sleeve and tugged. "He's posting it!" I said.

Andrew snapped to attention, and the ambient conversations ceased. We all waited, suspended, while Lucas stapled the cast list to the corkboard. Then he walked through the glass door and into the lobby. "It's up," he said. "You all can feast your eyes."

Lucas jumped out of the way as the mob moved towards the cast list. I was at the back of the horde and couldn't get close, but Andrew wormed his way up to the front. It didn't take him long to see the list and find me.

"Congrats, girl! We're both pages in the forest of Arden!"

We whooped and gave each other high fives. It wasn't a speaking role, but I was cast. "Our first role in a real college production!" I gave Andrew a hug.

Later, back in my dorm, excitement chased away sleep. My first professional-level play. And this was just the first step.

Another realization kept me awake, and my dizzy eighteen-year-old heart celebrated.

I'd have more opportunity to run into Jed.

Wednesday, September 20, 2000

I did run into him.

On the night of my third rehearsal, Catherine dismissed the actors with non-speaking roles early. I grabbed my bag, knotted the corners of my men's white shirt over my tank top and stretch pants, and started back to the dorms. Then I heard his voice.

"Hey!" I turned, and there he was, sitting in the theater lobby with a book in his lap. "It's Robin, right?"

"Yeah." I walked closer to him.

Jed squinted and stared at my chest. "Then why are the letters

37

'PGM' monogrammed on your shirt?"

I felt my cheeks flush. "I got this shirt at a thrift store. 'PGM' must have been the first owner's initials."

"What do you think his name was?" He crooked his jaw and let his eyes roll towards the ceiling. "Okay. Pacey G-Money. He was a ghetto teen-soap character."

I bounced on my feet. "Nah. He's Pierce Gerber Manchester, handsome European baby food heir."

Jed laughed, a delightful sound echoing through the quiet theater. "I like that. Very sophisticated." He pointed to the shirt. "It suits you better, anyway."

I offered a silent smile in response.

Jed looked away, flipping his book open and shut. It was the screenplay for *Being John Malkovich*. "And, erm, sorry about interrupting your audition monologue. I thought you did well."

"Thank you." I wanted to say something else, but my tongue was paralyzed. My eyes couldn't get over how good-looking he was. Those eyelashes, those lips . . .

Something warm bubbled inside me. "I haven't seen you since that audition. Where have you been?"

"Why? Did you miss me?"

I stepped closer to him just as more actors emerged through the theater doors. "Hey, Robin," Andrew said, "we're all going to hang out at Pete's. You should come."

"Umm . . ."

"You make friends easily, don't you, Robin?" Jed's question was a challenge. It took me a millisecond to decide.

"That's okay," I called out. "Rain check?"

"Sure." They walked away without me.

I turned back to Jed. "Let's go somewhere."

Jed stood, leaving his book on the bench. "I know just the place. Follow me." He led me through the darkened lobby and around the moon-shaped building to a door at the very edge of the theater. We walked into the warm, breezy night.

"Where are we going?" I asked.

"Don't worry, Robin. It'll be fun." He took my hand. A shower of sparks coursed through me. "We're walking to Shelby Pond. It's on the edge of campus, right past the water tower."

"Do you bring all your dates there?"

"Oh." He raised an eyebrow. "So this is a date?"

"Well, we're holding hands."

Jed's voice cracked. "True." He tightened his grip, and we walked in silence for a couple of minutes. "Are you adjusting to college life okay?"

"I suppose," I answered. "I mean, things aren't perfect, but you know, it's all to the good."

"What does 'all to the good' mean?" He smiled. Those dimples lit up the night. "I've never heard that before."

"Oh yeah?" I smiled back, and warmth spread through my chest. "It's something my grandma would say. It means everything will work out in the end, even if it doesn't seem like it."

"All to the good," he repeated. "That's cool."

When we got to the pond, he led me across a bridge that connected one shallow edge of the pond to another. "Have a seat," he said.

We both sat down. "Why here? Is this your favorite spot?"

"Only at night."

I thought he would lunge towards me and we'd start making out, bypassing the chitchat that often comes before initial lip contact. I would let this happen because I'd imagined what his generous mouth would feel like pressed against mine. But he made no move.

"What's it like, being the son of a theater professor?"

Jed coughed, and it was thick and labored. "Terrible. She always tells me to find my motivation and project my emotions."

"For real?"

He let out another cough. "No. That was a joke."

"Do you ever take theater classes or audition for the plays?"

"You ask a lot of questions, you know?"

"Do I?" I chuckled at my own joke, but he stayed silent. "So . . . *do* you ever audition for the plays?"

"No." Another cough. "But I like hanging out with theater students and the professors. They're more fun than most people on campus."

"How so?"

Jed shrugged. "Theater students have real conversations. At most parties, people just hook up. That gets boring."

"Especially if you're not slutty," I quipped.

"Oh, but I am slutty," he responded, all serious. "Aren't you?"

My heart lurched. "No . . . I'm not."

"Huh." He started hacking again. This time it seemed painful, as his body wrenched forward and he struggled for air.

"Are you okay?"

"Fine." He took a deeper breath, sat up straight, and poked me in the thigh. "But I'm disappointed you're not a slut."

His gaze met mine, and I got shivers. "*Is your soul alive? Then let it feed!*" Jed gestured towards the night sky, stars twinkling like scattered diamond dust. "*Leave no balconies where you can climb; Nor ecstasies of body or soul . . .*" His eyes burned into mine. "*You will die, no doubt, but die while living!*"

If he had been trying to unsettle me, he succeeded. "That's some pickup line."

"It's from *Spoon River Anthology*. Edmund Pollard," Jed whispered as though we shared a delicious secret. "You asked me before which one I would choose."

"And you memorized it? Why, if you haven't taken Voice and Movement?"

"I don't know." He blinked a couple of times and swatted away a mosquito. "The instructor, Elaine, told me about the book, and I memorized the poems I like."

"Oh." I let my shoulders slump. The night around us was sultry, attempting to pull Jed and me together. But either Jed wasn't into me, or he wasn't into the night. I straightened back up. "What other ones have you memorized?"

He shook his head. "Nope. Your turn. Which poem did you choose?"

"George Gray."

His face fell. "Ah, a popular choice."

My heart sank. "So I'm typical?"

"I didn't say that. But why did you choose it?"

I let my fingers graze the bridge's railing. "I liked the part about the boat longing for the sea and yet afraid."

"Yeah. That makes sense." Jed tilted his chin. "You've set out on your own for the first time. Of course you identify with it."

I was glad it was dark so he couldn't see me blush. "Says the guy who still lives with his mom." My voice was like sour orange juice, and it sounded harsher than I'd planned.

Perhaps I offended him. He brushed his hair from his eyes and looked out at the water.

Trying to make nice, I spoke in a gentler tone. "What do you like about that soul-alive poem?"

"The message." His focus was straight ahead, not on me. "We're all going to die someday, so we might as well enjoy life while we're here. There's no point in being afraid."

I stretched my legs so they hung off the bridge and over the pond below. "That's easy to say, but fear isn't rational. It's not like we can go to a grocery store and just pick our emotions off a shelf."

Jed didn't miss a beat. "Like ramen noodles, three packs for a dollar?"

"Right." Neither of us talked for a moment, but crickets chirped and a couple of fireflies lit up. Thinking back to his poem, I asked, "Okay, Jed. Do you let your soul feed?"

He ran his fingers through his straight, light brown hair. "I try to. As much as I can, anyway, since I live with my mom."

"Is that why you brought me out here?" I let my voice get raspy and low. "That 'ecstasy of body' thing?"

He scowled. Then, I was this silly girl who didn't get him. "It's 'estasies of body and soul.' And, yeah, I guess." He covered his mouth, seemingly resigned, as his coughing resumed. "I thought you might be fun. But you say you're not a slut, and you're afraid of taking chances."

My jaw dropped. "I never said that."

He rolled his eyes. "You're the boat, longing for the sea and yet afraid." Another cough. This time, his entire body shuddered.

"Are you all right? That cough sounds bad."

He glared at me like I'd said something offensive. "I'm fine. But I won't be the guy who brings you out to water. What if you sink? I'd never forgive myself."

I was no stranger to rejection; most of us have been stung by the time we hit eighteen. Still, it was like being hit in the stomach. "Wow. Okay, thanks. I'll walk home now."

"You're leaving because I won't make out with you?"

I crossed my arms over my chest. "Don't flatter yourself." Christ. He wasn't even offering to walk me home.

"You know what, Jed? I like the poem I chose. Nobody else in class picked it. Everybody else picked short ones."

He rolled his eyes. "Okay . . ."

"Just because I identify with a tied-up boat doesn't make me afraid of taking chances. I'm here, at Hoyt, where I don't know anyone. That's taking a chance. Going off with you tonight was taking a chance. But sometimes chances don't pan out. The waves are choppy and then you're puking overboard."

He didn't flinch. "I'm the waves in this scenario?"

I bit the inside of my cheek. *No, you're the puke.*

"See you around, Jed."

THREE

Saturday, June 2, 2013
6:00 a.m.

The hospital calls. "Your boyfriend is in the ER. Come quick!" When I get there, no one tells me anything. I run from person to person, looking for answers. Panic claws at me, leaving terrible scratch marks inside.

I find a woman in green scrubs and screech, "What happened to Nick Davies?"

"Car crash. He was driving while talking on his cell phone." Her voice and face are both cold. "You should have told him to be more careful."

Out of nowhere, Catherine appears. "We're late," she says. "Jed is waiting."

"Huh? But I have to find Nick."

She pushes me from behind, and we're in the Mayo Clinic, in the corridor that holds Jed's old room. "Get your priorities straight, Robin!"

Catherine makes me march toward Jed.

Startled into consciousness, I glance at the clock. But I don't need to. Every morning for the last few weeks, I've woken up at 6:00 a.m. And I'm never able to go back to sleep.

It's misty when I go for my run. Moisture clings in little droplets to my shirt, arms, and hair. It's sort of peaceful, like I'm running through a Chinese painting. But when I turn the corner and see Flashdance Girl, I'm yanked back to reality.

Today's headband is purple. She's stretching as I approach. Then she jolts up, shoots me a sanctimonious squint, and zips down the sidewalk, overtaking me.

"Showoff!" My winded gasp doesn't reach her ears.

As I round the corner towards home, my anger dissipates. Let her outrun me—I'm an adult with too much going on to care about our stupid rivalry. But deep down, I'm one step away from a pint of ice cream for breakfast or maxing out my credit card at the outlet mall.

7:30 a.m.

After my shower, I get dressed and call Nick. He has work this morning; Saturdays aren't off limits for real estate agents. But maybe I'll catch him before he's knee-deep in property listings and housing contracts.

"What's up?" he asks, rasping a little on the *up*.

I picture him clenching the steering wheel, his phone pressed between his shoulder and ear, driving with terrible posture and little attention to the road. My stomach flips over. "Are you in your car?"

"No, I'm in my office. Why?"

I need the release of scolding him. "Nick, it's not safe to talk on your phone while driving. Please get Bluetooth. All real estate agents should have it."

"Yeah, but I'm not driving." He laughs away my reprimand. "What's going on?"

Pressing my lips together, I wrestle for a response. "Why are you in your office so early? It's barely after 7:00 a.m."

He sighs. "We have an 8:00 a.m. meeting. It's my turn to bring the donuts, and I need to print out a report. Any other questions?"

"Yeah." I look over at my empty bed, with just one side mussed up. "Did you miss me last night?"

"Of course." The temperature of his voice rises a good ten degrees. "What are you wearing?"

"Perfume and an attitude," I sigh. "I'm buck naked in my living room."

There's a measured pause. "Are your curtains open?"

"No."

"Are you really naked?"

"Maybe."

"Okay." His voice scrapes. "I'll be over in fifteen minutes. Stay there, okay?"

"I thought you had a meeting."

"Crap." I hear him tap away at his keyboard. "And I can't miss it. Will you stay naked for the next two hours? I'll be over as soon as the meeting is done.

I go to the mirror and adjust the strap of my tank top. "I'll be cold. Besides, I have things to do."

"Then why did you call?"

"Flashdance Girl terrorized me again. I need you to stroke my ego."

"I'd rather stroke some other part of you."

"We're talking about me right now, Nick."

"Okay." He inhales, and I can hear him thinking. "You're the most dedicated runner I know."

"That's the best you can do?"

"Robin! I have to work. And now I need to erase the naked picture of you from my mind. What do you want from me?"

Standing in front of my mirror, I look into my eyes and cringe. Why does he put up with me?

I wouldn't.

"Sorry," I say, my voice as low and warm as I can make it. "I want you to say we'll see each other tonight."

"Yeah, of course. I'll meet you at eight."

"Okay." I tilt my head down, stare at my bare feet, and try to redeem myself. "Have a good meeting. And I missed you last night too."

7:20 p.m.

I walk into Tavern 33, the restaurant my cousin Jack owns. My eyes adjust to the dim lighting as my skin reconciles with the cool, dry air-conditioning. Maybe I'm underdressed in my semi-sheer blouse and blue denim miniskirt. At least I have on my crocheted beach boots; they'll keep my legs warm.

Jack's office is past the kitchen, so I walk back and knock on his already open door. He sits at his desk and looks up.

"Hey! I forgot you were stopping by." Above Jack's desk, there's a chalkboard with his daily schedule written in a sloppy scrawl. Jack scowls, realizing there's no mention of a meeting with me.

"Don't worry," he says, "I have the backroom reserved for your dad's party." But he reaches for a piece of chalk and writes "Uncle Peter, party room, 6/29" in large letters he can't miss.

"Great. Ian will be happy too." I smile. "How's it going?"

"Great." He clears his throat. "But I'm glad you're here. I've been meaning to call."

"What's going on?" I sit on the folding chair by his desk.

"Lucy's father had a massive stroke. He's alive but in pretty bad shape."

I lurch back. "That's terrible." Lucy, who's married to my cousin Monty, is one of my favorite family members, blood relative or not. "Is Lucy in town now?"

"Yeah, she called the other day at 5:00 a.m., needing me to pick her and the kids up at the airport."

Jack's brow line thickens as he gives me the details: Her father is in the ICU, and they're hoping he won't die. Meanwhile, Monty's far away for work, and Lucy's at the hospital every day, unable to care for their children.

"I've sat with her at the hospital as much as I can, but"—Jack sighs and rubs the top of his balding head—"I know you and Lucy are close. So I was wondering . . ."

"Yeah, of course. I'll help with the kids or sit with her, or"—I wave my hands around— "whatever. I'll call right now."

Jack rolls a pencil under the palm of his hand, up and down, along the contours of his desk. "Just leave a message if she doesn't pick up. They're not supposed to have cell phones in the hospital, so she's hard to reach."

Sure enough, I get her voicemail. "Hey, Lucy, it's Robin. Jack just told me about your dad, and I'm so sorry. I'd love to watch Noah and Abby, or I could visit you at the hospital, so, umm . . ."—I falter, and Jack meets my eyes with a shrug—"so call when you can. I'm thinking about you."

Ending the call, I notice the time on my cell phone. "I should go find Ian." I get up. "Are you joining us?"

"Yeah, but wait a second, okay?"

"What?"

Jack looks at me with a solemn face. "How's the play going?"

"Fine," I squeak. It must sound like a lie. "Why?"

"Well, I ran into Isobel the other day. She mentioned Jed's play, and with everything that happened, I'm curious how you're handling it." He pauses and twitches his nose. "Isobel is worried about you."

I make a conscious choice not to cringe. "Nope. I'm good."

"But have you told Nick that Jed wrote the play? Have you told him about Jed at all?"

I stare at Jack. Time to change the subject. "When did you and Isobel become such good friends?"

Jack gazes at his pencil and presses his thumb into its dull edge. "Who says we're good friends?"

"Okay." Nodding, I let my gaze drift toward the ceiling. "You ran into her and had an in-depth conversation about my life?"

He shrugs. "You're what we have in common."

The pieces of the puzzle fit together. Jack met Isobel last fall, when he stayed with me after his marriage fell apart. She was up early the other day, and she's never up early. It would have been around the time Jack left to get Lucy at the airport.

I give him my police interrogator stare. "You and Isobel are dating, aren't you?"

Jack throws his pencil in the air, watches it somersault above his head, and catches it, smiling at his party trick. "If you know so much, why do you have to ask?"

"Why can't you tell me what's going on between you and Isobel?"

He shoves the pencil back in among its friends, into a coffee mug with a picture of blue sunglasses and "Cool Dad" painted in black. "When there's something to tell, you'll be the first to know."

"But—"

"Okay." He points his finger at me. "This conversation was supposed to be about you. Maybe it's time to find Ian?"

My defenses sag as our gazes bump into each other.

"Fine," I say. "You'll be out soon?"

"Yeah." Jack returns to his normal self. "Let me finish up, and I'll be right out."

I leave his office and go find Ian, ruminating on all the secrets we all keep.

9:30 p.m.

Nick shows up at the tail end of my meeting with Jack and Ian. We all sit in a booth toward the back, adjacent to the stage, where bands can play. Nick's arm is slung over my shoulder, keeping me warm, while the four of us joke and drink beer.

"Did we ever tell you about when Robbie protested outside of Red Lobster?" Ian, his cheeks rosy from alcohol and laughter, is gleeful.

Nick shakes his head. "I haven't heard this one."

I cover my face with my hands. "Not this story again," I groan.

Ian takes a swig before starting in. "She was horrified when she found out the lobsters are picked from a tank and boiled alive. So she made a picket sign that said 'Don't murder your *diner,*' and she stood outside the Red Lobster for hours, hoping a news crew would come along. Nobody had the heart to tell her that she'd misspelled *dinner.*"

Nick, Jack and Ian all share a deep belly laugh at my expense.

"I was nine! It was an easy mistake!"

"Did a news crew ever come?" Nick asks.

48

"No," I say.

"But you were looking for your fifteen minutes of fame, huh?"

I push Nick in the shoulder, offended at his question. "I was worried about the lobsters!"

Ian looks at his watch. "I hate to say it, but I should go. I promised Eddie I'd be home by
ten."

"Oh, no." My voice is soaked in sarcasm. "Don't go home to your husband. Stay and tell more embarrassing stories about me."

Ian plops down a twenty and winks. "That's what big brothers do, Robbie."

"Put that away." Jack grabs the twenty and pushes it back to Ian.

Ian's face twists with indignation. "You don't always have to cover us just because you own the place.

"Then come over and help me fix my closet." Jack stretches in his seat. "It's falling apart."

"You want to put me back in the closet?"

It takes Jack a minute for the joke to sink in, and then they both laugh. As they do, Nick grabs my hand and whispers in my ear. "You're coming over, right?"

I nod and squeeze his hand back.

10:00 p.m.

Nick fetches me a glass of water from the kitchen. "Thanks for staying here," he says. "I know you prefer your place."

"No problem." I accept the water glass and take a long sip.

"You won't miss going for your morning run?"

"Flashdance Girl will be bummed that I'm not around to snarl at. But tomorrow's Sunday." I sigh and snoop through his living room. It's been a while since I've been here. "I take Sunday mornings off and do a mile-long swim in the afternoon."

"That's not much of a break." Nick leans against an armrest and watches me look around.

I shrug one shoulder. "I don't swim fast, so it's like a break." Gesturing to a large white envelope, I ask, "What's in here?"

Nick moans. "Oh God! Don't look at that."

I laugh. "Well, now I sort of have to." I reach inside the envelope and pull out some contact sheets. Every image shows Nick smiling and wearing a necktie.

"They're my real estate agent headshots. I was required to get them done."

"But you look so good!" I beam at him and point to my favorite. "I like this one. Your eyes have that glint. I would buy a house from this guy."

Nick steps towards me and takes the headshots from me. "I look like a douche in every single shot."

"Why would you say that?"

"Because it's true. I'm okay with selling houses, but with selling myself?" His shoulders sag, and his eyes are downcast. "Let's talk about something else."

"Sure . . ." I keep poking around. Then I spot some handwritten sheet music on his piano. "Is this what you played me the other night?"

Nick shakes his head in disagreement. "It's something new. On Thursday, when you were at rehearsal, Dave and I worked on this together."

"Will you play it for me now?"

Nick gives me his crooked smile and looks at his feet. "Nah. It's not ready yet."

"But I won't judge."

Nick takes my water and places it atop the piano. Then he wraps his arms around me and whispers in my ear. "I'll hum it for you instead." As he does, we sway together to the rhythm.

But the joke's on me. He sings the melody to *Oops! . . . I Did it Again*, so I push him away. "Does Britney Spears know you've taken her song?"

"I had to choose something you'd recognize." He lets out a self-satisfied chuckle. "Besides, you know what they say: 'Talent imitates. Genius steals.'"

I push his shoulder. "That was Oscar Wilde, and it's 'Talent *borrows*, genius steals.'"

Nick steps in closer, so we're almost eye-to-eye. "Aren't you a smarty-pants!"

"Well, if my theater degree couldn't teach me to quote Oscar Wilde, then what was it worth?"

As Nick's smile melts across his face, I picture us years from now, still finding joy in the fault lines of our personalities.

I tug at the frayed collar of his T-shirt. "When do I get to hear your song?"

"Soon. Dave and I are still working on it." He places his hands on the small of my back.

"We were thinking of putting together several songs and finding some place to perform them."

I pull away. "You mean like you're starting a band?"

"I guess. Wanna be a groupie?" I chuckle, and he takes that as a yes. "I mean, it's a while before we're ready." He sounds so eager, speaking in a tone he never uses for real estate. "Do you think your cousin might let us perform at his restaurant?"

"Jack?"

Nick narrows his eyes and smirks. "Do any of your other cousins own restaurants?"

"Not that I know of."

"Are you okay? You seem weird." Nick studies my face, so I remove any sign of negative emotions from it.

"I'm fine," I say while kissing him.

It's sort of true, but my mind drifts back to months ago, another time I wasn't upfront with Nick.

• • •

It was Sunday afternoon, a few days after our *Flashdance/Rocky* movie marathon. We were on my couch, me reading the paper and him doing the crossword. I was cozy in my oversized sweatshirt, flannel pants and knee socks, confident my sloppiness wouldn't turn him off.

"What's a seven-letter word for love?" Nick gripped the pencil between his teeth. "Passion?"

He examined the puzzle and shook his head. "No. It has a "d" in it."

"Are you sure?"

"Positive." He took the pencil out of his mouth and tapped it against his blue-jean-clad thigh. It was sleeting outside, but Nick wore jeans and his gray T-shirt. When I reached underneath to stroke his belly, his skin was warm.

"Hey!" he laughed. "Focus."

"What?" I let the Variety section fall to the floor and climbed into his lap. "It's research."

He kissed me, but after a couple of seconds, he needed his mouth to speak. "Maybe they mean it as a verb."

"Huh?"

"Passion is a synonym for love, but maybe they mean 'to love,' you know?"

"Umm . . ." I understood the difference between nouns and verbs, but it was Sunday, and thus, my brain's day off.

Nick's face lit up. "Adulate!" He wrote the letters into the little boxes, his arms still resting against my legs as he filled the crossword in.

"I adulate you?" I laughed. "Who ever says that?"

"I do," Nick joked. "All the time, to anyone who will listen."

It had been a few days since we'd each used the "l" word for the first time, and neither of us had repeated it since.

"Oh yeah? Who else have you adulated, Nick?"

Nick looked up from the crossword puzzle, his eyebrows raised at the somber tone of my question.

"I was just kidding." His gentle voice penetrated right through my chest cavity.

"But have you ever been in love before?"

Again, he tapped his pencil against his thigh and watched the motion. "No." Then he raised his gaze to my eyes. "Not until you."

Nick put the pencil and crossword puzzle down, and reaching for me, he cupped my face in his hands. He gave me a kiss that required all of his focus, and the rest of the world dissolved around us. After he pulled away, we sat there. The sleet pelted against the window. We memorized each other's breathing and this moment.

He swallowed. "It's okay if you can't say the same," he said.

"Wh . . . what?" Confused, I stuttered. Two days ago, I *had* said the same, and that had been a huge deal for me. "No, no, I can say the same. I haven't felt this way in a long—"

"No, I mean, it's okay if you've been in love before."

I stopped, paralyzed, dishonesty floating between us like a balloon waiting to pop.

"I, um . . . "

Nick's crooked smile conceded his acceptance. "I know you've dated a lot of guys."

"I wouldn't say a lot."

"Okay," he continued. "Then you've dated a few, and I'm sure you've been in love with some of them. For whatever reason, those relationships ended, and here we are."

"One," I stated, and Nick cocked his head in question. "I've been in love with one other guy, and yes, it ended, but—"

Nick held up his hands to silence me. "Wait, stop; don't tell me." He sighed. "You'll be surprised to hear this because I'm hot and perfect and all." His laugh was self-deprecating and sarcastic. "But I can also be jealous and insecure. I'd rather not know."

I looked down.

"Robin?" Nick stroked my arm. "Is that okay? Are you upset?"

Upset? No. But at some point, I would need to tell him about Jed. What's a four-lettered word for *complicated*?

"Of course not. Come here." I held Nick and felt the beat of his heart and the rise and fall of his chest, achingly aware that one day they would slow down and then finally stop.

. . .

Now I hold him again, on this summer night that's stretched out like the promise of a heat wave.

"You're sure you're okay?" he asks. "You seem sort of weird."

I can hear the vulgar wheeze of my conscience; it's like a decompressed whoopee cushion. What's my problem? I'm thrilled that Nick is pursuing music, so it's not that. But I can't open up to him the way he opens up to me.

"I think it's great that you and Dave are playing music together," I tell him. "Whenever you're ready, let me know, and I'll talk to Jack."

And before he can try to get me to talk more, I kiss him—hard. That will distract him.

Sunday, June 23, 2013
6:00 a.m.

I swim in the clear, sparkling ocean. It's so warm, and I never need to come up for air. "When did I learn to breathe underwater?" I ask myself. Maybe I've always been able to, and I just didn't realize.

There's a dark form up ahead, with flailing arms and legs. Jed. My strokes are swift and strong, but not enough. By the time I catch up to him, he's drowned. Jed could never breathe right—neither underwater nor on land. How could I be so selfish as not to save him?

Unshed tears congregate in my lungs, and then I'm drowning too.

I awaken, gasping for breath.

"What's wrong?" Nick mumbles, still sleepy.

My chest is pounding, and something more—I'm smothered with guilt. "Nothing's wrong," I pat his shoulder. "I had a weird dream. Go back to sleep."

"Come here," he murmurs and tries to snuggle. I push him away. "Sorry. But I need some water." I get out of bed and go to the bathroom, where I have to refill my glass three times, and even then, I'm still thirsty.

When I get back to bed, Nick is asleep, so I go to his living room and turn on the TV. TBS is playing *She's All That*, so I purge my psyche by watching uber-cute actors with three names. It sort of works, and I begin to nod off during the commercials. By 7:30 a.m., I've calmed down enough to climb back into bed, and when Nick wakes, he has no memory of me ever getting up.

9:30 a.m.

"Do you want your pancakes with or without chocolate chips?"

I look up from the newspaper. Nick stands at his uncluttered kitchen counter, holding a large mixing bowl. I roll my eyes. "Do you even have to ask?"

He smiles and turns to the freezer, which is where he keeps the chocolate chips. With his back to me, I get a nice view. His blue boxers save him from nakedness, and I marvel at my luck.

He's barefoot and bare-chested, making me chocolate chip pancakes.

Nick retrieves the chocolate chips and pours some into the bowl. "What's your day like today?"

I spread the Sunday paper out on the kitchen table and sit cross-legged on the white wooden chair. "I'm dropping off my outfit for the St. Jude's silent auction. That's about it."

"Oh yeah, that's tomorrow!" Nick's sleepy face registers surprise. "Are you still able to come?"

A children's hospital in Des Moines has their annual fundraiser tomorrow night, and Nick's office bought a table. When I heard about it, I offered to donate an outfit for the silent auction, and Nick insisted I come with him to the event.

"I have to be at rehearsal at eight," I tell him. "Maybe I can push it to 8:30 p.m. But either way, I can only come for an hour or two."

"Okay. Then let's meet there." Nick tilts the handle of the frying pan up, spreading the oil around, before he drops in the pancake batter. "Hey, I've been meaning to tell you, there's a great bungalow for sale on Woodland Avenue. Three bedrooms, two baths, and a huge basement you could use as a studio. We should think about it."

I rub behind my ear with long, slow strokes. "You mean, should we think about buying a house together? Since when?"

Nick's back is to me, but he shrugs with a forced nonchalance. "Do you realize how much money we both waste every month on rent? If we share a mortgage, our bills will go down, and we'll build equity."

"We'll build equity? The three most romantic words ever spoken." I laugh, hoping he'll laugh too.

My cell phone rings and I grab it. "It's Lucy," I tell him and press answer.

Lucy and I talk for a couple of minutes and agree to meet up later. I can tell Nick is listening while he flips pancakes, and when I get off the phone, I answer his questions before he asks them.

"Lucy's married to my cousin Monty, who you haven't met yet. They live in Seattle."

"But she's from here too?"

"Yeah." I roll my head around and stretch. Even though I've been up for hours, I'm still half asleep. "Lucy and Monty met in high school, but they didn't fall in love until years later. Now her dad's had a stroke and Monty's in Africa for work, so we're all looking out for her."

Nick uses his spatula to maneuver the pancakes, and the aroma of doughy, fried goodness fills the kitchen, making my stomach grumble. "That's tough. How's her dad doing?"

"Not good, I guess."

He shakes his head. "I feel for her. There's nothing worse than watching your parents die slowly."

I look at him. Biting his bottom lip, he flips the pancakes onto a plate. Then he turns, comes towards me, and puts the plate down beside the newspaper. "Do you want syrup?" he asks. "Or are the chocolate chips enough sugar for you?"

I'm still just gazing at him.

"What?" he asks.

"You never told me what it was like, with your mom at the end."

He shrugs and turns back to the stove. "There's not much to tell. It sucked. Of course it sucked. But you do what you have to do."

I look down. "Sorry. I didn't mean to upset you."

"You didn't." He throws me a smile before he pours more pancake batter. "It's fine." Now the corners of his mouth sag, and he stares at the frying pan. "You know, she was home, diminishing for weeks before she died. I stayed by her as much as I could. But one day I went out to school so I could pick up my diploma. I wanted the chance to show it to her, to make her proud. Driving home, I was hungry, and I hadn't felt hungry in weeks. So, I stopped at Taco John's for a root beer and Potato Oles, and I ate them while I drove. Then, when I got home . . ." He rubs at his eye. "Well, if I hadn't stopped for food, I would have been there when she died. But that's not how it turned out. I got home, and my mom . . ."— his voice cracks—"my mom was dead, and I'd lost the chance to say goodbye." He flips the pancakes over. "And I'll never be able to stomach root beer and Potato Oles again."

Nick turns off the stove and tops the pile of pancakes with the final one. When he shudders, I long to fill the hollowness inside him.

"I'm so sorry."

He gives me a sad little laugh. "Don't be. Potato Oles are terrible for you."

"You know what I mean." I get up. He's so exposed, baring his soul in his underwear. But when I wrap myself around him, I'm surprised by his warmth and sturdiness. He sort of hugs me back.

"You're going to make me burn my pancakes."

"You turned the stove off." I hug him harder. *Tell him*, I say to myself, *tell him you understand what it's like watching someone you love slowly die.*

Nick pulls away, and when he sees my face, he uses his thumb to wipe my tears. "Hey," he whispers. "Robin, it's okay. Bad things happen. We know that. But good things happen too. Like right now, this moment is really, really good."

His smile glows like sunlight, and it's just as warm. I stroke his cheek. "Yeah, this moment is great."

I kiss him, choosing love over honesty, which is a choice nobody should ever have to make.

1:30 p.m.

When Lucy called, she asked about using a guest pass at my health club. "My muscles are starting to atrophy," she said on the phone. "Would you mind taking me for a workout?"

So I pick her up at Aunt Natalie's house, with an extra swimsuit in my bag. I'm sure it's way too big, but it will do. On the drive, Lucy is quiet, staring forward, expressionless; her hair is pulled back, pinching her forehead and making her eyelids droop.

"How's your dad?" I ask.

Lucy's eyes flit around, not resting on any one place. "His stroke was massive. It's going to be a long haul. But it looks like he'll pull through."

What do I say? I swallow a "that's great" because it's not great. It's not even approaching great, although there is comfort that he's still alive. At least I think there is.

"When's Monty getting back?" I ask.

Lucy closes her eyes, and her head rests against the seat back. "I've only talked to him once, when I was half asleep. With the time difference, it's hard to get a hold of each other. Plus, neither of us can get phone reception. It's sort of hopeless."

"Oh." What it would be like having a family crisis while your husband is unreachable, thousands of miles away? "That's too bad," I say, making the understatement of the year.

"Yeah," she replies, "but your family—Monty's family—is great. You all have been so supportive."

"Well, of course. We're your family now too."

At the gym, Lucy swims with the vigor I reserve for weekdays. Her petite form moves faster than my elongated one. It's as if she's on a mission to splash away all her negative thoughts. I tell myself to chill, to maintain a slower pace. But I wind up competing with an oblivious partner, like she's a nicer, more benign version of Flashdance Girl. Meanwhile, I improve my time, even though it wasn't my goal.

I finish my mile, get out of the pool and sit in the vacant hot tub. Lucy keeps swimming. I watch until she gets out and walks, limp-limbed, over to me. She sits down in the steaming pool and wrings out her dripping hair. My too-large swimming suit puckers and inflates around her, as bubbles push air around. But she doesn't seem to care.

"That felt great," she says, smiling for the first time. "Thank you so much. I needed that."

"You swam for an hour! That's impressive."

"What time is it?" She looks around for a clock and sees one on the opposite wall. "I guess I have a few minutes to relax." Wiping chlorine from her eyes, Lucy rolls her shoulders back. "I have to be at the hospital again this evening so my mom can go home and rest. I'm worried about her. She seems lost."

"Yeah, it must be hard," I respond.

My mother died young, and my father never remarried. I've had no model for what two people share—their children sleeping in another room while they whisper about fears, bills, and the tedium of growing old.

Lucy rolls her shoulders again and stretches her neck. "They've been together for almost fifty years. What's she going to do now?

I don't want her entire life to be about taking care of him." She wipes her cheek, and I can't tell if it's a tear she's swatting or just pool water.

"I can't even imagine that level of commitment."

Lucy presses a finger to her temple, peering at me. "What about Nick? Or aren't you two that serious yet?"

It's like my head is filled with helium, so I get up and sit on the edge of the hot tub, with just my feet submerged. "I love Nick. But just this morning, he's talking about buying a house together."

"And you're not ready?" Lucy asks.

"That's not it. I'm not good at intimacy. What if there are parts of me I can't share?"

Lucy's face billows with longing. Or maybe I'm projecting.

"I'm not sure," she says, "but I believe in you." She tilts her head and reaches out to touch my hand. "There's no rush, Robin. Don't worry if you need more time."

"That's not what I'm worried about," I tell her.

"Oh. What are you worried about?"

I raise my foot and spread my toes. The bright pink nail polish from my last pedicure has chipped. "I didn't bring you here to talk about me."

"It's fine. I could use the distraction." She sits on the edge of the hot tub and offers me a smile full of undeserved sympathy.

I accept it nonetheless. "I need to tell Nick something, but I don't know how."

FOUR

Thursday, September 21, 2000

During rehearsal for *As You Like It*, I was on the lookout for Jed, but he didn't appear. We were on break when this sophomore girl, Miranda, sat across from me.

"You left with Jed Reardon last night?"

Her tone carried the hint of accusation, and I leaned away.

"Word travels fast," I said. "It wasn't any big deal. We walked down to the pond, talked for a while. That's it."

She nodded like we shared some big secret. "Sure," she bubbled. "That's what all the girls say."

"No, really."

"Oh, don't lie," Miranda teased. "I've been with him before. Last fall, we went down to the pond. Then I took him back to my room. He's hot and sort of forbidden. You know, since he's Catherine's son."

I watched her stretch, trying to ignore the uncomfortable twist in my stomach. The image of Jed with Miranda was hard to swallow. It was clear she had come from dance class because she wore a leotard and tights, and she had beautiful feet. She also had thin legs, big boobs, and a head of gorgeous, thick red hair. Like Ariel in *The Little Mermaid*, but without the fish tail.

No wonder Jed was attracted to her.

She kept talking. "You should be proud. You're his first conquest in a while. Last year, his health got bad, so he had to stop being a man-whore."

"What was wrong with his health?"

She raised both eyebrows. "He didn't tell you? With me, it was the first thing out of his mouth." Legs stretched out, she waved her hands as she spoke. "He uses the 'sexy dying guy' thing to its full advantage." She shrugged. "Can't blame him. There are few perks to having cystic fibrosis."

Cystic fibrosis.

I knew very little about it, except that it was something bad. My heart sank all the way to my pelvis. All that coughing, and I was too self-involved to notice. No wonder he'd discarded me.

That night after rehearsal, I looked up cystic fibrosis in my Health Psychology textbook.

Adolescents face many challenges during the formative years, including physical and social changes. These obstacles are exacerbated when a youth is faced with a chronic illness like cystic fibrosis, which can lead to thrill-seeking behaviors that extend beyond the norm. Healthy teenagers often have anxieties about sexual maturity and body image that may be exaggerated by a chronic illness. Another worry for youths with a chronic illness is how their futures will be affected by their disease—finishing school, starting a career, pursuing romantic relationships, and even starting a family are all questions rather than attainable goals. Unfortunately, adolescents with cystic fibrosis report having fewer friends and/or relationships with people of the opposite sex, and may require a great deal of reassurance and sensitive exploration of these issues.

I slammed my book shut. One paragraph in my freshman health psychology book was not enough to analyze Jed. I scolded my brain as it leaped and cartwheeled with all its conclusions. But then there was the term "chronic" rather than "terminal."

Miranda said he was dying, but was he?

After turning on my computer, I did an internet search. I learned it was a hereditary disease involving a lot of fluid in your lungs. People with cystic fibrosis often get pneumonia and are used to hospital visits. They live to be around thirty.

Jed was probably nineteen.

Tuesday, September 26, 2000

The next time I ran into Jed was on my way to health psychology class. My backpack slid off my shoulders, its straps slick against my damp trench coat, which was like Audrey Hepburn's in *Breakfast at Tiffany's*. It was the first cool fall day, and as I stopped to pull my backpack up and onto my shoulders, all I could think about was getting to the lecture hall and getting dry.

But then he was walking towards me. He didn't wear a jacket. He held neither a book nor a bag; it was just Jed in his jeans and soaked T-shirt, wet hair plastered to his forehead.

"Hi!" he said. "So you made it back to your dorm okay the other night."

"Yeah." I nodded. Then my mouth started working faster than my brain. "Miranda Hayes told me that you took her down to the pond last year. That you take girls there all the time. Do you always use that poem to get laid?"

He raised one eyebrow and smiled. "You don't waste time with chit-chat, do you?"

I shrugged. "Not when it's raining. Besides, I hear you don't waste time either."

He blinked and reared back like I'd slapped him. Those powerful blue eyes infiltrated me again, and I ordered my heart to stop beating so fast.

"No," he said in a low voice. "I don't waste time." He cleared his throat and spoke louder. "So Miranda told you all about me, then?"

I tilted my chin. "She just sat down and started talking. I didn't know it was some big secret."

"No, no. It's not." He grinned and those dimples appeared. "But to answer your question, yes, I use the poem all the time. First, I explain my illness, and I follow with those lines about living life to the fullest. By then, they're inviting me back to their dorm room."

"Okay then." I sounded like a life insurance salesman. "Thanks for being so upfront." I started to walk away, but he grabbed my arm.

"Wait a second. I have a favor to ask."

"Seriously?"

"Yeah, seriously." He shook some raindrops from his head. "Come on. What did I do that was so awful? Sure, I started to hit on you, and I changed my mind. I was trying to be a nice guy."

"Your nice guy impression needs work."

He laughed. "Fine. Okay, you're right. But please, help me out?"

I shrank underneath my raincoat and pulled on my hood. "What do you need?"

"A towel and maybe some dry clothes."

"Why are you out in the rain?"

"I stayed over at this girl's room last night, but she kicked me out before her boyfriend could find me. I haven't had time to clear my lungs, and the rain is bad for me." Jed coughed and blinked away the raindrops clinging to his lashes. "Please?"

I puckered my forehead. "I was on my way to health psychology."

"I took that course last year. I still have my notes, and I'll give them to you." The rain started to fall harder. "Please?" He coughed more, and his ribs strained against his wet T-shirt.

Damn cystic fibrosis. What kind of monster could say no?

"Fine," I told him. "Follow me."

I took him to my dorm, and as we walked, there was no hand-holding or giddiness. Just an effort to escape the weather. Once we were in my room, I gave him a towel and a pair of navy blue sweatpants.

"These should fit," I said. "We're about the same height."

"Thanks." He took off his wet T-shirt and jeans and slid the sweatpants on. They fit him fine.

"I can run these down to the dryer for you." I picked up his wet clothes and made for the door.

"Aren't you going to change into something dry?" He stood in the middle of my room, bare-chested and unselfconscious. I shivered, but not because I was cold.

"Yeah, I'm going to change." I grabbed a black sweatshirt and some waffle weave long underwear. Stopping to change in the girl's bathroom, I ran down to the laundry room, where I put all our clothes in the dryer. Except for my green velvet blazer; it would have to air-dry.

Upstairs, I found Jed sitting on the edge of my bed, coughing and awkwardly hitting himself on the back. "What are you doing?" I asked.

"Airway clearance. I do it every morning to get the mucus out of my lungs." He smacked himself on the back again as he coughed some more. Then he closed his eyes in frustration. "I need my meds for it to work right, and it's hard to do this to myself." More coughing. More smacking. "My mom will kill me. If I don't just die on my own, that is." He took a break from the coughing and smacking and looked at me. "I'm sorry. Last night, I was supposed to meet my mom after rehearsal for a ride home, but I didn't, and—" He coughed again. "I've got no excuse. I shouldn't impose on you like this. As soon as my clothes are dry, I'll go."

I draped my damp blazer over the back of my desk chair. "Can I help?"

Somehow, even through his gagging, Jed managed an ironic lip twitch. "Well, if you're still pissed, here's your chance to literally beat the crap out of me."

It was an intriguing proposition. "Okay. What do I do?"

He got off the bed, put his knees on the floor and raised his butt in the air so that his head and chest tilted downwards. "Start pounding my back. Hitting underneath my shoulder blades is especially helpful."

I did as told. He was shirtless, so the skin on my hands made direct contact with the skin on his back. And he had a nice back. But his coughing was horrendous, like choking on Jell-O. Soon, my fists made ugly red marks up and down his spine. The more marks I made, the easier he could breathe. Yet the task of hitting him took on a life of its own.

"You can hit me harder," he rasped. "Don't be gentle."

"Don't worry, I won't." I thought about the vocal warm-up every day in Voice and Movement—how committed we were during the chanting and yoga stretches. With each punch, I added more vigor, as if commenting on all the things I didn't want or need.

"You're good at this," Jed cried. "Keep going."

"I'm not hurting you?"

He coughed. Something thick and moist rolled out of him and into a tissue I'd given him. "Nope. It's helping."

I continued to hit him, hard, for at least ten more minutes. "Is this another part of your pickup routine?" I asked. "If so, you're into some kinky stuff."

He laughed and coughed at the same time. "Would you believe you're special? That you're the first girl that I've ever done airway clearance with?"

I hit him smack in the lower back. "Nope."

Jed wheezed out a chuckle. "Okay. What if I told you that you're not the first, but you're the best?"

Pound, pound, pound. "That I would believe."

Then my lock turned, and the door opened wide. April stood there, jaw dropped, staring, while I hit Jed. Jed still had his butt in the air, but he turned his head toward my long-lost roommate. "Oh, hello," he said. "Do you live here too?"

"Uh, yeah."

I bolted up. Jed lowered his behind and raised the rest of his body so that he was sitting cross-legged on the floor. "Nice to meet you." He was still shirtless. "I'm Jed, a friend of Robin's."

April raised her eyebrows. "Okay. Sorry to interrupt . . ."

"We were just hanging out," I said.

"Right. Um, if you want privacy, maybe put a sock on the door-knob from now on? That way, I won't walk in on you guys while you're . . . hanging out?"

"Oh! Sure." I flipped my hair over my shoulder. "I can do that. Will you be living here now?"

"I'll stop in from time to time. I mean"—she scrunched up her face—"I'm paying rent. So I was hoping to get some studying done."

Jed smiled. "No problem." He turned to me. "Do you think my clothes might be dry?"

"We can go check. Nice seeing you, April." I grabbed my keys, Jed and I both put on our soggy shoes, and we left April alone to study.

"The laundry room is this way."

I led the way downstairs, and as Jed followed, he continued to cough and chuckle. The chuckling gained in intensity, so by the time we were downstairs, his laughter was frantic and out of control.

"What did she think we were doing?" No exaggeration. He was gasping for air.

"She thought I was hitting your bare back while you waved your butt around."

Jed laughed some more, loud enough to make the girl folding laundry on the far side of the room give us the evil eye.

I used an exaggerated whisper. "You're helping me make all sorts of friends this morning. And you made me skip my class."

Jed swallowed his giggles and talked low enough to match my tone. "Sorry," he said, his blue eyes dancing. "But at least I won't die. Probably not today, anyhow."

"Don't pull the dying crap on me." I squinted at him, and my jaw set. "You say that stuff to get girls to sleep with you. We've already determined I won't do that, so enough."

"Again, I'm sorry." He looked at me, his lips parted and his head back. What would happen if he came closer and took me in his arms? If I grasped his bare shoulders and we kissed?

I stepped away.

"Your dryer is over here. Let's see if your clothes are done." I opened the dryer door and examined his shirt and pants. They were still a little damp, but much better than they'd been. "I don't know. You might want to wait."

He glanced at the clock. "There's a bus in ten minutes. The

sooner I get home and take my meds, the better." He coughed as he moved past me, grabbed his shirt and put it on, and without pretense, pulled off the sweatpants I lent him. His boxers were plain white. I looked away as he put on his jeans.

"Do you have bus fare? And where is your house key?"

He shook his head, as if to scold. "Didn't you check my jean pockets before you threw them in the dryer?" He reached in and pulled out a single key, unattached to any sort of chain, and a one-dollar bill. "I'll be fine." He looked around. "But how do I get out of here?"

I picked my sweatpants up off the floor. "I'll show you out."

He followed me back upstairs, and I led him to the front doors. "Do you know how to get to the bus stop from here?"

Jed brushed his hair off his forehead and grinned. "Yeah. I'll be okay now." Then, for the first time ever, he acted shy. He shifted his weight, and his eyes darted around the room. "Thank you, Robin. I owe you."

"Don't worry about it," I said.

"No, let me repay you. Like if you want to grab dinner some-time . . ."

"It's not necessary." I rolled my shoulders back, anxious for him to go. "Don't you need to catch your bus?"

He blinked a couple of times and pressed his lips together, like he was about to smile but wasn't happy enough to manage it. "See you around, then."

"Bye."

He was gone.

Monday, October 2, 2000

I sat in the audience during rehearsal, watching Rosalind, Touchstone, and Celia as they traveled through the Forest of Arden. In a few minutes, I'd be on stage, and Jacques would recite his famous "All the World's a Stage" speech. For now, I scrunched down in my seat, my legs propped up on the chair in front of me, wishing I was someplace else.

From two rows behind, I heard coughing. Jed sat down next to a freshman girl who, like me, was cast as a page in the Forest of Arden. "Hey," he said, "you're Amanda, right?"

"Yeah," she replied.

"I'm Jed."

"I know." Amanda giggled.

Jed lowered his voice by an inch. "I know somebody who likes you."

"Really?" she gushed. "Who?"

He coughed. "I'd tell you, but I'm too shy."

I almost groaned in disgust. That old pickup line?

It took Amanda a moment. "Ahh, don't be shy. You're too cute for that."

More coughing, more giggling.

"What are you doing after rehearsal?" Jed asked. "Do you want to hang out?"

Why didn't he straight up ask her to have sex with him? Why be coy? I lowered my feet and straightened my posture. It was hard not to turn around and glare with condemnation. But if I did that, he'd think I cared.

"Sure," said Amanda. "Let's hang out."

They discussed logistics until Catherine called everyone onto the stage for the next scene. Using all my focus, I listened to Jacques' speech as if hearing it for the first time. Moving around the stage, I tried to stay in character, even though I didn't have a name, lines, or anything distinguishing me from the fake trees in the scenery.

Still, I felt Jed's gaze. During a two-second break, I succumbed to temptation and looked at him. Sure enough, those piercing blues met mine. And he smiled.

I looked over at Amanda and gave him the judgmental head-shake that had been vibrating inside my brain for the last hour. Jed

69

smiled again and shrugged.

"Whatever," I mouthed.

He mouthed something back, maybe "Don't be jealous" or perhaps "Can't be callous."

Same difference.

Wednesday, October 4, 2000

Rehearsal got out late after a long day. I had a health psychology test to study for and costumes to sketch for my technical theater class. I grabbed my long, belted blue cardigan, putting it on over my print blouse and my tight men's Levis. It was cold, and I needed the sweater for my walk home.

"Have a good night, Robin."

Lucas, the stage manager, flipped through his script and notebook as I made my way up the aisle. He was always the last to leave. I liked how responsible he was and how he wore his headphones around his neck whenever he wasn't using them. When he was stressed, he ran his fingers through his hair, making it stick up a little. His nose was the biggest part of his face. It gave him character, and this imperfection was appealing—a bit of salt with sugar.

"Thanks, you too," I said.

"Hey. Some of us are going for coffee, if you want to stick around."

This was a surprise. Lucas was a junior, and he hung out with all the stars of the theater department, the chosen ones who got big parts or designed the sets or costumes. Going for coffee with them would be intimidating, but my stock would go up.

I looked at the clock on the wall. "I wish I could, but I still have a ton of studying to do."

He gave me a devilish smirk. "You're a good girl, huh?"

His question spurred the beginning of a headache. "I've been told that I am."

We said goodbye. Once outside, my feet dragged on the walk home. My dorm loitered in the distance, sterile and humdrum. Any hellos from my floor-mates would be sterile and humdrum too. I was to blame; balancing my drive to succeed with the need for friends didn't come easy.

I longed for someone to read my expressions and moods like a headline. Who'd understand my story without laboring over the fine print?

Thursday, October 26, 2000

Time picked up. Soon, rehearsals were over, and the performances began. On opening night, we got a standing ovation. After the applause faded away, I ran downstairs to change out of my page costume and wipe stage makeup from my face. Andrew found me in the green room.

"I got us a ride to the party," he said. "Miranda said she has room."

Miranda, Jed's mermaid-like former conquest, stood behind Andrew, coat on and car keys clutched. "Are you ready?" she asked.

"Sure," I said. "Thank you."

After all, if I never accepted rides from Jed's past hook-ups, I would stay on campus most of the time.

The cast party was at Lucas's apartment. People chipped in to rent a karaoke machine and to get a keg. When Miranda, Andrew, and I walked in, drunken singing of show tunes and power ballads bounced and shook the walls. After Andrew and I performed "I've Got You, Babe," I went to the kitchen, hoping for a drink of water and a bag of Doritos. Then I saw that the back door was ajar.

Jed stood on the porch, alternately breathing and coughing. He didn't have a beer, just a bottle of water that rested against the railing. I stood next to him. "Hey. What are you doing out here all by yourself?"

"Too smoky in there. I need a break."

"Yeah . . ." It was a cool night; fall was resigning to winter. Hugging myself, I pulled on the sleeves of my belted sweater, worn over a black T-shirt and stretch pants. My beatnik look.

"What'd you think of the play?"

He coughed so he could speak. "You were brilliant."

"Right."

"No, really."

"I'm pretty much the scenery, Jed."

He shook his head. "That's not true. During Jacques' 'All the world's a stage' speech, you have this great look on your face. I love how you respond to him."

"Why?"

Jed yanked the strings of his gray hoodie, which was attached to a denim jacket. "Because that speech is a load of crap. Your face rescues the entire scene."

"It's a load of crap?" I searched his watery eyes for a sign that he was joking, but his face held firm. "It's one of Shakespeare's most famous speeches."

"Yeah, and it makes this assumption that everyone's life is the same. That we're all male, we'll all live to be old, and we all experience the same stuff at the same time." Jed cleared his throat, and up came indignation. "People are more unique than that."

I shivered. Time to tread lightly. "Well, sure. But some of what we experience is universal, isn't it? We all have our exits and our entrances, and we all play many different parts."

"Some of us get more parts than others." He coughed again, so hard that my own chest tightened.

"I don't know what to say."

"That makes you the first." He coughed again, a mad, racking sound that echoed in the night. "People always have something to say." Jed squeezed his eyes shut with a wince. "Sorry. I try to be more than just my illness. I don't want CF to be the most fascinating thing about me."

"It's not."

His voice was flat. "Oh yeah? Then what is?" He looked me straight in the eye, daring me to answer.

I blew out a steady stream of air. "Your attitude. You're not afraid of anything. You find almost everything interesting, and I've never met anyone less shy than you." I gripped the porch railing and stared at my cold fingers. "If you were a boat, you'd never be tied to the harbor."

"If I was a boat, I'd sink." He hacked and took a swig of water. The night air was static, but we could hear the boisterous party noise coming from inside. I put my hand on his shoulder, and he turned towards my touch.

"Wanna know a secret?" he whispered. "I'm just an actor, like everyone else." Then he closed his eyes, and when he opened them, I thought I saw longing. Like the beginning of a tsunami.

"All the world's a stage, right?"

Jed tilted his head. "Yeah."

We hovered for a moment, moving towards each other. When our lips met, his mouth was soft, inviting, and powerful enough to make my toes curl. He let out a little sigh, like he was relieved to be kissing me, but before I could wrap my arms around his shoulders, he stepped away.

"No," he said. "This is a bad idea."

"Why?" I tried to sound jokey . . . light. "You'll sleep with any-thing that moves."

He matched my tone. "That's not true. I'll only sleep with human females who are in my age range and attractive."

"Don't I fit that requirement?"

He looked me up and down, his nostrils flaring. "Yeah, of course you do."

"Then why?"

Jed stepped back again, creating new space between us. "I just think we're better off as friends."

I squared my shoulders to pretend I wasn't wounded. "If it's because you think you'll corrupt me, don't worry. I'm not a virgin."

"Okay." He raised his hands in defeat and kept his voice steady, like I'd bite him if he wasn't careful. "Look, I'm not in a relationshipy place right now; I can't be, with all my health issues. If we were together, you'd have high expectations because that's how you are."

"You don't know that."

"I see you, Robin. You don't hide or lower your standards. I like that about you, but it also makes us bad for each other." Lines crumpled his forehead as he held my gaze. "Tell me I'm wrong."

I leaned against the side of the house. How had I gotten to this point, practically begging Jed to have sex with me? I was a pathetic cliché.

"No, you're right." I forced out a weird, strained laugh. "We'd regret it, you and me . . ." I tilted my head towards the stars and groaned. "Never mind. Delete the last couple of minutes from your memory."

I turned to go inside.

"Robin . . ." He grabbed my arm, and I let him pull me towards him. The yearning on his face told a different story than the one he'd just recited. I put my hand at the base of his neck but withdrew my fingers in shock.

"Oh my God. You're burning up." His forehead was clammy and hot and not the way a healthy forehead should be.

He ducked from my touch. "I'm fine," he growled.

"No, you're not."

He started to hack. "Just tired."

"Can I help you get home?"

"I don't need your help. And I'm not ready to leave yet."

He slammed the door as he went back into the party.

As soon as I returned inside, Lucas spotted me. "There you are," he slurred and glanced down at my empty hands. "Why don't you have a beer? Come on." He pulled me toward the keg. "I noticed you a while ago." Lucas used an elastic voice. "And I thought, 'Who is that pretty blonde? I want to get to know her.'" He pumped out a drink.

Jed walked in from the living room. Had he come back to find me?

I ignored Jed and spoke to Lucas. "Thanks for the beer. And for calling me pretty."

Lucas lapped up the encouragement. "Any time. But what will it take to get you to smile?"

A genuine smile felt impossible. "Would you settle for a kiss instead?"

"Sure."

I kissed him. Though Lucas held his beer, he returned my kiss with more enthusiasm than Jed had.

Jed.

Was he spying on us with clenched fists and a wounded heart? I was afraid to look and see.

I pulled away. "Can I have that beer now?"

"Of course." Lucas handed it to me, and I gulped it down. Then I went for another. It would take several more to enjoy the evening.

"Wanna tour of my apartment?" Lucas spread his arms, gesturing to the dingy space he shared with a couple other guys.

I took another swig of beer and grimaced at the foamy bitterness. "I'd love that."

Lucas took me by the hand and led me upstairs, and I turned off my inhibitions for the night. I'd have a good time if it killed me.

FIVE

Monday, June 24, 2013
6:30 p.m.

I rush into the low-lit banquet room of the downtown Hyatt. I'm late meeting Nick, and I'm cursing myself for it. I scan the room, but he's hard to find because everyone is dressed in black. The only splashes of color come from bottles of rosé.

I'm regretting my outfit: a brown vintage shirt with a poofy bow, a purple short-sleeved shrug, and a high-waisted brown skirt from a 1960s business suit. Compared to everyone else here, I'm like a comic book character. Lois Lane in search of Clark Kent. I need to find Nick, but I also need a glass of wine. So I grab one and take a healthy swig.

"Aren't you Robin, from *The Holdout*?" A woman approaches, laughing with people who stand behind her. Everything about her is sleek: her delicate frame, her shiny black bob, and her black, sleeveless blouse tucked into a perfectly tailored skirt.

"That's right," I say.

She laughs some more. I'm not in on the joke. Maybe I *am* the joke.

"You were so fun to watch! Your naïveté' was just charming."

Her posse giggles, and I look at the floor. She has on black patent leather pumps, the type with red bottoms. "I like your shoes. Three years ago, I wanted a pair, back when they were in fashion."

"Robin!"

Nick appears by my side, and the sleek woman smiles. "Well, hello, Nick," she says. "I wondered if I'd see you here."

"Hi, Jane. Good to see you." Nick places his hand on my back as he turns to me. "Have you met Jane?"

"Can't say that I have."

Jane extends her hand. "Nice to meet you."

I return her limp-wristed handshake.

"How do you two know each other?" I ask Nick.

"Jane's in real estate law," he answers. "We give each other referrals."

"And Nick's been teaching me Portuguese," Jane drawls. "*Você gostaria de um pouco vinho?*"

Nick's cheeks turn pink. "That's pretty good. Your accent's great."

"No, but really. Would you?" She purses her lips and scrunches her precious little nose.

He runs his hand through his hair, shaking his head. "I'm good."

"Does someone want to translate?" I look from Nick to Jane and back again. Nick knows some Portuguese from his mother, who lived in Portugal until she married Nick's father, a military man. Every now and then, Nick tries to woo me with a phrase, but I'm already wooed.

"I asked him if he'd like some wine." Jane smolders and squints. "I'm surprised he hasn't taught you Portuguese. If he was my boyfriend, I'd insist on it."

I look at Nick, so handsome, with his hair slicked back and a shirt that matches his eyes. He wears a tie, and he fits well with everyone else in the room. Like Jane, who is shorter than him even in heels. If this was a movie, she would be his girlfriend. No casting agent would pick me to go with him.

I shift my weight. "I wonder how the silent auction is going. Has anyone bet on my outfit yet?"

"You mean bid? Yeah, I think so." Nick looks at me, hopeful.

77

"Should we go check?"

"No, no. Stay and teach Jane more Portuguese."

Stalking off, I silently congratulate myself for being so immature.

I go to the auction table to locate the ensemble I donated. It has a plum, pink, and gray taffeta skirt with floral embroidery, a pink silk camisole, and a gray shirt-jacket that ties with a plum-colored sash. The sign next to it reads, "An original by designer Robin Bricker, from *The Holdout*."

Nick comes up, and I point to the card.

"What does *The Holdout* have to do with anything?"

He puts his arm around me. "Des Moines is short on celebrities. They want to exploit you however they can." He peers at the bid sheet. "Hey, you're already up to $75. That's great."

I shrug. "The outfit cost more than that to make. And if you count all the time I spent on the embroidery . . ."

"I'm surprised you went to so much trouble."

"Well, it's a good cause. When I think about what families with sick children must go through—" I cut myself off. "Anyway, I was happy to do it."

Nick hunches his shoulders. "What's wrong, Robin?"

I gesture toward where Jane stands. "Why were you teaching her Portuguese?"

"A year ago, she was planning a trip to Portugal, so we went out for dinner—it was sort of a date, I guess." Nick shoves his hands in his pockets, like he's trying to be casual. "And I taught her some phrases. Nothing ever came of it. She must have bought a book or those Rosetta Stone tapes." He shrugs. "I don't know."

"How many times did you go out with her?"

"Twice. Then it fizzled out."

"Did you guys ever—"

"No." He lowers his volume. "I kissed her once. She has cold, floppy lips. Nothing like yours, which are very warm and firm."

He puckers up and leans in, but I tilt my head back. "I don't like her, and I don't like that you kissed her."

"It was before I'd met you."

"I don't care. You should have thought ahead."

Nick laughs, because I have to be joking. So I sort of laugh too.

Then we mingle, surrounded by the tinkle of laughter and ice, but I have one foot out the door all evening. Every time I see Jane, heat rushes to my face and I clench my fist. Nick notices and after a while, he pulls me aside.

"You're having a terrible time, aren't you?"

"I wouldn't say that. A terrible time was my high school reunion, when my date got smashed and made out with the guidance counselor. Tonight is just below average."

Nick's face is stony. "Wait—why was your date making out with the guidance counselor? How old was she?"

"Late thirties, but *she* was Zach, the cool young counselor who the girls all had crushes on."

"Wow. Yeah, that's unfortunate." His face relaxes, and his eyes grow warm. "You're just full of surprises. Did you know your date was gay when you took him to your reunion?"

"Sure." I blow a stray hair out of my face. "I brought him so people wouldn't judge me for being alone." I sigh, glance down at my skirt, and then I scrutinize Nick's black pants, black tie, and dark brown shirt. "Why is everyone here dressed in black, including you? Was there some memo I didn't get?"

Nick smiles so hard that his eyes squint. "Yeah. I hid it so you'd dress like you. You're like a walking piece of art."

I resist the warmth his words bring. "Okay, but why are you such a conformist?"

"Hey, if you'd made me that corduroy suit, I'd be wearing it instead."

With a smile, I step in close and tug on his tie. "I'll make you a corduroy suit. But I'm calling your bluff, Nick Davies. Once it's done, you'll have to wear it. All the time."

"Deal."

We both laugh.

"How was your day?" I rub his shoulder with a flat palm. "You haven't even said."

Nick's whole body loosens, and he opens up. "It was okay. Dave and I rehearsed for a couple of hours this morning, before work. I think we're going to go the contemporary classical route, and—"

He's cut off when a balding man with a thick neck slaps Nick on the shoulder. "How's that listing out on Pine Street doing?" he asks, his voice booming.

The light in Nick's eyes goes out. "Fine. We'll have a showing soon. Probably next week." Nick turns to me. "Robin, I don't think you've met my boss. This is Phil. Phil, this is Robin, my girlfriend."

"Nice to meet you," Phil says, barely looking at me. "Look, Buddy, I think we need to up the urgency here. How about you schedule it sooner rather than later, huh? Let's talk about it tomorrow. I'll pencil you in for five."

Phil gives him another back slap and saunters off without waiting for a reply. "I was supposed to Skype with Andrea tomorrow at five," Nick mumbles. "She has to schedule a time since her camp's only Wi-Fi is in the office."

Hearing about schedules reminds me of the time. "Nick, I'm sorry, but I have to go. I promised Isobel I'd be at rehearsal by eight."

Nick's lower lip juts out. "Yeah, okay."

"What? You knew I couldn't stay long."

His look digs into me. "Knowing doesn't mean accepting."

"Nick . . ."

"It's okay, Rocky. Go. I know you have to." The right side of his face melts into a smile, but the left side is still a little frosty. "I'll be glad when the play is over. When we can spend entire evenings together. I don't mean to be unsupportive, but—"

"You're not unsupportive. Come here."

I grab his arm and lead him into the hall, where we won't be seen, and I kiss him hard. Suddenly, I need his proximity and affection, like I need a deep breath when coming up for air. His arms slip around my waist, and his embrace is just the antidote I need. When he pulls away, he tucks a lock of hair behind my ear and strokes my cheek.

"Have a good rehearsal," he says. "I'll miss you."

"I'll miss you too." I kiss him once more. "We'll talk tomorrow, okay?"

"Sure." He smiles with his whole face, and then he lets go and re-enters the party.

I resist the temptation to watch and see if Nick finds Jane. He'll just blend in with the mass of black business attire anyway. So I walk towards the parking garage, towards a time in my life that ended years ago.

Tuesday, June 25, 2013
6:00 a.m.

I don't know anyone. I'm not even sure why I'm here; maybe I came to the wrong party by mistake? But it's fancy. There's a pool outside, strung paper lantern lights, and waiters carrying trays with mini-quiches and pastel-colored cocktails.

So I mingle. I spot Grace Kelly, who's always seemed very accessible, and I'm on my way over to introduce myself, when someone grabs my arm.

"What are you doing here?"

It's Jed. He's clutching me, hard, his nails digging into my flesh.

"You're hurting me," I tell him.

"Robin, you're not supposed to be here! You have to go, now!"

"Don't you want to see me?"

He loosens his grasp, and his face softens. "More than anything," he answers. "More than anything. But it's not time yet. You have to go."

After that, things get blurry. I want him to explain, but he gets mixed in with other people—other conversations. After looking for my mom, I'm caught in this bustle that ends with me being pushed out through the backyard gate.

Then I wake up and go running.

The soles of my shoes slap the pavement like they're angry, but even still, I'm holding back. I haven't gone full speed yet, and my legs are just two restrained animals on a leash. Because today, I'm waiting for Flashdance Girl to set them free.

I turn the corner, and she's doing squats against the large oak tree in her front yard. Her head is down, and since I'm a little early, she doesn't know to watch for me. A second goes by, maybe three. It's just me and her and the dandelion fuzz blowing through the air. The quiet is commanding, but it's broken by an airplane that flies overhead.

She looks up. Our eyes meet. Today's headband is pink. Light pink, like a girl's baby blanket.

I start sprinting down the block, but soon she's at my heels. Her breathing is so steady, like she's never wasted a breath in her life. "On your left," she calls out.

She isn't even winded.

But I refuse to yield. In fact, when she tries to pass me, I block her, and we go back and forth on the sidewalk like awkward square dancers. When she jumps off the curb and starts running in the street, she passes me easily.

And she laughs as I fall behind.

12:20 p.m.

"Thanks for bringing me food," I say to Isobel.

"No problem! It's a small price to pay for all these costumes."

I sit down on my paint-chipped stool; it wobbles, but I adore the blue Erte' girl that's etched on the seat. My table is cluttered as usual, but I clear a space to eat my lunch.

I point to a rack a few feet away. "There they are; tell me what you think."

She looks at the clothes while I eat my bagel sandwich. I almost drop a dollop of jalapeño cream cheese onto my pink skull T-shirt, but I intercept the fall with my paper napkin just in time. Isobel notices and raises her well-tweezed eyebrows.

"Close one," she says.

"I know. And I got this at a thrift store, so if it had a big, greasy cream-cheese stain, I couldn't replace it."

"Don't you get all your clothes at thrift stores?"

"No." I point to my long black skirt, which has gray roses printed all over it. "I got this . . . God, I don't even remember, but it was some store at the mall." I take a huge bite and wipe my mouth as I chew.

Isobel gives me a crisp nod before turning back to the clothes rack. "Well, I like the ensemble. I could never pull off your outfits, but you totally do."

"Oh yeah? I'm starting to wonder if I'm kind of weird."

She laughs. "I could have told you that a long time ago." Isobel examines the sleeve of a red chiffon blouse, eagerness vibrating out of her fingers.

"So, am I weird?'

"Of course. But that's why I love you." She holds up a gray blazer. "This would be perfect for when Grayson goes job-hunting."

"Yeah," I answer, my voice deflated, "that's what I was thinking."

Isobel turns and squints at me. "Are you okay? You know I mean good-weird, right?"

"Sure." I take another bite of my sandwich—a smaller bite this time—and consider telling Isobel about my Jed dreams. They've got to be a result of the play. Isobel would understand, and she'd tell me I'm capable of being a real adult, someone with a real job and a real relationship. That this is just a phase and I'll stop regressing once the show is over.

But Isobel's face is buried in the clothes, so I look at her black hair, which is pulled into a bun, soft tendrils escaping in waves. Her lack of hairspray triggers a memory.

"Hey," I say to her back. "Do you remember our camping trip several years ago?"

"At Lake Louise? Of course. Why do you ask?"

One lazy summer, Isobel and I took off for a weekend and pitched a tent at a state park a couple of hours away. It had a lake with a swimming beach, so we read novels and sun-bathed, and at night, we roasted hot dogs and drank cheap wine from paper cups. It was so humid, but when the mosquitoes circled, we stayed up anyway, stargazing and soul-searching. I confessed my jealousy of how she could take charge. She said she thought I was a Barbie doll for the first few months she knew me. Then we laughed, cried, and hugged each other's sun-burned shoulders, promising to always be friends.

"I was just thinking about it," I tell her. "Maybe once the play is over, we can go again."

"That's a great idea! I'd love to." Isobel studies a cream-colored blouse. "Oh, I forgot to tell you, I talked to someone at the *Register* today, and they said they'd send a drama critic to opening night. All I had to do was mention that you're in the show, and they were interested."

"Did you mention Jed?"

"Yeah, of course." Isobel steps away from the clothes rack, pulls up a stool with the Eiffel Tower painted on the seat, and sits down. She widens her eyes, attempting to see through me. "Robin, I know you're struggling with this—all the attention and the emotional repercussions from doing Jed's play. And I can tell myself that I'm doing you a favor, but I know it's the reverse." She squeezes my shoulder. "I've been in a slump, but the tides are turning. I have you to thank."

The undeserved praise makes me recoil. "I haven't done anything."

"You're doing this show, and working on it together has been awesome." Isobel smiles with her special brand of affection. "I haven't been this excited about theater since I left Hoyt."

"Yeah, me too." I brush away a stray sesame seed and sip my diet coke. I wish I felt as happy as Isobel looks. But I wonder what's behind her new-found exuberance and why she hasn't told me about her romance with my cousin Jack.

My phone rings.

I pick it up, and Isobel goes back to the costumes.

"Hey," I say into my cell. "How was the rest of the party?"

"Okay. Your outfit went for $150."

My left eye starts twitching, and I press a finger against my lid. "That's cool."

"The only thing that went for more was the family fun-pack to Bacon Fest."

Nick's voice relaxes me into a smile. "How's your day going?" I ask.

"Pretty boring and tedious. I have a client who refuses to consider houses built before 1980 because they have bad energy."

"I don't understand."

Nick sounds breathy, like he's trying to do two things at once. "He thinks the older the house, the more likely it is to be haunted."

"Oh." I wrap what's left of my bagel sandwich in the white paper it came in, deciding to save the rest for later. "That's not boring and tedious, Nick. Perhaps unusual and exasperating? You need to work on your descriptive words."

Silence looms for an entire four seconds, and when he has no clever retort, I grow suspicious. "Hey, you're not driving, are you?"

"I'm at a stoplight."

"Nick!"

He groans. "I called to find out if you had another run-in with Flashdance Girl."

"Yup. Every morning. Like a bad infection resistant to penicillin."

"Maybe you should take a different route?"

"Never!" I make a tsk, tsk sound. "Do you know me at all, Nick Davies?"

"I like to think I do."

"Then you should realize I don't back down. Ever."

He takes a deep breath. "Okay, Rocky." His voice turns airy.

"Hey, do you want me to schedule a showing for that house I told you about . . . you know, the one I thought we might buy?"

Underneath Nick's breeziness, I hear a bundle of nerves. Meanwhile, Isobel has finished looking at the clothes, and she turns to me, holding the garments she's planning to green-light. She mouths the words *I have to go.* I nod, extending my finger to indicate that I'll be done in a second, and speak to Nick. "Nick, let's talk about it later, okay? Please hang up the phone before you get all squished in a three-car pileup."

"Okay," he says, and I can breathe again.

Isobel grabs her purse and holds five outfits by their hangers. "These are great. Thanks, Robin." Her eyes dart toward the door. "I'd better run. My class starts at 1:00 p.m., and if I'm late, there will be a bunch of unsupervised twelve-year-old theater geeks on the loose."

"Thanks for lunch," I say.

"Of course. I'll see you tonight, okay?"

She hustles out, unaware that I didn't reply.

8:15 p.m.

"How can you say that? We know what she's like, Grayson. If you're connected to Lea on any level, things will *never* be okay."

"Wait!"

I stop moving when Isobel barks her order, and I let the hand holding my script drop down. "What?" I ask. "Am I supposed to move stage right on 'things will never be okay'?"

"No. I want you over by the bed on that line," Isobel says.

"Sorry."

"It's fine, Robin. But this time, can you try playing strength?"

I let out a puff of air. "Wasn't I? Strength is sort of what I was going for."

"Oh." Isobel taps her pencil against her director's notebook. "You're coming off as sad. Which is understandable! But if you

86

could just—"

"No, no. I get it. I'll be strong."

If Isobel wants strength, that's what she'll get.

I say the lines again, and as I walk towards the bed, I imagine I'm a steel tower, indestructible and shiny even when it's cloudy outside.

And to keep my focus from taking extreme twists and turns, I study my surroundings: the paintings, the double bed, and the rehearsal props. Andrew speaks his lines. "Just because I'm taking the deal doesn't mean I'm connected to her. The only person I'm connected to is you."

I inhale, noticing how Andrew's hair is in his eyes. And he's dressed for walking in a cool Midwestern evening, with his sweat-shirt and jeans. If we were outside, he'd offer to give me that sweatshirt. We'd hug me as we walked, laughing and tripping over each other, using my body heat to warm us both.

Except we're inside, where it's air-conditioned, and Andrew is not Jed. I know this like I know that Gandhi was good and Hitler was evil. But Andrew speaks words that came straight from Jed's head, and it's easy to get confused.

What was I thinking, wanting to do this play?

"Can we take a break?"

Isobel looks at me like I just asked for her kidney.

"Sorry." I wilt under her hardcore director's stare. "I need to look over these lines. If I could take a second and read them again, maybe I'll stop being so distracted."

"Yeah, of course," says Isobel. "Why don't you take a breather, and Andrew and I can go over his monologue?"

"Thanks." I hit my script against my thigh and walk off stage, aware of everyone's eyes on me. Once I'm outside in the parking lot, I exhale in relief. We're kitty corner from a bowling alley and next to a TGI Fridays. I lean up against the side of the building and try to remember when I last went bowling or had a mudslide.

It doesn't matter.

I hold up my script and read through the lines, telling myself that they don't matter either.

But they do. Of course they do.

Grayson: *I just need you more than you need me, Georgie. (He gets up and kisses her.) Show me your painting.*
Georgie: *I haven't done much to it.*
Grayson: *I still want to see.*
(Georgie gives in and leads Grayson to her easel.)
Georgie: *Last night I added color, but I still can't get the face quite right. (She moves Grayson so that he stands by her painting.) I don't have the dimensions right. And the shadows. (She traces the contours of his face with her fingers.)*
Grayson: *You can feel my shadow?*
Georgie: *Of course.*

I lower my script and focus on breathing. A steady rhythm of in and out. In and out. I think of all the times Jed struggled for air and how I would place his hand on my chest. I'd tell him to breathe with me, and he would scuffle through his panic until he got his lungs to obey. I'd squeeze the fingers that rested right above my heart.

We were united.

• • •

After rehearsal, I'm packing up my stuff when Isobel comes over. "Hey, good job tonight."

"Thanks." I stuff my water bottle and my script into my bag.

"Sorry I'm intense. But I'm banking on this show. A lot of people might come just to see you."

I offer her a smile, trying to exude warmth even though I'm chilly on the inside. "I know, and I want the show to succeed as much as anyone."

Isobel's fingers drift down, absently picking at the frayed red velvet seat cover of the chair she's next to. "Are you okay? You seem sort of down." She uses the back of her other hand to rub her nose, and her green T-shirt has a coffee stain. I blink a couple of times, unsure why her lack of composure bugs me.

"I'm not down." We both know that's a lie, but I don't have the motivation to deal with the truth.

Isobel leans against the chair's armrest and exhales. "Look, Jack mentioned you were upset we talked about you." She squares her shoulders as if preparing to get shoved. "I'm sorry. I shouldn't have said anything to your cousin, but I'm worried about you."

"Okay, but why—"

Isobel twists her mouth. "But why didn't I tell you about Jack and me? I wanted to. But even though my divorce papers are signed, Karl has some legal troubles, and he might get me involved."

"Legal trouble? What kind?"

Isobel squeezes her eyes shut for a moment. "It's nothing to worry about." She opens her eyes, and they seem full of fatigue. "I wanted to keep things simple and not bring Jack into it."

I grin and slap my thigh. "Isobel! You've been dating my cousin, and you're just now telling me!"

Her laugh sounds natural, and we revert back to girlfriends sharing a secret. "He's so sweet, Robin! I like him, and I didn't want to jinx it."

"Yeah, Jack's a good guy."

"And I'm all about dating a good guy for a change." Isobel tilts her chin to the side, her thoughts so heavy they're weighing down her head. "You and I are both dating good guys. When was the last time that happened?"

"Umm . . . a week before never?"

She laughs, convinced that my little joke means we're good. And I suppose we are. But I'm still sort of angry, even though it's not Isobel's fault that life and love are so unpredictable.

The only thing you can count on, for sure, is death.

Wednesday, June 26, 2013
5:30 p.m.

When Isobel calls to cancel rehearsal, I rejoice.

"Don't you even want to know why?" Isobel asks.

"Why?"

"I had an allergic reaction to some strawberries, and my body is covered with hives."

I know I should ask if she needs anything. But resentment from last night still lingers in the worst parts of my personality. I say, "Hope you feel better," and then I hang up.

Man, can I use a night off.

I woke up at six again this morning. At least I didn't remember my dream. But both my run and my run-in with Flashdance Girl left me tired, and I haven't recovered all day. Instead, it's like I'm hung over. At my sewing machine, I made mistakes and had to pull out crooked seams. I drank a second cup of coffee, which dehydrated me. I drank extra water to make up for it, and then I needed to pee a lot.

But now, I can offer Nick the uninterrupted evening he pined for the other night. I call him, and he picks up right away.

"I'm coming over, and I don't care if you have plans," I say. "And if you have a showing, cancel it. I need some couch time with you."

"I love it when you're bossy," he replies.

When I arrive at his door, I hear music. Beethoven's *Moonlight Sonata*. I'm holding a takeout bag of Chinese food and a bottle of wine, and opening the door quietly is a challenge, but I'm good at performing under pressure. Nick's at his piano with his back to me, so he doesn't notice my presence.

His thick fingers glide over the piano keys, and the notes are as fluid as water, or, I suppose, moonlight. He looks up and out, with a high chin and arched neck, like he's driving down a beautifully familiar road.

I want to ride shotgun with him.

As the song winds down, I move with soft feet towards the

90

kitchen to place down the food and wine. When the last note is played, I come back to the living room and tap the wall. He turns to me with a start.

"When did you get here?" Nick asks.

"A couple of minutes ago. Your playing was so beautiful, and I didn't want you to stop." I sit next to him on the piano bench. "Why didn't you tell me you could play classical like that?"

Nick rests his hands against the edge of the piano. "I don't know. It's not a big deal."

"Nick, that was fabulous."

His smile humors me. "*Moonlight Sonata* is not a challenging piece. Everyone learns to play it in piano lessons."

"Yeah, but you were really good."

"Thanks." His face goes blank.

"What is it?"

Nick takes a deep breath. "I'm happy you think I'm a good musician, but Robin, I'm barely above average. There was a time when it was all I wanted to do." He skims the piano keys with his fingers. "I love music because it's this universal language that everyone can understand, and I thought if I could just create it or perform or . . . I don't know. Reality set in, and now I'm a real estate agent who plays when nobody's around to hear."

I lift one of his hands, press his palm to my mouth and kiss it. "I'm around and I'll always listen."

Nick answers me with a kiss on the mouth. "Thank you . . . And Robin?" His dark eyes drill into mine.

"Hmm?" I prepare myself for another confession, but Nick's confessions are like music itself.

"Robin, I need you to know that"—he swallows roughly—"that I'm very hungry. If you think you're getting my eggroll tonight, think again." He laughs at his own joke, and I push my shoulder into his.

"You're lucky I brought you food at all." I grasp the collar of his shirt, letting my fingers slip against his warmth. "And I also brought wine."

"Good." He tucks a lock of hair behind my ear and speaks in a raspy and affectionate tone. "There's ice cream in the freezer. Chunky Monkey."

"Awesome." I stand, reach out my hand, and pull him up. "I'm starving. Let's eat."

We settle on the couch, eat from the containers, and drink wine from the bottle as we watch our latest favorite show, *Battlestar Galactica*. After a while, the food is pushed aside, and our bellies expand into something round and satisfied.

"Do you think there's any chance that Gaius Baltar is a Cylon?" Nick asks. We're well into the third episode of the evening. "What if he is and he just doesn't realize it?" Nick's arm is around me, and when I don't answer, he gives me a sideways nudge. I bury my face into his neck, and he presses the pause button on the remote.

"You okay?" he asks.

I nod without looking up. But he places his fingers under my chin and lifts my gaze to his.

"What's up?" he asks.

"I'm tired," I say. And it's the truth.

"You've been busy between work, the play, and your crazy exercise routine."

"Yeah," I whisper, suddenly tearful. Nick stares at me, all warm and gooey, hot fudge against frozen vanilla me.

I stroke his cheek and kiss his forehead. "I love you," I say.

"I love you too."

I know that he does. So I don't make him promise that he'll always stay, that he'll always be here, that he'll never, ever leave. Even if he said the words, they'd be meaningless. Nobody can make a promise like that.

I just snuggle down and put my head against his chest, and soon I'm more aware of his breathing than I am of the TV. And when I fall asleep in his arms, Nick just lets me dream.

Thursday, June 27, 2013
8:00 a.m.

It's one of those rainy summer mornings, with thick gray clouds blocking the sun. It takes Nick's alarm clock to rouse me from a dreamless slumber. I roll over and sit up. Then I nudge Nick, whose head is still buried underneath his pillow.

"Aren't you getting up?" I ask.

"Haven't you ever heard of the snooze button?" he responds. His arm shoots out, as if it has a sensor to find me, and he grabs and pulls me down. "Cuddle," he grunts.

"We have to go. Come on."

With a belligerent groan, he rises from bed and prepares for the day. Soon we're both ready to leave—him to work and me to my apartment to change before I go to my studio.

"Well, at least you didn't miss Flashdance Girl," Nick says as we descend the stairs of his building. "Only someone with a death wish would run in this storm."

"Some people have them, you know."

"Huh?" he asks.

"Some people have death wishes," I clarify.

The rain comes down in sheets, and when we get to the outside door, he brandishes his umbrella. "Come on, I'll take you to your car first."

"You'll be soaked by the time you get to your car." I peer through the glass; the rain is so thick, it's like looking through a blurred lens. "It's fine. I'm going home to change anyway. I don't need your umbrella."

"Are you sure?" Unease outlines his face.

I kiss him dryly on the lips, knowing I'm about to get super wet. "See you later. Have a good day." Then I bolt out into the rain. It takes mere seconds to get to my car, but I'm drenched by the time I reach it, so I relax as I unlock the door and climb in. If there's a point beyond sopping wet, I've reached it.

But when I turn the key in my ignition, nothing happens. "No!"

I cry. "Not again!" I bang my head against the steering wheel. This is the second time this month that my car has given me trouble.

I call Nick, who has already pulled away. "This better not be a test," he says.

"A test?"

"You're always nagging me about not talking on my cell phone while I'm driving."

"No, no. My car won't start." I sigh. "Sorry, but can you circle back and pick me up? If you let me into your apartment, I can call a mechanic and wait there."

"Sure, I'm on my way."

He clicks off, and in a moment, his car approaches. But there's another car, which is barreling down a perpendicular road way too fast, on a collision course with Nick. A scream forms at the back of my throat, but I'm at once mute and paralyzed.

I find my voice right as the other vehicle punches Nick's fender and sends him spinning. "NO!" I jump out of my car and run towards Nick. The other car continues down the road, unconcerned with being the villain in a hit-and-run.

"Nick!" His car squeals to a stop, crooked in the middle of the road. I bang on the window. He's face down against the activated air bag. "Nick! Are you okay?"

My heart hammers in my chest. I pull and yank on his door. Like a miracle, there's a click, the door opens, and I fall back in surprise.

"Sorry!" Nick mumbles. "I didn't think unlocking the door would make you fall."

I'm sitting in a puddle while Nick stares down from his driver's seat.

"Are you okay?" I ask again. I stand back up and lean in, checking for a heartbeat, profuse bleeding, or signs of a brain injury.

"Yeah, I'm fine. Just winded from the airbag."

I gulp down a sob. "Stand up! I need to see that you can stand!"

He maneuvers his way past the airbag and out of the car. We're face-to-face.

94

I hold up three fingers. "How many fingers do you see?"

"Robin, I'm fine."

"Nick—"

He lowers my arm and pulls me in. The rain pours down, plastering his hair to his head and his shirt to his body. He takes my hand and puts it over his heart. "See? Still beating."

Pounding is more like it. I'm not the only one shaken. "That will teach you not to talk on your cell phone while driving."

Nick's mouth drops open, and his cheeks turn pink, despite the rain. "You make no sense! You know it had nothing to do with—"

I silence him with a kiss.

Adrenaline, fear, and relief swirl into a perfect storm inside me. I am flooded with desire as his mouth hungrily covers mine. Soon my heart pounds to the same rhythm as Nick's, and I must come up for air.

"Let's go." It's all Nick needs to say.

We break apart, he manages to deflate the airbag and park his car, and we run back up the stairs to his apartment. His door slams behind us, and he wastes no time. He grabs me and kisses me like his life depends on it. I wrap my legs around him as he carries me to the bedroom.

"Get our . . . wet clothes . . . off!" He struggles more with the words than with my blouse because his mouth is too busy with kissing to talk. He grows hard against me, and I sigh with relief when we've both stripped down to being naked, and his strength allows my trembling body to relax.

Then we're in bed, and his touch makes my back arch and my jaw drop. He's on top of me, and our eyes meet.

"Promise you'll never scare me like that again."

He gives me that crooked smile and shakes his head. "No way. You're hot when you're scared."

I grab his face in my hands. "I mean it, Nick. Promise!"

"Rocky . . ." He turns gentle and sweet. "I promise. I'd promise you anything, okay?"

Nothing has changed since last night. If anything, I'm even more aware that "permanent" doesn't exist. Yet I need to believe otherwise. "Just promise me that."

"I promise you that," he whispers.

Pleasure wins out over panic, and as the rain pounds against the window, we stay warm, dry, and rooted to each other.

Friday, June 28, 2013
3:30 p.m.

I quit working early so I can take Lucy's kids, Noah and Abby, to Blank Park Zoo. Like a trooper, Nick changes his schedule and comes with. We're in the animal yard. Nick soothes little Noah as he timidly offers a leaf to a baby giraffe.

"Good job, Buddy!" Nick says. Noah squeals with pride as the giraffe takes the leaf from his hand.

Why is a guy holding a toddler so sexy? Some primal part of my DNA makes me melt at the sight.

"Robin?" Four-year-old Abby tugs on my hand. "I'm thirsty. Can I have something to drink?"

She does look droopy. In this heat, I can't blame her. "Sure," I say. "Let's get lemonade."

I call Nick over, and after putting Noah in his stroller, we stand in line. I wipe my forehead with the back of my hand and pull the fabric of my patterned tank dress away from me, a fruitless attempt to cool down.

"Do you think they need more sunscreen?" Nick asks.

"I don't know. I hadn't thought of it."

Nick looks through the bag that Lucy packed, finds a bottle of baby sunscreen, and squirts some into his hand. "Here, Abby," he says. "Let's smear some beauty cream on your face." She giggles while he puts the sunscreen on her cheeks, nose, and arms. Then he does the same for Noah, who's falling asleep.

"You're going to be a great dad," I say once Nick is back,

standing next to me.

Nick grunts.

"What?" I ask. "Why did you make that noise? Don't you like kids?"

"Yeah, sure." He shrugs and I see sweat stains on his black T-shirt. "I'll want kids one day."

"But?"

Nick looks at me from behind his sunglasses. "But I have one more year before Andrea is in college, and then I'll have a little freedom. I'm not sure about new responsibilities, at least not right away."

"Oh." The sinking sensation in my stomach is like being on a twisty car trip and needing to roll down a window.

He raises an eyebrow. "That's okay, right? If you're not ready for a house, you can't be ready for kids."

"That's not quite true, and I never said—"

"I can read your evasion tactics, Robin." Nick grins, scratches at his second-day beard growth, and sets his jaw, like he's waiting for me to contradict him.

"Well, isn't a house a new responsibility? A really big responsibility?"

"Sure, but buying a house would also make life easier, and moving in with you would be . . ." He searches for the right word and smiles when he finds it. "It would be amazing. But I'm not ready for kids, not with all the new stuff I've taken on."

"What new stuff?"

Nick widens his eyes. "Nothing," he blusters. "I'll tell you later, when we have a chance to talk. You'll understand why I shouldn't have kids for a while." He runs a finger down my arm.

"Is that a problem?"

I lean forward with the stroller, trying to right a crooked wheel, moving away from his touch. "No. I mean . . . well, I am in my thirties. But that's okay. If I want to have kids, I can do it on my own."

Nick pivots his head, aware that others in line for lemonade might overhear our conversation. "Don't you kinda need a husband?"

I laugh, as if this conversation could become a joke through force of will. Looking him up and down, I let my eyes rest on his crotch. "Nope. All I need is someone to knock me up." Then I raise my eyes so they peer into his shades.

Nick pushes his sunglasses up onto the top of his head just as he turns away. "You just want my sperm? Wow. It's nice to know what I'm good for."

A cloud of tension settles over our heads, but it creates no shade from the sweltering sun. I don't know what to say.

But Abby isn't at a loss for words. "What's sperm?" she bellows.

Nick pats her head. "Something to stay away from. For a very long time."

Then we order lemonade.

8:30 p.m.

Nick has plans to rehearse with Dave again, so I drop him off before I take the kids back to Aunt Natalie's house. Lucy and the kids have been staying with Monty's mom, and I stay for dinner at Natalie's insistence. Now that the kids are down, Lucy and I sit on the back porch while dusk settles in. Everything Lucy says and does is delayed somehow, like she can't operate at full speed. But if Lucy is anything like me, a good morsel of gossip will cheer her up.

"Hey," I offer. "Did you hear that Jack has a new girlfriend?"

Lucy doesn't look at me but runs her fingers along Natalie's potted sweet potato vine. "He does?"

I shift towards her. "It's my friend Isobel, who is as nice as Jack is, if that's even possible. But she also has a lot of baggage. She just got through a messy divorce, so . . ." I shrug. "Maybe that means they're perfect for each other."

"That's great." Lucy takes a sip of water and wipes the condensation from her bottle. "Did you set them up?"

"No. They met through me, but I never encouraged anything."
I shift my position and stretch my back. "They've been keeping it
a secret, but I figured it out when Isobel spilled all *my* secrets to
Jack, and he said something to me." I shrug. "Oh, the tangled webs
we weave, right?"

"Yeah." I can't tell if she heard me or not. Her eyes don't change,
even when I mention having secrets. Now she holds up her water
bottle and examines it. "I could go for an ice cream sandwich." She
speaks from somewhere far away. "Do you want one?"

"Sure."

She gets up, goes inside, and returns with two rectangles
wrapped in white paper. As Lucy sits back down, she hands me
one, and we both unwrap our treat.

"I used to get these when I was in grade school," she says,
licking the vanilla ice cream sandwiched between two dark brown
wafers. "Once a week, my mom gave me a quarter so I could have
dessert. Usually on Thursday." She whispers out a laugh. "It always
seemed special."

"Natalie constantly has a box of these in her freezer." I take a
huge bite.

Lucy's sluggish with her ice cream, eating like she doesn't have
the energy to enjoy it. I'm bummed my news about Jack didn't
elicit more of a response, so I search for a new route that doesn't
include prying.

"I haven't managed to talk to Nick," I tell her. "I will soon, but
today at the zoo, he said he doesn't want kids for a while."

Lucy swallows her latest bite and sniffs. "But he's so great with
them. Abby went on about how funny he is."

"Did she mention Nick's sperm joke?"

"Huh?"

I wave my hand like I'm shooing away bugs. "Never mind."
Then I curl my toes against the pavement and describe the conversation Nick and I had earlier.

"I see his point," says Lucy. "But give him time. I bet he's ready soon." She finishes her ice cream sandwich, wipes at the corners of her mouth, and takes a sip of water.

"You're quiet tonight," I say. "Anything new with your dad?"

"He should be able to leave the hospital in a week or two. My mom and I are looking for rehab programs." Lucy scoops her thick, curly hair up into a messy bun, and she rubs at the back of her neck.

"How's that going?"

"Fine, I guess." A mosquito buzzes, and she swats it away. "It will be a tough road, and my mom will need help. I'll have to move here."

The mosquito has left Lucy alone, but now it circles my toes. I kick at it. "Wow. Well, it would be nice for all of us if you and Monty moved here. I'd love that."

"I don't know if Monty would come."

I tilt my body towards her, waiting. You don't drop a bomb like that without cleaning up the rubble. But she stares at Natalie's bird feeder, which hangs from the large oak tree in the middle of her yard. As a kid, I climbed that tree more than once, waiting for Thanksgiving dinner to be ready.

Those were simpler times.

"Lucy, what are you saying?"

She sighs like it hurts to breathe. "I haven't talked to Monty in over a week. But I know he won't want to move to Des Moines and get some boring lawyer job, representing Wells Fargo or Target. He loves to travel, and he needs a purpose." Lucy wipes away an invisible tear and sniffs. "Too bad his old girlfriend, Evelyn, left him years ago. They'd still be in Africa together—happy, sweaty, and altruistic."

She's not trying to be funny. I suppress my smile and pat her knee. "We all disliked Evelyn. I met her at Ian's Fourth of July barbeque years ago, and she was a piece of work."

Lucy doesn't respond, so I spew out what she must already know. "You're the best thing that ever happened to him, Lucy. But you two should make major life decisions together."

"Yeah." She takes a deep sniff. "But that's the thing about

marriage. You have conversations and think they went one way, but the other person remembers something different. Even when you try to communicate, it gets messed up. Now he's thousands of miles away, and I'm sick of needing him. I'll handle things myself."

She's still not looking at me, and everything about her seems numb.

I place a hand on her shoulder. "Lucy, you need to call him."

"I don't know," she whispers.

Monty and I have never been super close, but he's my cousin and a good guy. That makes me bound by blood and loyalty. And there was that time he helped me fill out my college applications. I should do what I can to try and save his marriage.

"You do know. You want to keep your family together." Lucy starts to answer, but I cut her off. "I understand what you said the other day, about wanting the same things. But I'm calling your bluff about true love. It does exist, it's rare, and it's worth fighting for."

The porch light bounces off her face, creating shadows and exacerbating stress lines caused by stress. "Of course you're right. But it's complicated."

I massage her back. "Just promise you'll call Monty and tell him to come home."

Lucy leans back and looks at me. "You sound so authoritative, Robin. When did that happen?"

It happened the moment I lost my grasp on my own life. My perception of other people's relationships grows as my ability to handle my own problems diminishes.

"Sorry," I tell her.

"Don't be sorry. You're right. I promise I'll call him."

10:30 p.m.

When I get home, I'm tired, but I don't go to bed. All these thoughts about love, sacrifice, wishes, and longing are like espresso shots to my brain. I blame Jed.

After yesterday morning, I should be focusing on Nick. But there's this itch I need to scratch, and it's like I'm cheating when I turn on my computer. Going straight to my email, I click on the folder marked "J."

January 7, 2001

To: R_Bricker@Hoyt.edu
From: J_Reardon@Hoyt.edu
Subject: Please Read Me

Robin,

If you check your student email and if you get this, please don't delete it right away. I wouldn't blame you if you did; I haven't done much to deserve a second chance.

But second chances are why I'm contacting you. You may have noticed that I haven't been around campus for the last few weeks. Turns out that when I insisted I was okay at the cast party, I wasn't. I wound up in the hospital, and I'll be here for a while because I've been put on the transplant list for a new lung. It was a tough decision because there are a lot of risks that come with lung transplants. But if it works like my doctors say it might, I'll have several healthy years ahead of me.

For now, there's a lot of waiting around while they poke, prod, and get me ready for something that could take months or even years to happen. However, I've had a lot of time to sit in this bed and stare at the same movies over and over, and I find myself thinking about you. A lot.

I know you're into Lucas, and I want you to be happy. But I'm sorry for being a jerk and getting scared. I liked you the first time I saw you, and I still like you now.

So if I don't die from CF or from a lung transplant,

I'll probably die from embarrassment after sending you this.

Hope you're well.

Jed

January 10, 2001

To: J_Reardon@Hoyt.edu
From: BrickerRobin82@hotmail.com
Subject: Hi

Jed,

I check my student email sometimes, but this address is a better way to contact me.

Sorry it took me several days to get back to you.

Anyway, I already knew about your lung transplant. Your mom mentioned it to a couple of people, and word spread through the Hoyt theater department. Everybody is rooting for you.

That must sound lame. Like you're a sports team, and we made signs, put on spirit sweatshirts, and bet in an office pool about which date your new lung will come through.

I mean that people are thinking about you, for whatever that's worth. Do you feel alone? Does knowing that people care make you feel any less alone?

Here I am, with more questions.

As for me, I'm doing fine. It's second semester, and I like my classes. A few weeks ago, my roommate stopped by (her third visit ever, including Welcome Week and that time you were there) to give me a Christmas present. I felt bad because it never occurred to me to get her something! She gave me a snowman-shaped jar filled with red and green skittles. Too bad they weren't M&Ms, but I can't complain. Do you like skittles? If so, I'll save them for you.

Because I hope that you're doing well. Really, really, really.

Robin.

January 11, 2001

To: BrickerRobin82@hotmail.com
From: J_Reardon@Hoyt.edu
Subject: Re: Hi

Robin,

I'll take the skittles. Will you deliver them yourself?

I'm at the Mayo Clinic. Room 1224.

-Jed

P.S. I guess I'm not as good at asking questions as you. So are you and Lucas a couple?

January 11, 2001

To: J_Reardon@Hoyt.edu
From: BrickerRobin82@hotmail.com
Subject: Re: Hi

Jed,

Lucas and I aren't a couple. We made out the night of the party. The next day, I found out he has a girlfriend. She's an early education major. Forest animals help her get dressed in the morning, while tiny birds braid her long, flowing locks. Everyone knew about her but me, and now I'm the home-wrecking harlot of the Hoyt theater department. Lucas is just a poor victim of temptation.

Maybe, as a guy who has slept around A LOT, you can explain this double standard. I have never heard anyone say anything bad about you. Surely, some of the girls you've had sex with had boyfriends. Meanwhile, all I did was let Lucas go to second base, and I'm a whore.

As for the skittles, I'd be happy to deliver them to you, but I'll need a ride. Do you think if I made out with Lucas again, he'd drive me?

January 12, 2001

To: BrickerRobin82@hotmail.com
From: J_Reardon@hoyt.edu
Subject: You're not a whore

Robin,

Please don't make out with Lucas again. I'm already working hard, trying to forget that you kissed him.

I'm such an idiot for pulling away from you.

Now I'm waiting for a lung, but what kind of monster am I? Several healthy people will have to die in sudden, violent deaths for me to work my way up the list, and then one more will have to make the ultimate sacrifice before I'll get the possibility of a few healthy years.

Meanwhile, I could die before any of it happens. And who will I have been? Just that sick kid, Catherine's son, who had sex a lot because girls felt sorry for him.

I decided that I must come up with something brilliant. Then, it won't matter as much if I die, because I'll have written myself back into existence.

But then I think, "Let me just check my email first." And there's an email from you, and it's way more important than some stupid play that will just be added to the world's undiscovered crap pile. Nobody will ever read my play, but I'm fairly confident that you'll read this email.

So I need you to know something: screw everyone who says anything bad about you. (Please don't take that literally.)

If it's too hard to adopt such a subversive attitude, just remember, it will all blow over soon. And yes, life is full of double standards and nothing is fair.

That said, some red and green skittles in a snowman-shaped jar would improve my outlook on this unjust world we live in. Please find a way to get to Rochester that doesn't involve letting anyone touch your ta-tas.

-Jed

January 12, 2001

To: J_Reardon@hoyt.edu
From: BrickerRobin82@hotmail.com
Re: You're not a whore

Jed,

My mom died in a car accident around 16 years ago. She was an organ donor. I don't know who got what, and we never received a thank-you letter, and my dad never fell in love with the person who got her heart, like you see sometimes in sappy movies or on TV shows.

But I like that parts of her are still out there, helping others. I don't remember much about her, but from what I hear, she always looked for ways to help people. Also, like you said, nothing is fair. Don't blame yourself for wishing for a new lung. I'm wishing for your new lung, and I've been on the other side, having my life turned around by one awful phone call.

As for all the self-pity and defeatist thinking, screw everyone! (I say this because you're in a hospital, and it would be difficult for you to take that literally.) Write your play. I'll read it. And if it's as brilliant as you want it to be, I'll get others to read it too, or maybe even find people to perform it.

I think I have a way to get to Rochester this weekend. There's a message board by the cafeteria, and somebody wants a passenger to contribute gas money. It's a girl, and she didn't mention wanting to touch my breasts, so I think we're safe.

January 14, 2001

To: BrickerRobin82@hotmail.com
From: Reardon_Jed@hoyt.edu
Re: thanks again

Robin,

These skittles are delicious; your snowman jar is
smiling at me while I eat his insides and type my
email to you.

It was great seeing you yesterday. I know I look
different, and you did a great job pretending not to
be shocked at how puffy the steroids made me. I've come
to the conclusion that getting a transplant is just a
giant test for the people I care about. When/if the
surgery ever happens, will I have managed to drive
everyone away? Will I be alone?

Please don't read an attempted guilt trip into that.
It's not my intention. No, I've been thinking about
our mothers—how hard it must have been to lose your
mom, and how hard it is for my mother to know she's
losing me.

Life is short. People say that all the time, but few
accept it as truth. Yet I've always known that I would
die. I was five when I understood that you can't beat
death. Most people hit old age before that sinks in. I
bet that's the only meaningful difference between me and
a healthy person. Still, I refuse to be chipper about
CF, claiming that it's made me who I am. Even if I'm
angry at fate or at all the imperfect people I know for
not giving me what I want when I want it, I'm still glad
to be alive. I still need to live as if I wasn't dying.

We all do.

We dive in and hold our breath while we're underwater.
We have faith our lungs will work when we come back up
for air. We love and hope to be loved back.

Someday, I will die, but so will you. I pray that,
in the end, we'll remember the wonder and pleasure of

living. Like an instant replay of our best moments
right before we go.

Love (don't freak out that I'm using the word),

Jed

P.S. I know this letter was rambling. When I get into
a mood like this, I go with it. So I'll start writing
my play now.

Forcing myself back to 2013, to a world where I can't hit "reply" to an email from Jed, I look at the clock. It's after midnight, but she was always a night-owl.

I pick up my phone and dial. If I'm wrong and she's asleep, hopefully her phone will be on silent and I won't have disturbed her.

She answers after the second ring. "Robin," she says. "It's been way too long. I've been meaning to call you. What's up?"

"I need to see you. When can I drive up to Hoyt?"

11:45 p.m.

Catherine pours cream into her coffee and stirs. We sit at a diner in between Hoyt and Des Moines. She drove south and I drove north, choosing this roadside restaurant as our meeting place.

Catherine flips through the script of Jed's play, which I brought to show her. "Does Isobel need anything? Sets or costumes? I could loan you stuff."

"It's pretty simple," I reply. "Costumes are just street clothes, but I get to be in charge of what everyone wears."

"Of course you do." She smiles. "You always were a costume designer at heart."

I laugh and let out an embarrassed "I suppose," aware of how badly I'm propagating my image. I have on a pair of knee-length sweatpants and an *Arrested Development* banana stand T-shirt, which belongs to Nick. If I was a therapist, I'd say that wearing something of Nick's to meet Catherine is significant. Like I'm trying to stay true to him while meeting with Jed's mother.

"I can't believe you're performing this," Catherine says. "How is Isobel managing the staging?"

"We have a loft, and the scenes in Grayson's head are performed up above, and the 'real life' scenes are below."

She scoots the script towards me and points. "I always liked that line," she says. "*Whatever exists in fiction, exists in reality. It just gets twisted up.*' It's a comforting idea."

"Yeah . . ." I sip my coffee and take a half-hearted bite of my cherry pie. Catherine narrows her eyes, displaying new wrinkles and the beginnings of crow's feet. If ever a woman earned a few wrinkles, it's her.

"I'm sorry I've been unavailable," she tells me.

"What are you talking about? You've been pretty available for teaching in Northern Wales." Catherine and I texted while she was abroad, like on Jed's birthday. And she called at the end of May, once she was back in the States. We just haven't found a good time to truly catch up. "I've been dying to hear about your trip."

"But that's not why we're here." Catherine's voice is warm and flat, like the pancakes she's eating.

I stretch in my seat and pull back my shoulders. Being in Catherine's presence makes me aware of my posture. "I've had an interesting year."

"Oh, sweetie, I'm aware. A friend recorded all the episodes of *The Holdout,* and I watched them first thing, soon as I got back. You were fabulous, but that Grant guy was a jerk! Tell me you're not still seeing him."

"No, not him. Someone else."

"Good. It's about time." Catherine pours a little bit of syrup onto her pancakes, replenishing what's already soaked in. "What's he like?"

"He's great. He's . . . so sweet and strong. Most of the time, I think he's way too good for me."

She takes a delicate bite of her pancakes, places her fork down on the side of her plate, and weaves her slender fingers together. "What about the rest of the time?"

I clear my throat. "Ever since we started doing the play, I can't stop thinking about Jed."

"Oh, Robin." Catherine's face droops. Her eyes drift to the postage stamp artwork that hangs on the wall.

"It's not always bad," I qualify. "Most of the time, I remember old conversations, like he's somebody I haven't heard from in a while."

Catherine nods and silently prods me to continue.

"But then I stop and ask myself, *What the hell am I doing?* Who sets out to be an actress but settles down in Des Moines because she's too afraid to sever ties? Who goes on a reality show, makes herself vulnerable, and returns to real life, only to repeat the cycle? It's like rinse, repeat, rinse, repeat, but I'm running out of shampoo. Or I need conditioner." I shrug. "I don't know. Am I making any sense?"

"A little." She reaches across the table and takes my hand. "When you say you're repeating the cycle, do you mean doing Jed's play? Or that you've fallen in love again?"

"Both." I clear my gunky throat. It's amazing how congested talking to my near-mother-in-law makes me. "I don't know if I can be with Nick *and* do Jed's play. But I have to do Jed's play. I've made a commitment, and it's too late to back out. Besides, I don't want to back out."

"The play will end in a few weeks. Then, you can focus on your relationship with Nick."

"Maybe." I push away my cooling coffee cup. "Jed's been making appearances in my dreams, and I can't escape this guilt cloud hovering over me." As I raise a hand to my throbbing forehead, exhaustion hits. "It's been eleven years. I should be past it all. If you'd asked me months ago, I'd have said that I was. And here's Nick, the first guy since Jed whom I love. Yet I can't tell him the truth about . . . everything. Now, Nick wants to buy a house together. How can I do that when part of me is still tied to Jed?"

"Oh, I see."

I try to find judgment or indictment in Catherine's face. But this woman has made her living in theater. She knows how to choose her emotions.

"None of this is easy to talk about. And things with Jed . . ." My voice trails off. I don't need to finish for Catherine to understand.

She's a living witness to how things were between Jed and me.

SIX

"Do you want any?" I reached across the tiny diner table and offered my nearly empty plate to my dad. He fought with himself for a moment before he grabbed a few French fries.

"You should eat these." He shoved them into his mouth and talked as he chewed. "You're the one with the fast metabolism."

"Please," I replied. My tall, thin genes came from him, as did my need to stay active. If my dad always had a sprained wrist or a busted knee, it was because he's incapable of sitting still. "You need to beef up before your bike trip. How many countries will you travel through?"

"Just the wine country of Germany and France."

"Oh, that's all?" I said with a smile. "Sounds fabulous."

Here I had been worried about my father being alone, but he'd joined a mature single's bike club. They would cycle through European vineyards in the middle of May, only getting back to the U.S. in time for him to pick me up at the end of term.

"It will be great," he said. "But I need to get in shape, and that doesn't include eating French fries." He took a sip of water to wash down his last bite. "But you're right, these are good."

My dad was visiting to see me perform in a student-directed comedy show, and I'd taken him to this off-campus diner for lunch. Now there were several hours to kill before show time, and I had to figure out what we could do. The only tourist attractions that Hoyt boasted were its small-town bank, which was built in the 1800s, a community park, and the swimming pool at the hotel where my dad was staying.

"Should we walk back to the hotel and go swimming?" I asked. "The bank is on the way, and we could stop and take a look."

"Sure," he said, "but you don't need to entertain me. If you have to study, we could just meet up later."

"No, no. Let's hang out." I took a final, loud sip of Coke through the straw and placed the empty glass against the red gingham table-cloth. "Are you ready?"

"You bet. Do I pay at the register?" My dad got out his wallet. I didn't even pretend to offer because I knew he'd refuse. Either way, it would have been his money.

"Yeah," I answered. "Thanks for lunch, Dad."

We gingerly walked through the tiny diner, with its many tables packed into the limited space. I stood at the register while my dad settled the bill. My back was to the door. When there was a gust of cold air, I turned and discovered Jed and Catherine had entered.

We may as well have stood in an elevator. Instantly claustro-phobic, I backed up, almost tripping over the sandwich board that listed the day's specials.

Catherine was the first to speak. "Well, hello, Robin. Is this your dad?"

"Yeah," I managed. "He's here to see the show tonight."

My dad finished paying and turned as he put his wallet in his back pocket. I introduced him to Jed and Catherine. Then there was this awkward silence when I wanted to pull Jed aside, ques-tions ready to leap from my lips. Why hadn't he told me he was out of the hospital? Why hadn't he answered my last email? Would he get his lung transplant? Was he up for going out some time?

I didn't need to ask. One look between us communicated every-thing. "Sorry I haven't been in touch," Jed said, his gaze as intense as always. "They discharged me, and a lot has been going on, but I was going to call and see if you wanted to hang." He coughed. "I could use a distraction while I wait for my beeper to go off."

He lifted the beeper from his jacket pocket and pressed the 'test' button. It lit up and beeped out a little tune. "I do that all the time," he said, smiling. "I can't help myself."

I laughed and reached out my hand. "Let me see it." He gave it to me, and I inspected it. "It's like you're waiting for a table at the Cheesecake Factory."

"I know!" Jed grinned. "Every time I look at it, I think about avocado eggrolls."

"I LOVE avocado eggrolls!"

"Yeah, me too."

Everything around us slipped away. It was just him and me . . . until my dad cleared his throat and turned, a question mark plastered on his face. I handed the beeper back to Jed and spoke to my dad. "Jed's waiting for a lung transplant," I told him.

"Too much smoking," said Jed.

Catherine gave him a light smack on the shoulder. "That's not funny, Jed." She looked at my father. "Jed was born with cystic fibrosis."

Two more people came into the diner, making the space as cramped as Marshall's clearance aisles. "We should go," I said, though I wished to stay and talk to Jed. "You should come to the show tonight," I offered. "I'm hoping it will be funny."

"Yeah, maybe," said Catherine, as if it was her I'd invited. "Break a leg tonight, and have a good afternoon."

"Nice meeting you," said my father. He guided me out the door. Jed gave me a tight-lipped smile and a wave, so I waved goodbye back.

Once we were outside, Dad zipped up his jacket, hunching his shoulders against the cold. "Poor kid," he said. "I can't imagine being that sick. Are you good friends with him?"

"We've exchanged emails. He wrote to me while he was in the hospital, and I went to visit him."

Dad and I walked down the narrow sidewalk, stepping over

114

piles of slush and patches of ice. "How come you never mentioned him before?"

"I don't know." I straightened my stocking cap, raising it further up my forehead so it wasn't quite so itchy. "I guess . . ." I sighed. "Dad, would you think I'm a bad person if I told you that I'm sort of scared to get close to him? I like Jed, but I have awful thoughts, like, what's the point of being with a guy who's going to die soon? I'm sure to get hurt."

Dad stopped in his tracks. Close, personal discussions were never our strength. Maybe this was too much for him and he couldn't balance his feelings with walking. "You're human for thinking that way, honey." He placed his hand on my shoulder. "But none of us know when our time is coming; your mother certainly didn't. And I wouldn't change any of my choices, even knowing she'd die young."

I looked both inward and down, at my emotions and at my black Doc Martens. It was easier than looking Dad in the eye. Then I hugged him—another form of escape.

"Are you okay, Robin?"

"Yeah." I took a long breath, in and out, aware that Jed couldn't do the same. Not with the same depth, anyway. "Thinking about Mom makes me sad."

"Me too." Dad released me and tugged on my sleeve. "Shall we go look at that bank museum?"

We hooked our arms and walked. I pretended to be comforted by my dad's words, yet the opposite was true. Almost seventeen years after my mother died, talking about her still made him sad.

How could he say he'd still do everything the same way?

• • •

The comedy show was called *Exquisite Corpse.* It contained a bunch of sketches created through improvisation, all of them having to do with death. But yes, it was supposed to be funny.

For example, I had a melodramatic monologue about a plant that had died. In another sketch, I claimed to be possessed by dead celebrities.

When I encouraged Jed to come, I hadn't thought about the death scenes. I was aware of it now, on stage. Hearing his hacking cough from the audience, I tried not to let it throw me. But I may as well have been a Frisbee.

I wasn't in every scene. While backstage, Miranda, who was also in the show, saw me peeking out at the audience.

"Who are you trying to find?" she whispered.

"My dad and Jed."

"His cough is coming from house left," she mumbled into my ear. "I don't know why he came. He can't sit through the show without hacking up blood."

Hot anger leapt out as I spun to face her. "That's mean!" My whisper was fierce. "Have some compassion. And he isn't coughing up blood."

She held up her hands in surrender. "Sorry. I didn't know you two were so close."

I shook my head and backed away from the curtain. Then I closed my eyes and rotated my head, which is actor speak for "Leave me alone. I'm getting into character." And I was trying to concentrate. My monologue was coming up, and I had to funnel strong emotions into grief over a dead hibiscus.

When the show ended, I found my dad in the lobby. After he hugged me and told me how great I was, I told him to hang on a minute and that I would be right back. Then I approached Jed, who stood, hands in his jacket pockets, trying to blend in with the potted trees by the box office.

"Hey," I said. "I'm glad you came."

"I'm not," said a paunchy, middle-aged guy as he walked past us. Then he coughed in this overstated, schoolyard imitation of Jed. Jed's face turned bright red.

"Do you know him?" I asked Jed.

"No."

I pushed up the sleeves of my cable knit sweater dress and started after the jerk. Jed grabbed my arm and tugged me back.

"Don't, Robin."

"He has no right to act that way!" I said. "And I'll tell him so."

The flush of Jed's face receded, leaving his cheeks pink and matching his lips and the faded red sweatshirt peeking out from under his jacket. "What else will you tell him? That I'm sick? You'll make him feel guilty?"

I threw my free hand in the air. "What's wrong with that?"

Jed loosened his grip. Now his fingers felt almost like a caress. "It's wrong because it's a waste of time." He looked up at the clock on the wall. "I have to get going soon, and I have something to ask you."

The inside of my chest trembled. Why couldn't my heart beat in a regular rhythm when he was nearby? "What?" I asked.

"Do you still swim every day?"

I pulled back in surprise. This winter, I had described my afternoon routine of swimming laps to Jed in an email, but until he mentioned it, it had been at the bottom of my brain's slush pile.

"Yeah," I said. "Why?"

"I need to exercise more," he answered. "CF patients are supposed to exercise a lot; it helps with treatment. So I was wondering what time you usually go to the pool and if you'd mind if I joined you."

A chance to see him every day in an environment where we'd be wet and close to naked? I envisioned us as Brooke Shields and Christopher Atkins in *Blue Lagoon*, except we wouldn't be surrounded by sand and palm trees, and we'd be separated by those thick, plastic ropes that divided the lap lanes. Still . . .

"Sure," I said. "I'd love some company. I get to the pool around 3:00 p.m. Does that work for you?"

"Yeah. I'm not taking any classes this semester, so my schedule is pretty open. Plus, I have a car now, so I don't need my mom to drive me back and forth from campus."

"What? How?"

He cleared his throat. "It's a guilt gift from my dad. He thought it would be good for me to get out more while I wait for my lungs. My mom isn't thrilled, but I promised her I'd put it to good use, and I think driving to the pool qualifies."

"That's great." I looked over at my dad, who stood in the middle of the lobby, reading his program and waiting for me to come back. It would be monstrous to ditch him and ask Jed to take me for a drive.

"So Monday, three o'clock?" Jed asked.

"Yeah, great." I beamed at him. "What are you doing right now? Do you *have* to go?"

Jed nodded and coughed simultaneously. "I'm pretty tired."

"Sure." I swiped away a lock of hair that had fallen onto his forehead. "Take care of yourself."

When he smiled, unfazed by my intimate gesture, my heart trembled again.

"I'll see you Monday."

Tuesday, March 6, 2001

Doing the breaststroke, my goggles fogged as I lifted my head in and out of water. The echoes in the room faded, and my ears got clogged from chlorine, but with the sunlight shining through the windows, I could have been anywhere. It could have been June, at the lake, instead of late winter, here at school. Plus, Jed was in the lap lane next to me, and that made this, without a doubt, the best part of my day.

But it would get even better. Every afternoon, when we were done with our laps, we'd sit in the sauna. Today he finished first, and I found him sitting on the wooden bench nearest the grate that covered what looked like hot coals, but it was really just an electric heater.

"How was your swim?" I asked.

"Good," he murmured. "You?"

"Great." I sat down next to him, flipping my hair and spraying him with drops of water. The droplets landed on his smooth chest and traveled towards his belly button, which was surrounded by a little ring of golden-brown hair.

Then I noticed Jed was struggling for breath. He clutched the bench, arching his neck while his chest heaved up and down.

I put my hand on his back. "Jed, are you okay?"

"Just a little winded," he struggled out. His panicked eyes widened, and his face went pale. I looked around the sauna room, as if I could find something to help us. Should I call for someone, or did this happen to him every day?

I took his hand and put it on my chest. "Jed, try to relax and breathe with me." I inhaled and exhaled slowly and purposefully, like I'd been taught to do in voice and movement class. The heat of the sauna enveloped us, and the echoes from the pool room leaked in, but it was just the two of us, focusing on the most basic part of life, on the first and last part of living.

After a couple of minutes, Jed's panicked look was replaced by something a little more relaxed. The color returned to his skin.

"I think the medical profession has it all wrong," Jed said once he had the lung capacity to speak.

"Why? What do you mean?"

He smiled. "All CF treatments should involve saunas and beautiful girls in swimming suits who let you touch their chests." He gave me a thumbs-up. "You get a five-star rating from me."

"Good to know. If this theater thing doesn't work out, I have options." I leaned back and laid my head against the wall, pretending not to notice that Jed called me beautiful. "Hey. How's your play coming? Have you gotten any writing done?"

Jed leaned his head against the wall too, but he rotated so he could look at me. "A little. There's a competition I want to enter."

"What's the competition?"

"It's by the Princess Grace Foundation. They set it up to help emerging artists, and the winner gets $7,000 to produce their play."

"Wow." I stretched out my legs. "And it's the play about Chopin that you're going to enter?"

"Yeah."

Jed had told me about his play—how people believed Chopin suffered from cystic fibrosis before they knew what cystic fibrosis was. Jed wanted to focus on Chopin's drive to make music, above all else, and how this legacy had made him, in a sense, immortal.

But it took a lot of research, and the play was slow-going.

"When do you have to enter?"

"Soon. The deadline is coming up."

"Will you be done in time?"

He shrugged. "I don't know. Maybe. I'm going to try."

"Right." I nodded. "But if you're not, I'm sure you could get your play produced at Hoyt."

He bristled. "By my mom?"

"No, by a student. Like, as their directing project."

His head still rested against the wall, and he smiled and closed his eyes. "Maybe. Then you could be in it. You could be George Sand."

He was unaware of my gaze, so I indulged in studying his face. Then my eyes traveled down, and I watched the uneasy rise and fall of his chest. When I looked back up, his eyes were open.

"Has anyone ever told you that you're cute with wet hair?"

"No," I laughed. "I haven't heard that one before."

"You're like a seal, in your black Speedo with your hair slicked back."

"Is that a good thing?"

He put one hand on my neck, right below my head. "Definitely," he murmured. "Although, if you decide to wear a bikini sometime, I won't complain."

"Bikinis aren't very practical for swimming laps."

He shrugged. "So we'll just lounge in the pool. Float and stuff."

I let my fingertips graze his chest. "Sounds fun."

He put some pressure against my head at the same time that he leaned towards me, and I was just about to wrap my arms around his shoulders and spoil myself with a sauna make-out session, but the door opened and somebody else walked in.

We pulled apart.

"Hey," Jed said to me after a moment. "I can't meet you tomorrow. I have a doctor's appointment."

"For what?"

"Sinus irrigation." He coughed. "My least favorite thing in the world—they're really painful."

"That's too bad." I put my hand on his thigh, aware we had company but still needing to touch him. "Thursday, then?"

Another cough. "Maybe. I hope so."

But Thursday came, and there was no Jed. Later, when I called his house and Catherine picked up, she told me he'd had a bad couple of days. On Friday, Jed emailed, saying the same—that I shouldn't expect him to come swimming for a while.

But he'd miss me.

There were no rules for courtship with a guy on the transplant list. When should you assume you're getting blown off? *He's sick,* I told myself. *He's not making excuses.*

But the more I told myself that, the more true fear gnawed inside my stomach.

Monday, March 19, 2001

The spring equinox was cold, but that's no surprise for northern Iowa. Slushy puddles of snow were everywhere, and gray clouds spilled out of the sky. But Andrew heard that you could stand eggs on end, and because of the equinox's special gravitational pull, they'd stay upright. Andrew did work-study in the cafeteria and stole as many eggs as he could fit into his pockets. He, Miranda, and I kneeled in the damp courtyard outside the theater building, trying to stand our eggs upright before we went back in for set building practicum.

My egg kept rolling over. "Dang," I say. "Why won't it work?"

"Robin, watch your language!" Miranda's chiding was playful as she attempted to stand up her egg. Months ago, when I was the Hoyt harlot for hooking up with Lucas, Miranda offered me a high-five. Now we were friends.

Frustrated and sore-kneed, I got up. "Aren't we supposed to do this at a certain time, like at noon? Because it isn't working."

Andrew kept trying. "You have to balance them right."

"But isn't the whole point of this that they'll stand on their own?" Miranda let her egg fall, and she got up too. "This is stupid. I'm hungry. Let's make an omelet."

"Oh my God! Look!" Andrew yelled and held out his hands in this "behold" sort of way. Like rays of light shot from his fingers to highlight his egg, which balanced on its end.

"Wow, it worked," said Miranda, her voice full of wonder. "I have to get a camera. This is awesome."

"Robin!"

I jumped when an adult voice called my name. When I realized it was Catherine, I stumbled, smack, onto Andrew's egg.

"Hey!"

"Robin!"

"I wanted to take a picture of that!"

"And I wanted to make an omelet!"

"Sorry!" I cried.

While trying to wipe the egg yolk from the bottom of my worn black boots, I hustled over to see what school-type thing Catherine wanted. She stood in the arched doorway to the theater building, wearing a maroon turtleneck sweater with brown corduroy pants.

Fall colors. With her complexion, I'd have gone for winter.

I slouched, because if I stood up straight, I'd tower over her, and this moment seemed to call for self-diminishment. "What is it?" I breathed.

"Do you have plans tomorrow night?"

My throat went dry. I'd expected some theater-related question. Like why I made the inane decision to play joy rather than anger in my *Heidi Chronicles* monologue. But she was worried about my social life? It was like picking up a textbook and finding the pages of *Vogue* inside.

"Um, no."

She blinked a couple of times and smiled, the edges of her mouth fighting with her eyes. "Tomorrow is Jed's birthday, and I'm having people over. His lung function hasn't been good, he's had this fungal infection, but he doesn't want to be back at the hospital . . ." She attempted a smile again, this time managing a more convincing job. "Jed would be furious if he knew I told you all this. But can you come? It's just some family friends. He said not to do anything, but, well, it could be his last birthday. We should celebrate the time we have."

"Yeah, of course," I said.

"Wonderful. I can drive you back and forth, if you want to meet me here, say, at a quarter to six?"

"That sounds great. Thank you."

Catherine nodded, and then she turned and walked back inside. Meanwhile, Miranda and Andrew had watched our interaction, and they approached.

"What was that about?" Miranda asked.

"Catherine is having a birthday party for Jed, and she wants me to come. She's even going to give me a ride."

"Wow. That won't be awkward," said Andrew, his voice low and sarcastic.

I looked at him. "You have egg yolk on those gorgeous gabardine pants."

He lowered his gaze, horror spreading across his features. Miranda took my arm and steered me inside. "We're skipping set-building practicum to go shopping. You have to bring the perfect birthday present."

"Good idea," I replied.

But I wondered, *Do any of the stores at the mall sell lungs?*

Tuesday, March 20, 2001

I sat, buckled into the passenger side of Catherine's Hybrid Prius, with Jed's present in my lap. For a moment, Catherine took her eyes off the road and looked down at my leopard-print boots.

"I like your boots," she said. "They look like something from the Mod Squad."

"Thanks. That's what I was going for."

"You made them?"

"Oh, no." I scratched my wrist even though it didn't itch. "But I found these canvas boots at the Army/Navy store and attached fabric to them."

Catherine took another look, squinting and thinking hard. I had the sudden urge to tuck my legs underneath me and hide them from sight. The leopard print fabric was used in a play we did this winter. Catherine must have recognized it.

"They said I could use the fabric because there wasn't enough for anything practical."

"It's fine, Robin." Catherine smiled as she steered. "I'm impressed by your resourcefulness and creativity."

"Oh, thanks."

"But you're a performance major and not costume design?"

"Yeah." I laughed. "I've always been an attention whore." I cringed, internally hitting myself for using the word 'whore' to describe myself to Jed's mother.

But Catherine just stared ahead, unfazed. "There are lots of ways to get attention. If you have a gift, you should nurture it."

"I never thought of it as a gift. I just like clothes. But I have other interests too."

"Okay." She shrugged. "It's better to have too many interests than not enough. What else do you like?"

I shifted in my seat. "The usual stuff. Theater, movies, books, television. I like to swim. I was on my high school's swim team. I also did track in the spring. Other than that, spending time with my friends and family. Sleeping. Eating chocolate."

"I'm with you on that," Catherine said, a chuckle skipping out. "Is there anything else?"

Was she fishing? If this was a test, I wanted to pass. "I like Jed."

Her eyebrows shot up.

"He likes you too," she replied. "I'm happy. For most of his life, Jed has seen himself as an imposition. It started after his father left. He couldn't deal with Jed's illness. Ever since, Jed hasn't let himself get too close to anyone. He seems different with you."

Had she read our emails or overheard our phone calls? Had Jed talked about me to her? He must have said something. I used caution, as if clutching the rails at a roller skating rink.

"Is that why he wanted me to come tonight?"

"Oh . . ." Catherine's face muscles twitched. "You're a surprise. The whole evening is. Didn't I mention that before?"

"No, I'm pretty sure you didn't." I looked out the window. Should I fake a headache and demand to be taken back? But the wheels were in motion. I let go and mentally skated into the center of the rink. "I hope he likes surprises."

Soon we pulled into the driveway of her pale-green ranch-style home. She got out first, then me. I ignored my roiling stomach, regretting the sloppy Joe that hours ago, in the student cafeteria, had seemed like a good idea.

"The other guests won't be here for a little while." Catherine walked up to the front door. "So Jed will see you first, and he'll get used to the idea of having people over. It will be perfect."

She unlocked the door, and we walked into a darkened living room with drawn shades and a weird, medicinal smell, like Pine Sol and Band-Aids.

"Jed?" she called as she turned on the lights, revealing a charming set of beige furniture and a dark red patterned rug. When there was no answer, Catherine turned to me, her face neutral, like a dentist who's promised that this won't hurt.

"Have a seat." She pointed to the couch. "Make yourself comfortable. I'll just go check on him."

I sat on the edge of the couch, not wanting to get so comfortable that I couldn't jump up and sprint out. I heard Catherine's footsteps above me, and then a knock and the squeak of a door.

There was unintelligible talking back and forth, which soon gave way to angry yelling. "You had no right to do that!" and "I'm not going to let you just sit around here and rot!" and "It's my life, Mom!" and "Well, I'm not telling her to go. If that's what you want, tell her yourself."

Soon there were more footsteps, and Catherine came downstairs.

"He'll be right out."

"Umm, if you need to take me back, I understand."

"No, no." Flustered, she ran her fingers through her wavy hair. "We're going to have a nice dinner. You eat meat, right? We're having beef Wellington."

Then Jed called from the top of the stairs. "Robin?" His voice was soft and tentative.

"Yeah," I said, waving from the foot of the stairwell. "Hi."

"Hi."

Even in the shadows, I could see his face light up. His smile was all I needed. I walked up the stairs, and he walked down. When we met in the middle, he grabbed my hand and led me to his room.

Jed closed the door behind us, and then he took my gift and placed it on his bed. The lights were off; in the dusk, he removed my coat and placed it on his bed too. Then he kneeled down, stroked my legs, and said, "Killer boots."

"Thanks."

He put his hands on my waist, over the fabric of my fitted dress. His touch scorched right through to my skin. "Compared to you, I am very underdressed."

He wore jeans and a plain white T-shirt. In the fading light, he looked like a ghost of himself, a facsimile in faded denim and cotton. There was something endearing about his disheveled appearance.

"I wouldn't say that." My voice was barely above a whisper. "You look perfect."

"So do you."

His mouth met mine. Should I pretend to push him away? There was no point, and I became a vine wrapping around his trellis. We kissed until his lips seared a path down my neck to the hollow at the base of my throat, with a brief detour to nibble my earlobe. He tightened his arms, and heat traveled all over me, even to my hands and scalp.

Jed carried me over to the bed, and we lowered ourselves so that he was on top. Our clothes were still intact; he hadn't yet tried for second base. But he was rock hard and pressing against me. I was more turned on than I'd ever been in my life. His heart hammered against my chest. His breathing was hitched, a low, raspy sound that made my heart flutter.

Jed wasn't above trying to score. His hand crept up my thigh, and I had to sit up.

"What's wrong?" he asked, concern etched into his face.

"Nothing. But we shouldn't overdo it, right?"

He laughed and held me close. "Don't worry. I'm having a really good day."

We held each other for a moment, our pulses beating in tandem. Soon, Jed started kissing my neck, ready for round two. I put my hands against his chest to create space between us.

"Your mom is downstairs," I whispered. "And more people are coming soon."

"I know," he whispered back. "We're having beef Wellington. That's always been my favorite, but lately I can't eat, even when I'm hungry. You'll have to enjoy it for me, and in turn, I can enjoy you."

I laughed. "That's cheesy."

He laughed too. "But it's my birthday." He kissed me again, and I let his lips stay on mine for several seconds, aware that Catherine could walk in at any moment.

"Hey," I said as I pried myself from his arms. "You should open your present." I sat up, looked around his bed, and found it in the left-hand corner. "Here." I placed the present in his lap.

"You didn't have to get me anything."

I shrugged. "It's your birthday. I wanted to."

"Okay." Then Jed tore at the wrapping and found a boxed lava lamp underneath.

"Haven't you always wanted a lava lamp?"

"Sure." Jed bit the inside of his cheek, trying not to laugh and struggling to be sincere. "Thanks. I love it."

"No, you don't." I adjusted my mussed-up dress and tucked back my tangled hair. "But we went to Spencer's Gifts, and the choices were limited. There was a statue of two deer fornicating, and there was a T-shirt that said, 'Of course I love you. My dick is hard.' After considering both of those, I went the tasteful route and got you the lava lamp instead."

Jed took the lava lamp from its box and rubbed it like a genie might come out.

"It's the best birthday present ever." Then he reached over and caressed my cheek. "Thank you."

I shrugged. "You're welcome."

After walking over to his messy desk, Jed cleared a spot for the lamp, plugged it in, and turned it on. A purplish light illuminated the room. He turned towards me, the hollows in his cheeks made more prominent by the iridescent light.

"I never knew I needed this. It sets the mood perfectly."

"Sets the mood for what?"

"Writing my play, of course." He came back and crawled into my arms.

I stroked his chest and held him, and he rested his head against my shoulder. When he coughed, I wanted to tighten my grip and somehow protect and hold him down. But I rubbed his back instead. "Should I start hitting you?" I asked. "Would that help?"

He shook his head but continued to hack. "Just give me a minute." He wheezed and looked around the room. When his gaze fell on what had to be an oxygen tank, he got up and brought it over to the bed, and he hooked the little tubes around his neck and into his nostrils.

"This is a sexy look, huh?" He coughed some more, but already he sounded better.

"You carry it off." I scooted in closer, so our legs were reunited and once again pressed against each other. "Why didn't you want me here?"

Jed raised an eyebrow and coughed one more time, a baby-wolf-cub cough that was barely intimidating. "You heard me and my mom yelling?"

"It was sort of hard not to."

"Sorry. I do want you here; it's just that my mom doesn't understand how other people feel." Jed shifted and tried to flatten the charcoal-colored sheets twisted beneath us. "She's always taken care of me, and she doesn't realize how others are put off by what she deals with every day."

"And you think I'll be put off?"

"You will be put off, Robin. It just hasn't happened yet."

"Maybe, but I've never been the squeamish sort."

Jed kept not looking at me. "This isn't about being squeamish, though dealing with my digestive crap takes a strong stomach." He struggled to take a deep breath. "Once the reality of my condition sinks in, you'll be tempted to run. I'm not saying that you will. But if you do, I'll understand."

I placed one hand on top of one of his, wove our fingers together, and squeezed. "I have no idea what to say," I whispered.

Jed met my gaze. The soft, sad curve of his lips reached his eyes. "I'm glad you're being honest. That's one of my favorite things about you. No pretense." He pulled me onto his lap, and we sat there, arms wrapped around each other and breathing together.

"Can I ask you something?"

"Hmm?"

The butterflies in my stomach flapped wildly. "Do you still sleep with a lot of different girls?"

He pulled away. "No." Jed's voice was urgent and hushed. He pressed his lips to my collarbone. "I haven't been with anyone since we kissed at the cast party." His eyes met mine. "Do you believe me?"

"I don't know." I adjusted myself in his lap. "I mean, I realize that in the hospital, you didn't have much opportunity. But it's not like we're in a relationship. You have every right to do what you want."

His hand crept up, and he combed his fingers through my hair. "Now I know you don't believe that." Jed smiled. "Come on, how big of a jerk would I be if I slept around these last few months and didn't even tell you?"

I shrugged. "You never promised me anything."

"But I want to. And as soon as I get my new lungs, I'll promise you all sorts of things. Okay?"

I nodded and smiled at his optimism, but then I rested my chin against the top of his head. That way, he wouldn't notice if a stray tear escaped or if my face betrayed my doubt.

Thursday, May 17, 2001

The days went quick, but the weeks were slow, and Jed's wait for a new lung was an unrelenting screech of nails on the chalkboard. Catherine was losing weight, and while every day she showed up to teach or direct, her presence diminished, like a bright color fading in the sun. Meanwhile, the rest of the world struggled through finals and prepared for summer. I couldn't put my life on hold even though Jed had been forced to do just that.

So I worked hard in my classes, and I hung out with all the kids who took their health for granted. And when the seniors in the theater department were putting together their final directing projects, I auditioned and Isobel cast me in her one-act play.

"Okay, which one do you think?" Isobel held up two dresses. One was black with wide straps and a scooped neckline. It would go great with both her hair and her graduation robe. The other was cobalt blue and knee-length, and the back plunged down almost as far as the waist line.

"The blue one brings out your eyes," I said. "But aren't you supposed to wear something traditional at commencement?"

"It will be under my robe!" Isobel scrutinized both dresses. "I think I like the black, though. It's very Greta Garbo, but a little long. Can you take it up for me?"

"Yeah, no problem. Go put it on, and I'll do it right now."

Isobel left for the girl's changing room, and I organized my sewing tools in preparation.

When I got a work-study job in the costume shop, it became like my second home. And Isobel became my strongest ally, other than Jed. But he wasn't on campus much. His lungs hovered at around 40 percent capacity, and his energy was too low for anything other than watching his beeper, hoping it would go off.

Isobel came back out, wearing her dress.

"You look amazing," I said.

"Thanks." She offered a bashful smile. "But it needs shortening. Can you take it up to just below the knee?"

"That short? Didn't Greta Garbo wear her dresses long?"

"Greta Garbo was a beanpole. I'm a woman, with hips and boobs, and I look better in something that shows a little leg."

"Point taken." I was on my knees as I pinned up her dress, trying to fold the fabric so it was even, but Isobel was a difficult subject. "Hold still," I demanded. "Do you have to pee or something?"

"Sorry." She stopped shifting her weight and sighed. "So I need to ask you something."

"What?" I spoke through the pins in my mouth.

"Do you remember Karl's friend, Alex? The environmental studies major?"

"Vaguely." A week ago, Isobel got me into a bar with a fake ID and introduced me to her adult-aged friends. "Was he at the bar?"

"Yeah. And he liked you."

I bit down on the pin heads, but then I thought better of it and spat them into my hand. "We talked for, like, maybe two minutes."

"Well, that was enough for him. What do you think? Double date? He's a good guy."

"Nah." I pulled on the fabric the way stylists do with hair, trying to assess if it was an equal length on both sides.

"But why?" Isobel asked. "Is it because of Jed?"

"Maybe."

Isobel stepped away so she could look down and meet my eyes. "Robin, have you thought this through?"

I grabbed the edge of the thick, wide table that served as the center of the room. It held tape measures, scissors, and countless pin cushions, but now I used it as an anchor as I rose to my feet. "There's nothing to think about. I'm just not interested in dating right now."

"But are you and Jed even a real couple?"

My blood pressure spiked. "Technically, no. But it would be weird dating someone else. And once he gets his new lungs, things will be different, and we'll define our relationship."

Isobel nodded and stood still so her dress wouldn't sway, and so she wouldn't stick herself with pins. "What if he doesn't get a transplant?"

I turned away. Confronting the mess in front of me, I grabbed spools of thread and fabric remnants. "Well," I said, trying to create order out of chaos, "then he'll be dead soon enough. And I can date anyone I damn well please." I made a big, impulsive sweeping motion with my arm, clearing the table of at least a pound's worth of crap, all in one fell swoop.

Isobel jumped back, avoiding getting hit by a pair of scissors. "Wow. When you get angry, you go all out."

Blood rushed to my face. "Sorry." I bent down to pick up what had fallen to the floor, including tissue paper pattern pieces, which floated around like fallen leaves from a tree.

"Let me help." Isobel leaned over. The pins in her dress had to be sticking her in the calves. "I'm the one who should be sorry." She placed the insurgent pair of scissors back on the table. "I didn't mean to upset you about Jed."

"It's okay." I picked up a stray spool of red thread, running it through my fingers in thought. The silence between us was heavy, filled with unspoken fears and implications. "I mean, I have to face reality." I placed the thread back on the table.

"Yeah, but knowing that doesn't make it any easier, does it?"

I blinked away tears and shook my head.

Isobel hugged me. "I'm here for you, okay?"

"Thank you." Now the pins in her dress were sticking to me, so I pulled away first. "Hey. Go change out of that dress, and I'll start hemming it for you, alright?"

Isobel did as requested, and I was glad to be alone. It was 5:30 p.m. on a Friday afternoon, and everyone had gone home except Catherine, who I'd passed right before she went into her office.

Still, when I heard noise behind me, I figured it was Isobel.

"Hey." I was still trying to put spools of thread back in their rightful place. "Where do you want to eat? I'm in the mood for Asian."

When there was no answer, I turned around. Tears streaming down her face, Catherine was smiling. And I knew.

I couldn't open my mouth for fear of puking out my heart. "Catherine?" I squeaked. "Is it Jed?"

"He just called. His beeper went off." She took both my shoulders in her hands. "We have to go, Robin. Jed's getting a new lung tonight."

SEVEN

Saturday, June 28, 2013
6:00 a.m.

We're building the set. I'm stapling a tarp to a platform. It keeps wrinkling and bulging, and it won't lay flat.

Catherine is beside me. "You're not doing it right."

"Yeah, I know. How should I fix it?"

"Get the spare set of lungs and use those. That should work."

I don't question her directive, but I do falter. "Didn't we already give the spare set to Jed?"

Catherine covers her face in her hands and weeps.

"Catherine, I'm so sorry! I didn't mean to upset you!"

I try to hug her, but she pushes me away, and her voice is muffled as she sobs.

"Oh Robin, we can never make this right. Just give up now."

The overwhelming sense of failure forces me to wake up. It was 2:00 a.m. before I got home last night, but I won't find sleep again. I put on my running gear.

Outside, the sun is strong and people are out in their yards, walking their dogs, and starting their cars. Weird. I checked the clock before I left, and it was my usual time.

A block ahead of where I'll see Flashdance Girl, I'm weighing the pros and cons of braving Whole Foods after I've showered. I'm in the mood for a lemon poppy seed muffin, and I could also buy produce and other healthy stuff. Or I could just shoot down to the

134

local bakery, buy a muffin *and* a coffee, and skip all the hassle.

My internal conflict is intense, so I don't notice when Flashdance Girl appears early. What's she doing here?

She reaches the end of the block and circles back, preying on me like a vulture. But I'm no roadkill. I ramp up my speed and run straight towards her. We're heading for a collision, and I won't flinch first. Maybe I'll knock her off her feet and displace her superior attitude.

She runs one direction down the sidewalk, and I run the other, competing in a game of chicken. My pulse sprints faster than my legs. Squinting and setting my jaw, I show her I mean business. Then I swerve, not to avoid her but to confront her head-on.

At the very last moment, right before we would slam into each other, she steps away.

"Yes!" I softly shout, and my speed accelerates as I run home. It's silly and petty, but it's better than defeat. So I'll take it.

11:30 a.m.

The buzzing table saw is earsplitting, and the smell of fresh wood is more stimulating than coffee. But I drink coffee anyway because I stopped at the bakery. I place down my electric screw-shooter, take another sip of glorious caffeine, and then put my cup on the worktable, next to a protractor.

Isobel says we're finishing the set today, come hell or high water. Des Moines rarely gets flooded, and the Bible never named Iowa as a lake of fire, so that means we're finishing the set.

"Hey! I'm here! What do you need me to do?"

Nick stands in front of me, wearing jeans and a T-shirt and holding a toolbox. He looks handyman-ready.

"Thanks for coming." I give him a hug. Then I notice he looks haggard, with shadows under his eyes and a clenched jaw.

"Late night?" The question is unfair. I'm not telling him about my midnight diner meetup with Catherine.

Nick shakes his head. "I went home early. It's what happened afterwards that wore me out."

"What?"

"My dad called. He was in one of his moods again."

After his mom died, Nick's father never recovered. He lives alone, and he spends all his free time online, either reading The Drudge Report or writing his blog, *Conspiracy News Today.*

"Did he criticize you again?" My chest constricts at the idea. How any parent could find fault with Nick is beyond me. But his father complains that Nick dropped out of college, likes music better than sports, isn't making six figures, and is still single. So something must be wrong. Oh, and Nick's disloyal because he won't watch football and he refuses to go hunting.

"Nah. He talked about the NSA. Dad's convinced his house has been bugged."

"For real?"

Nick's face sags along with his shoulders, aging him about five years in two seconds. "Do you think mental instability is hereditary?" There's a sweet, anxious edge to his voice.

I smile. "Sure."

"I'm not kidding, Robin. I don't want to end up like him."

"No way. You're nothing like your dad.

"But you don't know everything about me," Nick says, "and you know almost nothing about him."

There's a jolt of pain in my head, like an ice cream headache.

"What don't I know about you? Are you hiding a deep, dark secret?"

I expect him to laugh, but he chews the inside of his lip instead. "It's not deep or dark. My secrets are shallow and translucent."

"Okay . . ." I widen my eyes, telling him to go on.

Nick leans against the worktable, and his fingers graze the protractor resting there. He lifts it as he answers. "You're like my protractor, Robin."

"Huh?"

136

"Remember using these things in school? They measure and create angles, and they figure out points and distances. That's what you are for me. Otherwise, my life is just a bunch of parallel lines and nothing ever comes together."

I don't know whether to laugh or cry. "Nick—" I reach for him, but he steps away.

"I made it sound stupid," he says. "But that's my secret. Without you, things don't make sense. I almost called you last night, after I got off the phone with my dad. I was lying in bed, missing you. But then I thought about how tired you've been and how you're not getting enough sleep. I didn't want you to think it was a booty call, you know?" His self-deprecating laugh turns into a sweet smile, and my heart contracts.

If Nick had called me last night, I would have lied about where I was.

Around us, people are hammering and drilling, but the background noise is nothing compared to the roaring in my ears. I must tell him that I'm incapable of finding a radius or equidistant points.

But I want to be what he needs.

Isobel walks up and beams at Nick. "Excellent! You're here! We need some muscle to lift the bottom of the loft. Come with me."

Nick drops his solemn mood and, with a goofy grin, flexes his biceps. "That's right," he says. "I'm the muscle." He places the protractor back on the table and, walking off with Isobel, points at me. "Don't forget that, Rocky."

"How could I forget?" Nick may be more than an inch shorter than me, but he lifts me all the time to show off his strength. I find it charming, and okay, kind of hot.

Later, I'm painting one of the wall platforms red. I get a huge paint smudge on my baggy overalls, which will blend with other paint smudges from other shows. A door opens, and a flash appears, bathing the darkened theater with daylight.

The door closes, and my eyes readjust to the dimness. Jack's here.

"Hey," I call. He comes over.

"Are you here to be a good boyfriend and help Isobel with the set?"

Jack twists his mouth and rolls up his sleeves. "I may as well be, since the secret is out."

"Oh." I dip my brush into the red paint and make a stroke. "So Lucy said something?"

"Yeah," Jack huffs. "And she told my mom, so now I'm the hot gossip of the Harmony Central Women's Choir."

I laugh, but Jack doesn't. "I don't understand why it was ever a secret."

"Because things are complicated. I have custody and alimony to worry about." He looks around the room. "It's not a HUGE deal. But you're in no position to share my secrets when you can't reveal your own."

Stung, I focus on my brush work. "Sorry," I say.

Jack, who can never stay mad for more than thirty seconds, pats me on the back. "Robin, why can't you tell Nick about Jed? It's not like you've done anything wrong."

"Maybe not, but I feel like I've been unfaithful."

"To who? Nick or Jed?"

I let my chest rise and fall. "Both."

Nick comes over, holding a hammer.

"Okay, I hammered in over two dozen nails. I'm not sure what they were for or if they were necessary, but if I saw a nail, I made it my bitch."

Nick stands there, his hair messy and his proud smile emitting heat. My stomach takes a nosedive. He's devoted, loving, and ready to commit. Yet my heart's unavailable, vaulted away and hidden from daylight.

"I should go find Isobel," Jack says, and I point him in the right direction.

"What's wrong?" Nick asks.

Putting down my brush, I lead him through the theater doors

and out to the parking lot. We both blink away the sunshine, and I take a step backwards so we can make eye contact. I cross my arms over my chest, and then I let them fall to my side.

"Nick, I've been meaning to tell you something." I clear my throat as Nick draws his eyebrows together. "This play we're doing, it was written by my college boyfriend."

"Oh." Nick's face is dispassionate. "Have you been in touch? Is he coming to opening night?"

"No."

"Why not?" Nick tilts his head. "Haven't you told him that you're doing his play?"

Unable to meet his gaze, I shake my head. "I need to explain my relationship with him. Can we go sit somewhere?"

Nick's smile disappeared as soon as I led him out here, but now he scowls. "Is he the other guy you were in love with?"

His guilelessness squeezes my heart. "Yes."

I'm still searching for the right words to explain, but Nick's lower lip juts out. I'm tempted to use my fingers and spread his mouth into a smile.

"Why are you doing his play?" Nick's voice is hoarse. "Are you *still* in love with him?"

My throat catches and I look away, aware that I'm shaking. "He died." It takes all my courage to look back at Nick.

His jaw drops, and his foot taps against the handicapped symbol painted on the parking spot below. Nick seems as choked up as me. I go towards him, but he steps back.

"He died? That's terrible. Umm, how . . . ?"

"Cystic fibrosis. He always knew he wouldn't live very long."

Nick's eyes dart around and he nods. "How come you never told me before?"

"You said you didn't want to know."

I see him trying to wrap his head around this. "No . . . I said I didn't want to hear about . . . ." Nick blinks rapidly, so confused. "I didn't know he died."

"Please, Nick. Let's go somewhere and talk."

"No. Let's talk here." When Nick crosses his arms over his chest, it's like a door slams between us. "You're still in love with him, aren't you?" His voice is gentle, yet there's pressure on each word.

"Yes." My answer sails out, and Nick flinches like I slapped him. "I'm sorry; I know that sounds bad, but . . ."

"But you're just being honest, right?" He looks at his wrist and traces the rim of the watch his mother gave him.

I start to tell Nick that I also love him, but the words dry up. His face is a wall of anger and hurt. I wipe away a renegade tear and try to stay strong. "Nick, please, can't we go someplace other than this parking lot? I'll explain so much better that way."

He lets out an empty laugh. "What are you going to say, Robin? How will you convince me that I'm not the world's biggest tool right now?"

"What? No. You're not a tool. This isn't even about you, Nick."

As soon as I say it, I realize my mistake. Nick's eyebrows shoot up with incredulity. "It isn't? I don't play a major role here? Well, that makes it worse." He starts to walk away, but I follow him.

"No, no, that's not what I meant. It's just—it happened a long time ago. I wanted to tell you, but I couldn't."

He spins toward me. "Come on, Robin. You could've told me sooner, but you chose not to."

I'm grasping at straws, and I can hear the desperation in my voice. "You said before that I shouldn't tell you. I started to, and you stopped me."

Nick throws his hands in the air. "I'm building the set and professing my love, while you're wishing he was here instead of me." His voice cracks. "Did he write the play for you, like as a love letter to remember him by?"

I don't respond. Nick shakes his head. "Jesus Christ, he did, didn't he?" His laugh is empty. "Well, I'm sure it's a lot better than my stupid protractor speech."

"Nick . . ."

He brushes me off. "I have to go. I'm showing a house in less than an hour."

Nick gets into his car, slams the door, and with a squelch of tires, he's gone.

Sunday, June 29, 2013
5:00 p.m.

Everyone will be at my dad's surprise birthday party; even my brother, Ted, is flying in to surprise him. Since Dad's real birthday isn't until Tuesday, it's my aunt Natalie's job to deliver him to us under the guise of eating dinner at Tavern 33.

Isobel and I arrive together. I drove, since she'll go home with Jack and I'll go home alone.

"How many times have you called or texted Nick?" Isobel asks.

"I lost count." And with every unanswered text or voicemail, my desperation grows and burns like an ulcer.

We walk from the parking lot into the restaurant, which is nearly empty, save for a few customers in the front.

"Well, you look great," says Isobel. "If he does show, you'll be ready."

"Thanks." I'm wearing my red-print jersey wrap dress, which is not by Diane von Furstenberg, but I sewed it to look like it was. I've teamed it with sparkly dime-store flip-flops—my attempt at irony: teaming classy with cheap.

"Let's find Jack and help set up," I say.

We walk to the back of the restaurant, into the party room, where I expect to see Jack and Ian hanging streamers and pushing around tables. Instead, I find two extra family members—my cousin Monty and my brother, Ted. The four grown men gather around the pool table in the corner of the room.

Ian uses just one hand to control his stick and hits the cue ball so it bumps into several of the other balls. The solid yellow one rolls into a pocket.

Monty and Jack laugh and high-five, while Ted scowls and pushes Ian in the shoulder. "What are you doing? We're supposed to be stripes!"

"Don't get mad," Ian protests. "It's not easy to aim playing this way."

"Why are you shooting with one arm?" They all turn in the direction of my voice.

"It was Jack's idea," Ian says. "He said he could beat us at one-armed pool, so we're playing, brothers against brothers."

"And so far, I'm winning." Jack grins and walks over, giving Isobel a kiss on the cheek.

"We're both winning," says Monty.

"Yes, because I've sunk enough balls for us both," Jack retorts. Monty rolls his eyes.

Ted murmurs, "I'll sink your balls."

But Jack just laughs. "Hey guys, this is Isobel." He points to each family member.

"That's my brother, Monty, and my cousins, Ian and Ted."

I stand back, arms crossed, while the introductions are made.

"Hey, do you want to play?" Jack asks Isobel. "You can play with Monty and me, and Robin can join her brothers' team."

"Aren't we supposed to be setting up?" My voice is high and hard. "People will be here soon. Let's save one-armed pool for later."

They all look at me, chastened. "Geez, Robbie," mumbles Ian. "You're in a mood."

Shaking my head, I turn to my oldest brother. "Hi, Ted." We make no move to hug each other. "What's it been, six months?" Then I speak to Monty. "Aren't you supposed to be in Botswana?"

Creases form around Monty's eyes, though he's not quite smiling. "I came home for Lucy."

Then I'm fighting the urge to cry. Like a parody of a hormonal basket case, my voice goes from angry to tearful. "So she called you?"

"Um, I guess. There were a couple of hang-ups while I was on a plane. Flying here took forever." He leans his cue stick against the table and runs his hand through his hair. "Hey, your boyfriend is a real estate agent, right? Can you introduce me? We're looking for a house in the area."

I squeeze my eyes shut, and my whole face trembles.

"Robbie," says Ian. "What's wrong?"

"What did I say?" asks Monty.

"Nothing." My body pivots as my arm juts out. I shake my hand dismissively. "I just need some air." I exit through the back door.

A second later, Jack finds me in the alley, standing by the dumpsters. I hang my head in shame. "Sorry for my outburst."

"You weren't that bad," says Jack. "But are you okay?"

I breathe in and out through my nose, which is kind of gross, with the smell of spoiled food wafting through the air. "I have to be." I throttle out my words. "My dad will be here soon. I can't ruin his good time."

Jack nods. "Yeah . . ."

"By the way, if you hadn't pressured me to tell Nick, he'd be here right now, and everything would be fine."

"Maybe he'd be here, but everything would not be fine." Jack runs a hand over his balding head. Then, I'm caught off guard when he captures me in a tight hug.

"You're a good person, Robin. You loved Jed, and you were incredibly strong the whole time you were losing him."

"I wasn't incredibly strong," I mumble into his shoulder.

"Talk to Nick." Then he lets go of me. "There's no reason you have to lose him too."

I pull myself together, go back to the party, and apologize to everyone. One of the perks of a predominately male family is that they're good at ignoring emotional displays. So we set out trays of food and pitchers of beer, and we hang a banner that says "Happy 70th Birthday!"

When my dad arrives, he seems surprised and pleased, and

later Ian insists upon a second chance at the one-armed pool game. "Dad, you and Robbie can be a team," he orders.

"Then we get to be stripes." My dad picks up a cue stick.

"We'll need another team, to make it even." Ted scans the room. "How about in-laws?"

"The only in-law here is Eddie," I say, referring to Ian's husband.

"Isobel will play!" Jack grabs her hand and pulls her over. "Right?" Isobel shrugs. "Sure."

So Isobel and Eddie form an unlikely fourth team, and they're pretty good, or maybe they didn't get the memo about letting my dad and me win. Because despite my distracted, half-hearted effort and my father's arthritic shoulder, we beat Monty and Jack in the first round and play Eddie and Isobel in the finals.

It's my turn, and I'm holding my cue stick with my right hand, trying to get enough leverage to aim, when my cell phone vibrates against me. It's tucked into the folds of my dress and secured with the sash tied around my waist. When it goes off, I jump and my phone falls to the floor.

"Oops!" I cry and let go of my cue stick as I reach for my phone. It bounces off the floor and smacks Ted in the knee.

"Robin!" He grabs the stick and curses under his breath.

"Sorry!" I pick up my phone. There's a message from Nick. "Dad, you get my turn. I have to take this."

I scurry away to read the text in private.

Sorry about yesterday. Didn't mean to get so upset.

Thumbs flying, I text back. *It's okay. I understand. Are you coming to my dad's birthday?*

He responds right away. *You said before that you didn't need me to come.*

My fingers are poised over my phone. How do I answer that? Before I figure it out, I get another message.

But I'll meet you tomorrow for breakfast if you still want to talk.

I text him back, and we set up a time and place, yet my stomach is still in knots.

144

Later, Aunt Natalie brings out a huge sheet cake, lit up with seventy candles. My dad's face holds a bittersweet combination of joy and nostalgia as he takes a deep breath and blows out the candles.

"Thank you everyone for being here and celebrating with me." My father looks around the room. I follow his gaze and see Ian, his rosy face beaming, his arm draped over his husband Eddie's shoulders. Jack stands behind Isobel, his fingers in her hair and his chin resting on her head. And Monty holds Lucy while he listens to my dad. Since she's been at the party, she and Monty have been attached at the hip.

"Forgive me if I get emotional," my dad continues, "but tonight, I think I'm allowed. There is a lot of love in this room, and I'm a lucky man to be surrounded by it. If I've learned one thing over the course of seventy years, it's to count your blessings and to count them often. Each and every one of you is a blessing, and I'm happy to have you in my life."

"Here's to the next seventy years, Dad!" Ian shouts, and everyone laughs. "If anyone can make it to 140, it's you!"

While the party breaks out into little side conversations, I approach my father and give him a hug. "Happy birthday, Dad."

"Thank you, sweetheart." He hugs me back. "You put together a great party. But hey, where's Nick?"

I shrug. "He had a real estate emergency."

After a while, I find Isobel. Her eyes are bright and the light bounces off of her hair. "I'm taking off," I say. "Do you need a ride, or are you good?"

"I'm good," she replies, glancing at Jack. She leans in and whispers in my ear. "Jack introduced me to his mom, and she invited me for dinner next week!"

"That's great!" I try my best to beam and be happy.

And I am happy for Isobel. But as I walk to my car, I ruminate that while my dad is surrounded by love, he isn't *in* love. In this case, prepositions matter. As many blessings as he has to count, at the end of the night, he'll be counting them alone.

And so will I.

I start my car, but I don't drive home. Instead, I make a detour to Woodland Avenue and stop outside the little bungalow with a *For Sale* sign in the front. I try to picture living here—coming home to Nick every day and waking up to him every morning.

It could all be so wonderful, except for that little wrinkle of me still in love with Jed. I can't start a new life with Nick if Jed is going to haunt us. So I restart my engine and drive away from that lovely little house.

And my mind sprints back to the past—back to Jed.

EIGHT

Thursday, May 17, 2001

Catherine was too jumpy to drive, so she drafted Isobel. We piled into Catherine's Prius, with Isobel at the wheel, Catherine riding shotgun, and Jed and me in the back, holding hands. Thank goodness Isobel was there; her chattering made the eternal car ride bearable.

Catherine checked her watch again, and Jed rolled his eyes. "We're doing fine, Mom."

"They said we only had an hour to get to the hospital," Catherine retorted. "Between picking you up and getting to Rochester, we're cutting it close."

The car surged forward. "Don't worry," Isobel said as she wove in and out of traffic. "I'll get you there in time."

And she did. We made it to the hospital in just over thirty minutes, though it felt like thirty days. As soon as we got through admitting, Jed was whisked off for X-rays, and then they gave him a bed in the ICU. Meanwhile, we sat in the waiting room. We'd get a chance to visit before he went in for surgery.

Catherine was off filling out forms, so I was alone, staring at one of the televisions mounted to the walls. Isobel came in with two Cokes, a bag of Cheetos, and some Little Debbie oatmeal cream pies. "We never had dinner." She plopped down in the seat beside me.

"Thanks, but I'm too nervous to eat."

Isobel's mouth turned down at the same time her eyebrows shot up. "Aren't you happy? I thought this was what you were hoping for."

"Yeah . . ." I took a deep breath. "But," I whispered, "a lot can go wrong with lung transplants. Even if he makes it through, the first forty-eight hours are critical."

Catherine strode into the waiting room, clutching a clipboard with a stack of papers and a pen. "You would think, with all the forms I've already filled out, they'd have what they need. But no." She sat and stared at the papers on her lap. "I can't do all this now. I haven't even called anyone. Jed's father doesn't know yet, and I have to tell people at Hoyt, because there's no way I'll be in on Monday."

"I can call people for you," said Isobel. "Who should I contact first?"

Catherine stared at Isobel like she was trying to remember who she was and why she was here. "Isobel," she said, coming out of her fog. "I'm so sorry. I shouldn't have let you drive; I'm going to be here for hours and hours. Maybe you should call someone for a ride." Catherine's eyes darted over to me, and she rubbed and pinched her bottom lip, which was full, like Jed's. "What about you, Robin? Can you stay, or do you have a lot of homework?"

"Homework?" The word sounded as foreign as the concept. I shook my head. "I can stay." I reached over, took her free hand, and squeezed.

"I can stay too," said Isobel. "Please let me help; I'll call people so you can get those forms filled out."

Catherine nodded. After a second, she hung her head, pressed her eyes shut, and hiccupped. "Sorry," she murmured. "I'm happy. I am, but I'm also scared." I grasped her hand harder, but she didn't notice. "I can't fall apart, not until he goes into surgery. If you girls want to help, help me keep it together, okay?"

I scanned my brain. If Jed was here, in the waiting room, what would he say? He'd aim to obliterate that look in her eyes—the one that suggested sympathy for him or for herself. As if she could read my thoughts, Catherine raised her head. Her gaze bulldozed straight into me. I held my breath because I was too afraid to exhale.

"How are we doing?"

I hadn't noticed that Jed's transplant coordinator came in. She stood over us, wearing scrubs and a smile.

"Okay," Catherine answered. "How's Jed?"

"Relaxed, given the circumstances. You would think he'd had a lung transplant before!" She shifted her weight. "He's getting his nebulizer treatments, and the surgeons are preparing. Because"— she cocked her head—"the lungs are definitely a go! Dr. Rutland gave them medical clearance, so Jed should be in surgery within the next hour."

Catherine nodded rapidly, almost in a tremble.

"That's great," I said, speaking for Catherine. "I'm Robin, by the way."

"Jed's girlfriend," Catherine explained, and I tried not to glow at the label.

"Excellent," said the transplant coordinator. "It's nice to meet you. I'm Carol. And don't worry; we'll take Jed through here before he goes into surgery. You'll have a chance to wish him luck!"

With that, she strode off, her walk purposeful. Then Catherine handed me the clipboard. I recited questions, and she answered, her hands shaking in her lap. Meanwhile, Isobel called people at Hoyt.

An hour passed. A horde came streaming into the waiting room, professors and students, all from the Hoyt theater department. Isobel shrugged. "I only called a few people, but I guess news travels fast."

"We're here to support you and Jed," said Elaine, my Voice and Movement teacher and Catherine's colleague. She pulled Catherine out of her seat and gave her a hug.

Catherine returned Elaine's hug. But then Elaine started doing breathing exercises, like the vocal warm-ups she taught me in class. Soon, others joined in. "I always find this relaxing," Elaine said, between breaths. "We should center ourselves at a time like this, you know?"

In the corner, Andrew and Miranda ran lines from their scene for Acting I class. Others rehearsed choreography for an upcoming dance concert.

Catherine looked at me with arched eyebrows. "Well, it's a diversion, anyway."

Then Jed was wheeled in, and the room erupted in spontaneous applause. Jed looked shell-shocked, but he got out of his chair and accepted the high fives everyone offered him. I tried to lower the buzzing in my brain as Jed's hands made contact with girls he'd had sex with. He chatted and laughed.

There I stood, one of the few females in that waiting room who had never seen him naked.

It's not the time for jealousy, my inner critic reprimanded. *This could be the last time you'll see him. Make it count.*

Jed found my gaze from across the room, and his come-hither look drew me to him. He pulled me aside, away from everyone.

"Are you scared?" I asked.

"No." He smiled like he'd already been sliced open but it hadn't hurt. "If I die on the table, it will be a peaceful way to go. However, if I make it through the surgery but I'm in a coma or a lot of pain, I need you to tell my mom something. Okay?"

"Sure. What?"

"Tell her to think about Barry."

"Okay." I scratched at my wrist. "Who's Barry?"

"She'll know." He used his fingertips to trace my cheekbone. "I'll tell you later, unless I can't. Then it will be for my mom to tell."

"But—"

He tilted his head, leaned in, and kissed me on the mouth. His lips were warm and firm. I tried to return the pressure but was too paralyzed.

Jed whispered in my ear. "I love you. However brief or inconsequential our time has been, I love you. And I'll love you again, no matter what."

I buried my face in his neck. If I was a stronger, better person, I wouldn't have cried, but I was me and the tears flowed. "I love you too. And our time together hasn't been inconsequential, not to me. You changed my life. Please get through this surgery, okay?"

"Yeah," he said, giving me one more kiss. "Okay." His eyes lingered over my face like he was trying to memorize it. "I have to go now."

I nodded, let go, and stepped away so he could talk to Catherine and give her the final hug before disappearing behind the surgery room doors. Isobel came and put her arms around me from behind.

"He told me that he loved me."

"That's great," said Isobel.

"Yeah." Somehow, I was underwater. Saying goodbye to Jed was making me drown. "Don't let go of me," I said to Isobel. "Don't let me bolt from this room until he's gone, okay?"

"Okay."

Jed and Catherine talked with their heads close together, her nodding and him smiling. Then they hugged one last time before he released her and walked away. A nurse directed him to sit back down in the wheelchair, and with a final smile and a wave goodbye, he vanished from the room and into surgery.

"Okay," I wheezed. "I'm getting out of here for a while."

Isobel lifted her hands.

"Do you want me to come?"

I shook my head. And as I sprinted from the room, I remembered Jed's words from the night of his birthday. *You'll be tempted to run.*

Blindly, I loped through the corridors of the Mayo Clinic and made myself a promise. Two promises. One, I would never let Jed know that I was running. And two, I would always come back.

Friday, May 18, 2001

It was after 3:00 a.m. Most everyone who came to support Jed was still around, but the energy of the room slowed to a tender crawl. People slept in chairs or on the floor. Some talked in quiet whispers, and others watched *A Farewell to Arms*, which Andrew found by standing on a chair to channel flip.

Catherine sat next to me, less jittery than before, looking off at nothing. I was less jittery as well. My jog around the hospital had released most of my fizzy anxiety. Now my anxiety was of the quiet, serious sort.

"We discovered he had cystic fibrosis when he was just a few weeks old." Catherine spoke as if I'd prompted her. "He wasn't gaining weight, and something just didn't seem right, so I brought him in. The doctor examined him, did a skin test, and looked at his dirty diaper. I guess his poop was the giveaway. 'Oh, he has cystic fibrosis.' He said it like it was no big deal." She shrugged. "And he put Jed's life expectancy at twenty-one."

Catherine stared at the light brown walls. If I wasn't the only person close enough to hear her, I wouldn't have known she was talking to me.

"It's horrible to learn that you will outlive your child. He wasn't even a month old when the doctor told me. Just this tiny little baby. I wanted him to have everything. I still do."

I pulled up my knee-length socks, which kept creeping back down. It seemed impossible that less than twenty-four hours ago I woke up, got dressed, and went about my day without realizing how it would end.

"But," I said, "if this lung transplant is successful, he could live a lot longer."

"Another five years, *if* it goes well." She was so calm, like it was somebody else's son this was happening to. "Jed accepted that a long time ago. He said, 'If I could take just one deep breath, then the transplant will be worth it.' How could I say no?" Catherine used the back of her hand to wipe her tears.

"My mother was healthy, with everything to live for, when she got hit by a car and died." I rubbed at the knots along the base of my neck. "You would think I'd have a decent grasp on my own mortality. I sort of know that one day I'll die, but I don't *feel* like I will." I pressed down, hard, on the very top of my spine. "I'm not like Jed. He understands death and he's still brave."

She rotated her head and looked at me. "If Jed dies, there will be one silver lining." Her eyes were almost vacant. "I won't be afraid to die anymore."

I took her hand. She squeezed my fingers and we sat, silent and breathing, waiting for news about Jed.

Finally, Doctor Rutland came in. Dressed in scrubs, his heavily lidded eyes had purplish half-moons beneath them. He took off his surgical cap, which ruffled his hair. As he sat down next to Catherine, I noticed he wore a wedding ring. It was stupid to observe these details, but I had to distract myself in the seconds before he opened his mouth to tell us if Jed was okay.

Catherine and I clenched each other's hands.

The doctor smiled. "Jed's awake. I asked him if he wanted to see you, and he said yes."

"He can talk?" I asked.

"No. He blinked his answer, but that's fantastic. He's doing great." Doctor Rutland reclined in his chair with the look of an athlete who'd run a marathon. "The lungs he got are not the best I've ever seen, but not the worst either. Some signs of pollution and light smoking, but compared to Jed's old lungs, these are worlds away." He placed his hand on Catherine's shoulder. "I didn't realize how infected Jed's old lungs were until we removed them. He wouldn't have lasted more than a few months without this transplant."

Catherine burst into tears. It was like a dam breaking. She leaned forward and put her face in her hands, and I rubbed her back. "Sorry," she murmured as she cried. "That's great that he's doing well. I'm just emotional."

"Of course you are," the doctor said. "No need to apologize."

Catherine's face was still in her hands. He met my eyes and continued. "I can't let you see him for a little while yet, but we'll get you in there, okay? Just you two, though. We don't want to overwhelm him."

Catherine sat up, and as Doctor Rutland stood, so did she. Then she sort of leapt towards him and gave him a hug. "Thank you," she said. "Thank you so much."

He returned her hug for a moment, which was enough. "You're welcome." I thought I heard tears in his voice, too. "The next forty-eight hours are critical. Let's stay positive. There's every reason to be, and we'll hope for the best. Okay?"

Catherine stepped away, and with her hand at her throat, she wept and nodded simultaneously.

She had to sit. I spread word of Jed's successful surgery. Soon, most everyone, including Isobel, hugged us goodbye, sent Jed their love, and went home.

"Did Jed's father ever call you back?" I asked Catherine. "Is he flying out here?"

Catherine sniffed. "Probably not. He's in an off-Broadway production of *The Seagull*. It's one of his dream roles, or so he says, and if he left now . . ." Catherine waved her hand dully through the air. Then she sighed and pulled out her phone. "I'll call and let him know Jed's okay."

An hour later, a nurse took us to put on surgical gowns and masks. Then she chaperoned us into the ICU, where Jed was on a bed, hooked up to a million different machines. One seemed to be breathing for him. The sound was Darth Vader-like, with a loud, steady inhale and exhale. Jed's mouth was forced open by multiple tubes, and his lips were drawn back, like an animal baring its teeth.

It was ridiculous to have thought he might talk on his own.

Catherine went right up, but I held back, timid and terrified. How was I important enough to fill the number two spot in his life, invited to see him at his most vulnerable?

Someone had made a mistake.

"Hi, Honey," Catherine's hand crept up and out. I could see her struggle, wanting to touch him, but the nurse told us not to. Instead, she grasped the rails that surrounded his bed. "Congratulations! You made it!" Her voice was soft, like I'd always imagined my mother's would sound. "The doctor said you're doing great. I am so, so proud of you. And I love you . . . so very much."

Jed blinked rapidly, which had to be his way of telling her he loved her too. But then his eyes found mine, and he stopped blinking. My heart pounded in my throat.

"Hi." I whispered. "I'm glad you're okay."

He widened his eyes. That's when I saw that the real Jed was still inside his ravaged body. Shame pummeled me for ever having doubts. "You know," I said. "It's good the surgery happened now. By fall, you'll have recovered. So you and I can have philosophical conversations while drinking beer at frat parties."

Now he blinked.

Those beautiful blue eyes were telling me yes.

Tuesday, May 22, 2001

"Shouldn't he be awake by now?"

Doctor Rutland shrugged. "Everybody is different."

"But the high fever . . . and his color—he doesn't look right." Catherine's face was pinched, except for her mouth, which was fierce and pulled back.

"I'll admit I'm not encouraged," the doctor said, "but we have to give it more time. We're doing everything we can to bring Jed's fever down."

"If you're not encouraged, do more!" Catherine yelled and stepped into his personal space. "You can't just give up and do nothing. JED is fighting for his life. He's always had to fight for his life, and you need to fight for him too! He has to wake up! He has to!"

I wasn't sure if I should try to calm her, but I wrapped my arms around her shaking shoulders. She barely noticed. *"Please."*

Trembling, she glared at Doctor Rutland. "Do more. Figure out what's wrong with him and fix it."

The doctor sucked in a breath and nodded. "I'll do my best."

Then he walked away.

Catherine placed her head on my shoulder and sobbed. She allowed herself a half-minute breakdown before raising her head and sniffing back tears.

"I shouldn't do this to you," she said. "Leaning on you—it's wrong. Jed would be furious if he knew."

"It's fine."

She shook her head. "No, it's not." Catherine massaged her temples and paced in small circles around the hospital waiting room. I'd memorized every corner of it by now and had grown to hate it—the light brown walls, the magazine rack, which held only *US News and World Report* and *Good Housekeeping*. And the smell. Antiseptic, weak coffee combined with something sugary sweet.

"You must have schoolwork to do," Catherine said. "You shouldn't get behind."

"I can't concentrate on schoolwork right now."

Catherine stopped pacing and looked at me from across the room. "You have to. You have finals coming up. I won't let you throw away an entire semester's worth of work. That's another thing Jed would never forgive me for."

Did she think she was the only one who cared about Jed? He wasn't just some romantic idea to me; he was real. I couldn't drive off into the sunset while I waited for his credits to roll.

"Robin," Catherine said, though she was speaking to the floor. "Go home, get a good night's sleep, and attend your classes tomorrow. In the evening, you can pick up Jed's car and drive it back here. He won't mind if you use it while he's in the hospital. That way, you can get to and from campus."

Truth was, I'd love to sleep in my own bed and get out of this God-awful hospital waiting room. And I did have a ton of schoolwork to do. But how could I leave?

"What if I go and"—I sagged into the closest chair—"something happens?"

Catherine nodded, understanding the code. "Jed knows you've been here. If he dies tonight, I doubt he'll wake up first." She gasped like she'd been punched. "But if he does die, I'll tell him that you love him."

I circled my knees with my arms and pulled them to my chest. Right before his surgery, Jed said that if he wasn't doing well, I should remind Catherine of someone named Barry.

Should I mention him now? No, it wasn't time. Not yet.

I wiped my face with my sleeve and stood up. "Okay, I'll call Isobel and ask her to pick me up. You're sure you'll be okay?"

"I'll be fine. My best friend is coming, so I won't be alone." Catherine picked up her purse and pulled out a single car key on a leather strip. "Here you go." She handed me the key. "But don't let me see you back here before 6:00 p.m. tomorrow night. And that's at the absolute earliest."

"But what about you? When are you going to rest?"

Catherine placed a gentle hand against my cheek. "It's not your job to worry about me, honey. Let me be the mom, okay?"

Her words, her touch, her kindness—they were a trigger. But I couldn't succumb.

"I'll see you tomorrow," I mumbled and rushed out while I could still leave.

Saturday, June 2, 2001

Two weeks had passed since Jed's surgery. I had trouble thinking about anything but his health. Would I be this distracted for the rest of my life? Standing in the middle of my dorm room, I shifted my weight, ready to say goodbye to freshman year.

"Have a good summer." April picked up her oversized athletic bag, stuffed with the belongings she'd left in our room over the course of the year. "I'll see you next fall."

"See you next fall," I said.

I would have given my "roommate" a goodbye hug, but she held that bag. Besides, this was only the fifth time I'd ever seen her.

We'd agreed to share a room next year. She still needed to lie to her parents about her living arrangements, and I couldn't afford a single room of my own. So I gave her a warm smile and a wave as she walked out the door and away for the summer.

I kept packing. Shoes in boxes, clothes in bags, posters off the walls and rolled into tubes. I had twice as much stuff as when I'd moved in. It was all the clothes I'd made while working in the costume shop. I placed my leopard skin boots on top of a shoe pile, and since the box was now full, I shoved it into a corner.

My radio was on. I belted out "I Hope You Dance" along with Lee Ann Womack. While scrubbing away at my dusty venetian blinds, I didn't hear my dad's tentative knock. But my door was ajar. When he walked in and placed his hand on my shoulder, I jumped in surprise and knocked over the bucket of dirty, soapy water I'd been using to clean.

His shoes and pants were drenched.

"Dad!" He looked like he had just gone wading. "I'm so sorry."

"Guess I shouldn't have snuck up on you like that."

I put down my sponge and gave him a hug. "It's good to see you." Then I noticed how tan and vibrant he was. After spending lots of time at the hospital, I'd grown used to the pasty, wilting look, sported by patients, visitors, and staff alike. But my father was the opposite. He was like a superhero in comparison—Vitamin D Man. "You're so brown," I said. "And muscley. Your bike trip must have been amazing."

"It was! I can't wait to show you the pictures." He gazed around my room. "You seem to be almost done packing. Do you want to grab lunch before loading up the car and hitting the road?"

I tried not to stammer. "Umm . . . well, actually, I have a favor to ask. Can we, um, drive up to Rochester?"

"Rochester?" Dad narrowed his eyes. "But that's in the opposite direction. What's in Rochester?"

"Jed." I rolled my shoulders back and lifted my chin. "He got his lung transplant, Dad, and I promised I'd visit him in the hospital once more before going home."

Dad took a moment. I could tell his mind was racing. "You really care about him, don't you?"

"I love him," I said in a spineless sort of voice. But I said it nonetheless.

He nodded. "Okay. Then I guess we have to go."

We loaded up the car, I checked out and handed in my keys, and we drove north instead of south. I filled Dad in on everything he'd missed while he was unreachable during his bike trip. "We didn't know if Jed would make it," I said. "A couple of days after the surgery, he became septic, and he wouldn't wake up. Catherine wouldn't leave the hospital, and I didn't want to leave her."

"But how did you get through your finals?"

I shrugged. "Most of my finals weren't tests. I had an acting scene to do, a garment to construct, and a dance routine to choreograph, but Catherine pulled some strings and got me an extension. My only real exam was for astronomy, and I studied in the hospital waiting room."

"How do you think you did?"

"Fine." I looked down at my grubby knees, cursing myself for not changing. Now Jed would remember me in my pull-string shorts and gray V-neck T-shirt. That would be the photo plastered in his mind for the entire summer.

"But Robin," said my father, "you're still doing your best in school, right?" He cleared his throat. "I understand your concerns about Jed, about wanting to be there for him and his mother. But you'll regret it if you don't worry about yourself as well."

"I said I did fine, Dad."

He gripped the steering wheel and stared ahead at the road. Dad could have said I should do better than "fine," that I was capable of more than "fine," that he wasn't paying massive tuition bills if all I aspired to was "fine."

But he stayed silent.

When we got to Mayo Clinic, I walked us through the corridors like I owned the place and found Jed's room. He'd been switched out of the ICU and was lying in bed while a nurse changed a bandage on his left side. "What happened?" I asked.

Jed smiled when he saw me. "I went for a brisk walk down the hallway, and my sutures tore. I started gushing blood."

"He had to be stitched back up in the OR, but that was two hours ago, and he's still bleeding." The nurse shook her head while she finished with him. "You need to be more careful."

"I agree. Listen to her, Jed." I kissed him on the forehead.

Jed grinned and took a really deep breath. Then he breathed again. "I don't mind if I bleed a pint every hour. It's worth it if I can breathe like this."

The nurse finished bandaging him, still clucking her disapproval, and then gathered her tray and left. I didn't care that my dad was in the room; Jed's joy was so infectious that I had to give him a real kiss on the mouth. And I imagined jumping into bed and giving him a whole new way to rip out his sutures.

But I settled for the kiss.

"Jed, you remember Peter, my dad?"

He nodded and tried to sit up straight. "Thanks for driving Robin up here. I know it's completely out of your way."

I sat on the edge of the bed with my arm draped over Jed's shoulder. But it was Jed's hand, casually gripping my bare thigh, that my father's eyes landed on.

"Of course." My dad forced himself to meet Jed's gaze. You had to know him well to realize he spoke through gritted teeth, but I could hear it. "I'm so glad you're doing well. Robin was pretty worried."

"Pretty worried" was an understatement. Just thinking about Jed made my heart puff out and my pulse race, and the days after his surgery were the hardest I'd ever known. Now, sitting next to

Jed was an exercise in frustration. Who knew a guy in a hospital gown could be so scorching hot? Still, I wasn't about to swoon with lust in the presence of my dad.

After a few minutes of small talk, my dad excused himself and let Jed and me have a moment alone.

As soon as he was gone, Jed pulled me in for a kiss. His thigh thrust into my hip, which was delightful. We pushed the boundaries of propriety, since there's no such thing as privacy in a hospital room. I tilted my chin down and pressed my forehead into the groove of his neck. His skin smelled of generic soap and musk.

He stroked my hair. "What are you thinking?"

I wrapped my arms around his middle, careful of where his incisions were. "I'm thinking that I'll miss you."

Jed sighed, and that was so much better than a cough. "We'll still see each other. As soon as the doctors say I'm okay to drive, I'll come down to Des Moines and visit you."

I raised my eyes so I could look at him. "But it's going to take a while for you to heal. I don't want you rushing things on my account."

"I won't." He kissed the bridge of my nose. "Did you know that you are my first real girlfriend?"

A laugh rose up and out of me, from the deepest, warmest part of my center. "I don't remember ever agreeing to be your *girlfriend*. I thought this was a casual thing. You know I'm not the serious relationship type, right?"

Jed's face was blank for a split second—the amount of time it took for him to get the joke. Then he bit the corner of his lip, squinted maliciously, and tickled me. I squealed and pushed him away.

And he yelled out in pain.

"Oh my God," I cried, "did I hit you where your sutures ripped?"

"Only a little," he gasped.

"Jed, I am so sorry. But you were tickling me, and I just didn't think."

He was panting, trying to act like it didn't hurt, when the nurse returned.

"Everything okay?" she asked.

Jed looked down at the area she had just re-bandaged. There was a bright red spot. Horrified, I sucked in my breath.

The nurse waved a finger at both of us. "I don't even want to know how this happened!" Then she turned to me. "Young lady, it's time for you to go. Jed needs to rest, and you're not helping."

Chastened, I stood and hung my head nearly to the ground.

"I'm sorry," I told Jed.

He held out his hand. "Hug me before you go."

We both looked to the nurse, as if asking for permission.

She crossed her arms over her wide bosom and pursed her lips. But was she fighting a smile? "Please be careful."

I took baby steps back to Jed.

"I love you," he whispered as we hugged goodbye.

"I love you, too."

Wednesday, July 4, 2001

Standing at the island in the middle of Ian's kitchen, I mixed ranch dip and sipped lemonade. My cell phone rested against the chocolate-colored marble, refusing to make a sound.

A couple dozen guests were here for the barbeque, their laughter and the smell of charcoal drifting in from outside. Ian strolled into the kitchen. "There you are." He glanced down at the bowl of dip. "You don't have to do that. There's plenty of food already."

"I don't mind."

Ian leaned against the counter. "You should come outside. Monty's here with that girl he's going to Africa with."

"Evelyn?"

"Yeah, that's right. Evelyn." Ian raised his eyebrows, ready to gossip.

"What's she like?" I asked.

"Bitchy. Hot."

"How would you know?"

He huffed. "You think cuz I like guys, I can't tell when a woman is attractive?"

"No, how can you tell she's bitchy? Didn't you just meet her moments ago?"

He shrugged. "We were introduced, and she was like, 'Thanks *so* much for having us! I wish we could stay longer, but we're preparing for our departure.'"

"She said 'departure'?"

Ian nodded. "It's not a trip, since they're sort of moving there. I thought Monty was here to spend time with us. Nope! And he gave me this knowing look, trying to tell me she's worth it. But who announces they're leaving a party moments after they get there?'

Ian stood there, in his American flag T-shirt, waiting for me to agree with his thumbs-down assessment of Evelyn. When I didn't, he nudged me. "So get out there and catch a glimpse of the infamous Evelyn."

"Yeah, okay," I replied.

"Robbie, what's wrong?" Ian asked, tapping my shoulder. "Has Jed called yet?"

"No." I groaned with my mouth pinched shut. "He said he'd come today! Catherine was going to drive him! And I haven't heard from him at all."

"Didn't he just get out of the hospital? Maybe something came up?"

"Well, then he could let me know!"

Ian went to the refrigerator and grabbed a beer. Shutting the door with his hip, he used one hand to hold the bottle against the counter and the other to whack it, which sent the bottle cap flying.

"Isn't it better to use a bottle opener?" I asked. "Doesn't that hurt?"

He threw away the bottle cap and held up his spare hand, palm facing out. "Several years as a contractor built up my calluses."

163

"You're so tough," I said, rolling my eyes.

"And you need to get tough." Ian took a swig of his beer and wiped his mouth with the back of his wrist. "Love is not for the faint of heart, Robbie. And loving someone with . . . issues is even more challenging."

"Have you ever fallen in love with the wrong person?"

Ian looked at me, his face still. "You're talking to an ex-high school football player who realized he was gay in the mid-nineties. I could write a dissertation on loving the wrong person. Now come outside."

He came over and yanked on my arm. I relented, but not before I grabbed my cell phone. Then I followed Ian outside, where the sunlight bounced off the swimming pool, forcing me to shade my eyes.

Later, I was listening to Evelyn. "The reproductive rights of women in the Congo are a travesty!" Her skinny body pitched forward, and intensity emanated from her pores. "Abortion is illegal, birth control is unavailable, and the average woman has six children by the time she's hit menopause." She brushed her long, ebony locks off her shoulder and expanded her enormous, dark eyes. She was like Mother Teresa, only liberated and in a halter top. "Meanwhile, there's no recourse for rape victims." She waved her arms. "Can you imagine? Most Americans enjoy extreme excess, like all of us, drinking beer and eating barbecue at this party, ignorant and apathetic to those suffering and fighting for their humanity. That's why Monty and I are going—to help these women with their legal rights."

I nodded. Wait, did she just call my family and me ignorant and apathetic? "Don't you have to speak French in the Congo?"

She cocked an eyebrow and answered in a condescending tone. "That's right. We're both fluent."

"Oh. Wow. I didn't realize that." I made a mental note. *Learn a foreign language.* It was one more thing I needed to do if I wanted to be important and successful, like Evelyn.

My cell phone vibrated in my pocket, so I grabbed it and relief erupted in my chest. It was Jed.

"Hi!" I said into the phone. "Where are you?"

"We're outside your brother's house," Jed said. "Where are you?"

"Inside my brother's house," I answered, joyful. "Or in his backyard, to be more specific. I'll come out and get you."

I'd have excused myself, but Evelyn turned and joined Monty to chat with Jack while he flipped burgers at the grill.

I skipped out to the front of the house.

Jed and Catherine both looked twice as alive and healthy as the last time I'd seen them. I rushed straight into Jed's arms, and he captured me in a tight hug.

"Sorry we're late," Jed said. "You should see all the pills I have to take. We couldn't get out the door because I had trouble swallowing them all."

"I'm just glad you're here!" I gave him a proper inspection; he had gained enough weight to look strong, and his skin had an unfamiliar glow. "You look fantastic."

"So do you," he said.

I felt myself blush as his eyes passed over the outfit I had put together, hoping he'd see me in it. I wore a satiny black tank top with straps that tied around the back of my neck and pinstripe shorts, cut off and hemmed from a pair of pants I'd found at the thrift store.

"Yes, I like your outfit," said Catherine, smiling. "Although I'm not sure it's appropriate for the Fourth. You look more French than American."

"That's what Robin was going for, Mom." Jed's tone included a silent "duh."

I just laughed and gave Catherine a hug. "Thanks so much for coming. It's good to see you."

She returned my embrace. "Same here. It feels like forever, even though it's only been a few weeks." She kissed me on the forehead. "And thanks for the invitation. I haven't been to a barbecue in a while."

"Follow me out back. My family can't wait to meet you both."

After the sun went down, Jed and I sat by the edge of the pool, with lit sparklers in our hands and our feet in the water.

"How long have they been talking?" Jed asked as he looked over at the darkest corner of the yard, where Catherine and my dad sat on adjacent lawn chairs, leaning towards each other and laughing.

"I don't know. But they must have a lot to discuss. They're both single, around the same age, and they have the two of us to gossip about."

"You think that's all it is?"

"I don't know. Are you worried about it?"

Jed dipped the singed edge of his sparkler into the pool, and it sizzled. "It would just be weird." He spoke in a funny, horrified whisper. "What if they got married? Then you'd be my sister!"

I laughed. "I think you're jumping the gun."

"Am I?" He smiled, leaned back, and looked up at the starry sky. "I used to wish she'd find someone so she wouldn't be alone once I died."

Queasiness fluttered in my stomach. "But not anymore?"

"I don't know," Jed replied. "I want her to be happy. But she can only get together with someone if he's a good guy." He raised an eyebrow at me. "Is your dad a good guy?"

"My dad's the best sort of guy."

"Then I won't break up their private party." He scooted close and grazed my neck with his mouth. "Besides, I have my own private party planned."

Suddenly we were just two college kids, enjoying summer, fireworks, and being in love. I kissed him back, wishing we could stay that way forever.

Thursday, September 20, 2001

Once I got back to school, I was so consumed with living my life, I didn't even realize how happy I was. I liked all my classes, I got a speaking role in the fall play, *Picnic*, and because my elusive roommate, April, still loved her boyfriend more than she loved her alone time, I had our dorm room to myself. Still, I was busy with studying and rehearsals.

Jed was busy too. He had a full-time class load and a part-time job taking pills. There were dozens of horse-sized capsules he had to take daily. The task took on a life of its own. Yet the idea of us finally getting to be a real couple loomed on the horizon, like a sunrise.

Then two planes flew into the World Trade Center, and the entire country was in mourning.

Jed and I drove to Rochester for a benefit concert, and we waved flags and cried for the victims. I scanned the audience members' faces as the music played: toddlers sitting atop their dad's shoulders, students in jeans and hoodies, women with tears in their eyes, and I thought of my dad, saying he'd still marry my mom, even knowing that she'd be struck down by the maliciousness of fate. I thought of Catherine sobbing against my shoulder when she believed her son would die.

Yet here Jed was, alive.

We took the back-route way home to Hoyt. The country road stretched out, flat and peaceful, and the warm night air cushioned us as we listened to the radio. "Superman" by Five For Fighting was playing.

"When I first heard this song, it reminded me of you," I said.

"Why?" Jed swiped a glance at me. "I'm not heroic. There's nothing brave about just surviving."

"Sure there is, especially when it's easier to give in." I reached out and combed my fingers through his hair. "You held on because you had to, for Catherine."

He cleared his throat. "I suppose." I couldn't read his face in the dark.

"What are you thinking?" I asked.

He sighed. "That the world is one screwed-up place. I can't

make sense of it. I suppose nobody can. But now I have to try."

"What do you mean?"

"I got this set of lungs. Somebody died because I got these lungs."

"No, you got the lungs because somebody died."

"Isn't it the same difference?" he asked gently. When I didn't answer, Jed continued. "Anyway, now there's this pressure, and I need to do something big to make my life worthwhile."

"Or you could do a bunch of small things." I twisted in my seat toward him. "When I was little, I used to think the meaning of life was about having fun, but when I told my dad that, he said, 'I think it's about making the world a better place.'"

Jed let one hand fall from the steering wheel, and he placed it on my knee. My body grew warm. "Isn't your dad a systems analyst?"

"Yeah." I laughed. "So he hasn't spent his career working in social services, if that's what you're getting at."

"I wasn't getting at anything."

I put my hand over his, and our fingers entwined. "He tries hard to be nice to everyone. He loans our neighbors tools and shovels this widowed woman's driveway. He volunteered at my school while I was growing up, and he always donates to United Way. So imagine the world if everyone was more like him."

Jed picked up my hand, brought it to his mouth, and kissed each one of my knuckles. "I'd rather imagine the world being more like you." He put my hand on the back of his neck, and I began to rub. "Then again," he said, "that might be bad. I'd have trouble concentrating."

"And then you wouldn't be able to play chess anymore."

That was a joke. Jed told me how he learned to play chess as a child, during one of his numerous hospital stays. He was always in the hospital and always playing chess, and he came to hate the game.

But Jed didn't laugh at my joke. He scowled instead.

"What's wrong?"

"Nothing." His answer was hushed, but then he raised his volume. "Except that I need you."

"Okay . . ." I skimmed his shoulder with my fingertips. "Why is that a problem?"

The road was empty, save for a car here or there. Jed pulled over, gravel grinding under his tires. He turned off the ignition and faced me.

"There are many reasons." The moonlight lit half his face, adding to his vehemence. "I could die and leave you and break your heart. You could be in the next airplane that gets hijacked or the next building that gets bombed, and that would break me." He took a deep breath, and it was still so weird for him to be able to do that. "There are other, smaller reasons, but they all come down to the same thing—needing anyone is a fool's game, because nothing is permanent. *Permanent* doesn't exist, and needing you is like running into the wind." He placed a cautious hand on my shoulder. Then he leaned in and kissed me. "But I do need you," he whispered.

"I need you too." I kissed him back but pulled away after a second. "Jed, you're shaking."

"Yeah. Because the world is fucked up, and I don't know how to keep still."

"Then I'll show you." I took my shirt off, then my bra, and I placed his hand over my beating heart.

His eyes flicked down my bare skin. I could almost hear the thoughts whirling inside his brain. His hand traveled down and cupped my breast. Pleasure rippled through me in waves. I pulled at his shirt, and he took it off. "I should drive us somewhere more hidden," he said, chest bared to the starry sky.

"I don't want our first time to be in a car."

Finally, he smiled. "Don't be cruel." His words came out in a light, airy breath, but his body told a different story. He pressed his mouth to mine, and I returned his kisses with all the desire I had been pushing away for so long.

"Let's get out of here," I said. "I want to be outside."

He kissed me one more time. "Okay."

I pressed the fabric of my shirt against my chest as we got out. Hand in hand, we skulked through a field and the breezy, moonlit night. Soon we were far away enough from the road that he could lay me down, and we'd be hidden behind stalks of corn.

I laid my shirt against the ground, and then he was on top of me. We kissed and strained against each other, and I thought I would go crazy with wanting him. With his hips pressed into mine, he stopped and tilted his upper body towards the sky. "Are you sure you want it to be now? Because pretty soon I won't be able to stop."

"I've never been more sure of anything," I panted.

He moved back down and into me. Then, in the entire world, only three things existed: the earth, the sky, and Jed and me, together.

Monday, October 15, 2001

Acting Two class got out, and I sprinted up the stairs, from the basement to the lobby. I was starving, and all I wanted was to find Jed and make him come with me to the cafeteria. We could each devour a cheeseburger.

He was waiting for me in his usual spot, on the sofa-bench by the big picture window, right outside the doors to the main stage. Today, he was not alone. A pretty brunette wearing a tight sweater sat next to him. She kept jutting out her chest further and further, until I thought she might assault him with her double Ds. Jed's back was to me, nodding as she spoke.

"Mamet's genius is that his plays are allegations. But the audience is unaware of the resentment his dialogue sparks."

Jed tilted his head. "You mean Mamet's brilliant because he makes the audience feel like shit?

Insecurity pumped through my veins instead of blood. Maybe this girl's brain was as big as her bra size. How could I compete?

170

Then, as if he sensed my presence, Jed turned, saw me, and his face lit up.

"There you are." He motioned for me to come closer. "Robin, have you met Esther yet? She just transferred from Iowa State."

"Hi," I said, "nice to meet you."

Esther squinted. "You're Robin and Jed—the couple everyone refers to as *Red*?

Jed's smile grew. "That would be us." He stood and gave me a peck on the mouth. "Are you ready? I'm hungry."

"Yeah," I said, and we waved goodbye to Esther.

Outside, it was chillier than I expected, given the brightness of the day. I shivered. Jed noticed and draped his arm over my shoulders.

"She seemed nice," I said. "Like the type of girl who could analyze Mamet while drunk and naked."

"You got that from a five-second interaction?"

"Sure," I replied. "Didn't you?"

Jed stopped and his sweater-clad arms pulled me in tight. Then he tilted his face down. His mouth met mine—a now familiar gesture that always warmed me. "You know I only have eyes for you, right?"

I gave him a shrug-nod combo, accompanied by a goofy laugh, and we stumbled towards the cafeteria, tripping over each other's feet because we refused to let go.

Saturday, December 21, 2001

Slush hit the window. The clock read 2:47 a.m. I blinked and squinted at it again, making sure I'd read it correctly. I could sense his presence, all the way on the other side of the room.

Sitting up, I saw Jed's silhouette, outlined by the glow coming from his computer. He was typing away.

"Why aren't you in bed?" I asked.

He turned. "Sorry. Did I wake you?"

"No. But I could feel your shadow."

"You can feel my shadow?" He chuckled. "I think you're still half asleep."

Months ago, I abandoned my dorm room and pretty much moved in with Jed and Catherine. It was Catherine's idea. She didn't want Jed staying out all night and falling behind on his meds regimen. So I'd been encouraged to stay over often.

"Sorry," he said again. "I couldn't sleep. Then, I had ideas for my play; I figured I'd get them down."

"Is this the new play? Where the girl gets killed?"

"Yeah." Jed stood, stretched, and came over to sit on the edge of the bed. "But I don't know how he'll bring her back from the dead."

"I can see why. That's not an easy one. Why does he have to bring her back?"

"Because he's trapped in his apartment with his memories of her. He's stuck until he can find her again, in a permanent way." Jed twisted his mouth into a smirk. I reached for his hand, and when he gave it to me, I pulled.

"Spoon me," I said.

"Sure, but help me brainstorm."

"Fine."

He laid down and took me in his arms. "So Georgie's been murdered, it's Grayson's fault, and now she's haunting him. How can he bring her back to life?"

I snuggled in. He was so warm. "Hmmm . . . perhaps Grayson needs to revise the script he already wrote, the one that led to Georgie getting killed. Like in *Groundhog Day*. He just keeps going back for another revision until he gets it right."

"But he can't. Grayson has writer's block."

I turned over so our bodies faced each other. "He can if you let him," I stroked his hair. "It's your play. You're entitled to change the rules."

"Maybe not. The play is about acceptance and loss."

"That's not much fun. I thought you said it's a comedy."

"Comedy is tragedy plus timing." Jed kissed my hairline. "Do you have to go home for Christmas? How will I last two weeks without you?"

"I'm only a couple of hours away. Drive down to see me."

"You think your dad would be okay with that?"

I ran my hand along the contours of his torso. He'd gained weight since the surgery, partly because of the steroids. Jed hated that; he said he didn't look like himself anymore. But he was still beautiful.

"My dad will have to be okay. I can't go two weeks without you either."

Wednesday, March 28, 2002

It was spring break, and we sat across from Jed's dad in a low-lit restaurant. He'd been showing us around, taking us to tourist sites and letting us sit in on rehearsals at his theater company. Jed and I fantasized about moving to NYC after graduation, so when Zeke offered to fly us out, we prepared for something epic. But several days had gone by, and all the tense nerves were rubbing together.

Zeke held a dish toward me. "Robin, try some calamari. You won't regret it."

I took a bite of squid, to appease Jed's dad rather than my taste buds. It was like Kentucky Fried rubber band.

"Yeah," I said between chews. "Delicious."

Jed grabbed my knee from under the table and squeezed. I had a weird, scary moment where I wasn't sure whose fingers rested against my thin black pantyhose. Jed and his father looked so much alike; they reminded me of when an actor does flashback scenes and you're supposed to believe he's twenty years younger because the image is sort of blurred.

Only Zeke's features were more distinct. He was the rugged cowboy type, but with soft hands and a fleshy belly. Still, I could understand what Catherine once saw in him. Zeke seemed like the kind of man who turned a woman's name into his own romantic language.

"More wine?" he asked, and he refilled my glass before I could reply.

Jed stuck to water, and with all the steroids he was on, that was smart. But I felt like a traitor, drinking with his dad.

Zeke turned to his son. "I have some good news for you."

"What's that?" Jed asked.

"Your play about Chopin, the one that came in second in that competition . . ."

"*Simplicity*."

"Right. Why can't I ever remember the name?" Zeke smiled and shrugged. "It's so simple."

Jed remained stony-faced. "What about my play?"

Zeke took a bite of bruschetta, and he poked his fork in the air, jabbing it in excitement. "You'll never guess," he said right as he swallowed. "I just found out today. We're going to produce it!"

Jed's hand, which was still on my knee, balled into a fist. "What? How?"

"You remember Annette? She's terrific at writing grants, and the Cystic Fibrosis Foundation is going to pay for everything. I'm telling you, it's gold. You have CF. Chopin had CF. I mean, how could they refuse?"

Jed coughed and stared at the tablecloth.

"That's great," I said.

Jed's head snapped up, his enraged eyes battering me. "Really, Robin? You think it's great? Guess I don't know you like I thought I did." He stood up, threw his napkin on the table, and addressed Zeke. "If my play was any good, it would have won, and I'd be producing it on my own. And if you were any sort of decent human being, you'd have asked me first. Instead, you're prostituting my play and benefiting from my disease."

Zeke, the couple at the table next to us, and I all watched as Jed stormed out.

The silence was like ice melting on a late February afternoon. Zeke's impassive face betrayed no emotion.

"He's still temperamental," said Zeke. "Guess his lung transplant didn't change that."

I slid my chair out. "I'll go see if Jed's okay."

I strode through the restaurant, where everything blended with the red velvet and covered lamps. When I didn't see him, I pushed open the heavy front door and walked into the chilly, noisy evening. Jed stood outside, coughing and gasping for air.

"Oh my God, are you okay?" I rushed to him.

He shook his head. "Fine . . . Air pollution and stress, that's all." He coughed some more and struggled to breathe. I grabbed his hand and put it on my chest.

"Breathe with me, Jed," I commanded and forced my heart rate to slow down so he could keep up.

"Sorry," he murmured. "I didn't mean it."

"It's okay."

Jed closed his eyes and focused on the rise and fall of my chest. Soon, his breathing kept pace with mine. He opened his eyes. "Let's go home tonight. Do you mind?"

"No."

"I'm sorry, Robin. But I can't be around him anymore. And I need my mom."

"Hey," I said, my smile urging him to smile in return. "Don't worry. It's all to the good."

Then Jed laughed. "Yeah," he said weakly. "It's all to the good."

After dinner, we packed up our stuff and took a taxi to the airport, where Jed and I got a 10:00 p.m. flight. The hum of the engine and the ding of the seatbelt sign filled the silence, our hands clasped together the entire time. We were cushioned by the clouds.

I didn't realize it wouldn't always be so easy—delivering Jed to safety.

NINE

Monday, June 30, 2013
6:00 a.m.

I'm on stage, but I forgot my lines. Underneath these glaring lights, every face is hostile. I'm suffocating, collapsing on the inside, planning to run.

Someone taps my shoulder. I turn. It's Nick, smiling at me.

His eyes crinkle with love. "It's okay, Rocky. Explain life's mysteries, and you'll be fine."

"But I don't know life's mysteries, Nick."

He cups my cheek and I breathe again. "Sure you do," he whispers. "You know so much."

Opening my eyes, I'm aware that I'm waking from a dream. I groan. Why do I weigh so much this morning? It's a struggle to sit up, but I do, and then I rise and get into my running gear. Exercise will help relax me before I meet Nick.

But I don't run my usual route. *Just this once*, I tell myself. *Skip all the drama with Flashdance Girl. It doesn't mean you're running away. It means you're a grownup, refusing to cater to the obsessive, competitive nature of someone half your age.*

So, I cower and choose alternative streets, sprinting down unfamiliar blocks. Hoping I won't see her, praying she won't see me.

God, I'm pathetic.

7:50 a.m.

I get into my car and put the key in the ignition, but it makes this terrible grinding sound. What the hell? I just spent a ton on a brand-new battery. My head falls, so it hits the steering wheel. I fight the urge to open the door and puke out onto the parking lot.

I can't be late to meet Nick. It would be so wrong. I'm not the praying type, but now I plead, *Please, God, just let my car be okay. Let me be on time. Nick will never forgive me if I'm late.*

With a heavy sigh, I turn the key once more, and hallelujah, my car starts up. Should I be thanking God? Or was Jed watching down? Did he grant me this favor? I'm not sure about Jed as an angel, snapping his ghostly fingers to right some irrelevant wrong. He has better things to do, and hopefully stays busy in the afterlife.

8:15 a.m.

I sit in the cafe and wait for Nick, more squirrely than serene, despite my morning run. Every thirty seconds, I check my phone, making sure I don't miss a text.

Finally, he arrives, his hair damp, smelling like soap and resentment.

"Sorry I'm late." Nick sits down opposite me in our booth.

"You're never late," I reply. "I was worried you were standing me up."

His hands rest on the table, yet he makes two fists. And his eyes don't crinkle with affection, like they did in my dream. "I wouldn't do that to you."

"That's good." Already, I want to rewind or maybe just erase this bumpy start. "I was early, so it's on me. I should have planned my time better."

Nick nods, and his clenched hands remain on the table as he studies the menu in front of him. He doesn't argue or deflect, nor does he smile. His eyes rove over the printed words like it's an ancient manuscript rather than a breakfast spread.

I force my face to chill. "Hey, guess what? Last night, after my dad's party, I drove down Woodland Avenue, and I think I saw the house that's for sale. The one you'd been talking about. It's nice. I like the green shutters. Anyway, I don't know if I'm *quite* ready for such a big step, but I was thinking, maybe we should look into it, you know, figure out our options."

I'm like a dishonest politician, backtracking from a stupid mistake, ignoring my hot face and sweaty palms. Even I don't believe what I'm saying.

But Nick ignores my rambling. He presses his lips together before opening them up to speak. "I feel stupid about how I acted the other day. It was immature, thinking about myself and not about you."

"It's . . . it's fine. I should have told you about everything before. I'm sorry I didn't."

Nick's brown eyes grow dark, almost black. Then he stares down at his fingers. "I understand why you didn't. I'm sure it's been very hard for you."

"Yeah . . ."

"And you've been sad. I'm sorry about that too."

I thought I was sad before, but hearing him say that sort of drowns my heart. "Thanks." My voice is barely a whisper, but I know he hears me when he meets my eyes.

"I want you to tell me about . . ." Nick falters. "I don't even know his name."

"Jed."

"Jed was your boyfriend who died."

When Nick states this painful truth, it's like hearing it for the first time. A chill washes over me. "Yeah."

Nick grabs a cup and fills it from the carafe of coffee that the waitress brought earlier. He takes a sip without adding anything sweet or light, grimacing at the bitter taste, as if bracing himself for more pain. "I need to know what happened, and why, after so many years, you still love him."

Nick sits across from me, but he's like a mirage in the desert, unreal and inaccessible. The way to bridge this difference is by telling the truth. I look around. Families order breakfast, and senior citizens linger over their crosswords. I wish I was one of them.

"Okay," I say to Nick. "I'll tell you everything."

TEN

Summer came. The weather turned warm, and Jed kept experiencing shortness of breath. Leaving him for three months was agony, but my dad insisted, and besides, I'd committed to working at Tavern 33. So I tried not to obsess over Jed's lungs. That was like trying not to breathe.

"It's probably nothing. There's bound to be ups and downs." Jed coughed, and I squeezed my eyes shut, like that would make the horrible noise disappear. I gripped my phone so hard that had it been glass, it would've shattered.

"Put your mother on," I said.

"Excuse me?"

"Let me talk to Catherine." I kicked some gravel by my foot. I was on my break, standing outside by the dumpsters, watching the sun slowly set. This summer, I'd gone from hostess to waitress, and I had orders up.

There was a silent, tense moment. "You don't trust me?" Jed's voice was low.

"I want her perspective, that's all."

"Fine."

His terse response said it wasn't fine, but I couldn't worry about that.

In the last couple of months, Jed's lung function had decreased. He'd had a couple of short hospital stays and a longer one, where they'd operated to relieve his acid reflux. The doctors explained that his lung's small airways were obstructed and might be infected with stomach acid, so they went in to correct it.

We'd hoped that would fix the problem.

But now Jed had checked himself back into the Mayo Clinic. He was having trouble breathing and eating. It was much too soon for this. Statistics said that he should stay healthy for several years yet.

"Hi, Robin." Catherine's voice was heavy, like the weight in my gut.

"H . . . hi." Stumbling over words not even uttered, I cut to the chase. "What's his lung function right now?"

"Forty-five percent."

"That's all?"

"They're doing a bronch screen tomorrow, so we'll know more soon. But Dr. Rutland mentioned chronic rejection."

My lunch threatened to come back up. "But they don't know anything for sure yet."

"No, not yet."

"I'll find a ride to Rochester, okay?"

Catherine sighed. "What about your job?"

"This is more important."

"Robin, you should stay put. I promise I'll call tomorrow when we know more."

Jed yelled in the background. "Mom, if she wants to come, let her come."

Catherine ignored him. "You've missed a lot of work after his surgery last week." She sounded so tired. So collapsed. "Would your cousin give you the time off?"

I wrapped my arm around my stomach and squeezed. "I don't know, but I'm going back to school soon anyway. I could just quit."

"Don't you think that's a little extreme?"

"I wish the two of you would stop making decisions without me!" Jed rasped.

"Can you put Jed back on?"

Catherine handed the phone back to her son. "You're coming

181

up?" he asked.

"Do you want me to?"

"Yes."

No explanation, no qualifications. He just wanted me there. I took a heavy inhale. As I exhaled, I knew. It was the beginning of the end.

"Okay, I'll figure something out," I said. "My break was over ten minutes ago, but I'll talk to you tomorrow, okay?"

"Yeah."

"I love you." My words were a Band-Aid when I wanted them to be a cure.

"Me too," Jed replied. "Bye."

We hung up, and I moved like a zombie through the rest of my shift. At the end of the night, I pulled Jack aside.

"I have to talk to you." I avoided his eyes. They held too much warmth . . . too much understanding. Meeting his gaze would be like sticking freezing toes into hot water.

"Okay," he said. "What's up?"

"I'm handing in my notice." Pinching the bottom of my wrist to keep from crying, I searched for words to explain. I came up short. "Sorry."

Jack waited before speaking. I couldn't take the silence, so I looked at him. He peered at me with confusion, but not anger. "What's wrong?"

I tilted my eyes down. "It's Jed. He's back in the hospital. The doctors think it might be chronic rejection."

"And that's bad?"

I nodded and spoke through emptiness. "Yeah. It's bad."

Jack put his hand on my shoulder. "I'm sorry, Robin."

I rocked back and forth on the balls of my feet. "I think I'll pack up all my stuff and head back to school early. Dad will understand. I can stay with Catherine until campus housing reopens. That way, I'm there when Jed needs me."

"That sounds like a good idea." Jack leaned against the bar, tapping his pencil against his clipboard that held the shift schedule. "We'll cover your shifts. It will be fine."

"Thank you." I had no idea what else to say. So I turned to go.

"Wait a second. Who's driving you to Rochester tomorrow? Do you need a ride?"

"Really? Are you offering?"

Jack shrugged. "I don't mind."

Gratitude obstructed my voice. I grabbed Jack in a death-grip sort of hug. It was supposed to be an affectionate thank-you, but it turned into something else.

Desperate. Needy. Lost.

Thursday, August 22, 2002

When I got to the hospital, Jed was just waking up from his bronch screen, breathless and in pain. They had him on a ton of oxygen, but it didn't do much good.

So he went for an X-ray. As soon as he returned, a tall, broad surgeon came in, scary and intimidating in his green scrubs. "I'm here to fit your chest drain," he told Jed.

"What? Why does he need a chest drain?" Catherine's eyes grew wide and anxious. Stepping in front of the surgeon, she switched into mama bear mode.

The surgeon shrugged his massive shoulders. He reminded me a little of the Hulk.

"Unfortunately, Jed's lung collapsed this morning. The X-ray confirmed it. You know that's a hazard during a bronchoscopy, when lung function gets low."

Jed's face grew pale, and his eyes were large with fear.

Catherine stared at the doctor. "He's already in a lot of pain. Is a chest drain absolutely necessary?"

"I'm afraid so." He rubbed at the back of his neck. "We'll give him a morphine drip, so it won't hurt. We're hoping the chest drain will make him feel better."

Catherine blinked a few times, wavering. I made eye contact with Jed, and he crawled out of his pain and dread enough to nod his consent.

I walked over to Catherine and placed my hand on her lower back. "If it's going to help and it's not going to hurt, shouldn't we let him go ahead?"

Catherine's chest heaved up and down. "Fine." She spoke to the surgeon. "But if he has an ounce of pain, you've got me to answer to. Understand?"

"I do." Those two words seemed to be full of compassion. Maybe he really did understand.

Jed was fitted for the chest drain. I stayed in the room and visualized steel cords tying me to my chair so I wouldn't bolt. The sounds during this procedure were worse than in Halloween horror films. The tugging, heaving, smothering noise was too much to bear, but it wasn't me who had to bear it.

"I'm okay," Jed told me afterwards. "It didn't hurt." He reached out and patted my hand.

"You don't have to take care of me, Jed." My fingers brushed against his cool skin. "I should be taking care of you."

"Don't deny me the simple pleasures I have left, okay?" Jed tried to smile, but his face was burdened by the BiPap mask covering his nose and cheeks.

I sat on the edge of his bed and stroked his forehead. "Don't talk that way. You're getting through this."

Jed nodded and closed his eyes. "Really tired right now," he murmured.

I sat there while he slept, worried that if I looked away from his face, I'd never see it again.

Monday, August 26, 2002

It was just before 7:00 a.m. Catherine and I were with Jed in his hospital room, waiting for Dr. Rutland to come in during rounds. A Rochester TV station's morning show was on, with the anchors discussing fun Labor Day barbecue recipes.

"I never thought of using apples with ketchup," Jed said. He was the only one paying attention to the show. "I wonder how that would taste with chicken."

"Good morning!" Dr. Rutland walked in, his lab coat tails flapping. "How are we doing today?"

Jed answered. "I feel like I'm breathing through a straw."

"I'm not surprised," said Dr. Rutland, and his left eye twitched. "You have bronchiolitis, which means the smallest airways in your lungs are inflamed. You also have a chest infection, which further inhibits your ability to breathe." He studied the clipboard, avoiding eye contact. "And your lung function tested at twenty-eight percent."

Catherine gasped. "That's lower than right before his transplant."

"Yes, I know." Dr. Rutland pressed his lips together and inhaled through his nose. "I'd like to start you on radiation, Jed."

"Radiation? Why?" Catherine came closer to Jed so Dr. Rutland could address them both.

"If he has chronic rejection, radiation could help stabilize it," replied the doctor. "In the meantime, we'll run more tests and find out if Jed still has acid reflux. If the surgery did its job, maybe we can get Jed back on the transplant list."

"Another transplant?" Jed's mouth dropped open. "Will I last long enough for that?"

"I'm hoping the radiation will help." Dr. Rutland rubbed his eye, which wouldn't sit still. Neither Jed nor Catherine asked a follow-up question, probably because they were afraid of the answer.

"We'll schedule your first round for today and do more tests as well." Doctor Rutland relaxed his face and let his gaze rest on Jed. "I'm sorry I don't have better news. But there's still hope, okay?"

Tuesday, August 27, 2002

"You wouldn't believe what he's been put through." I was outside, in one of the hospital courtyards, talking to Isobel on my cell phone.

"He's exhausted from the radiation and his low lung function. But he's also had abdominal ultrasounds, bone scans, X-rays, visits with the psychiatrist and social workers, pentamidine inhalation, and required walks around the hospital. There's more, but I can't remember . . . Oh, they're collecting his urine twenty-four hours a day."

"Why?" asked Isobel.

"I'm not sure, but I think to see if he can go back on the transplant list."

The wind picked up, and dark clouds rolled in. A summer storm approached—the type where the air suddenly turns cool, sending you to your basement to wait out a tornado.

"It's possible Jed could get a new lung?"

"I don't know." A fat raindrop plopped down, hitting me on the thigh. I made no move to go inside.

"I'm sorry, Robin." Isobel's voice was flooded with concern. "Is there *anything* I can say or do? If so, tell me, and I'll do it."

"I don't know," I repeated, this time in a whisper.

"Do you want me to drive up?"

Several more raindrops fell. I could smell the clouds and rain. It was a million times better than the scent of the hospital, but if I didn't go inside, I'd be wet and cold once inside the air conditioning again.

"I should go," I said. "Thanks for listening. Love you."

"Love you too. Call me soon, okay?"

"Yeah."

When I got back to Jed's hospital room, he and Catherine were having a deep conversation. Both their heads snapped towards me. Catherine's chin was set with determination, but her eyes were pools of doubt.

"Sorry," I said, "I didn't mean to interrupt."

"That's okay," Jed replied. "You should hear this too. I could use another witness."

"It's too soon to talk about it, Jed." Catherine barely moved; she just stood in the middle of the room, like a post.

"It's not," Jed retorted.

I wrapped my arms around my chest. "Talk about what?"

"My living will."

My heart stopped for a second and then resumed at twice its normal rate. Jed motioned for me to come closer. I did, and I gripped the railing around his bed.

"I'm sorry to do this to you both," Jed said. "But if anything happens, and sometimes things happen quickly, promise you won't use drastic measures to save me. If I'm trying to die, please let me."

Catherine wrapped one arm around her stomach, and her other hand rubbed her mouth. "I really think it's too soon for this discussion."

Jed's vibrant blue eyes stared into me, reminding me of the day we first met. "Tell me you understand."

That was like asking me to understand the theory of relativity, or why black holes look white. My mind could not wrap around the concept of letting Jed die.

So I lied. "I understand," I told him.

"Mom?" Jed's voice was so strained, so desperate. Catherine dropped both of her arms in defeat. "Of course, sweetheart. I'd never let you be in pain."

Later, the three of us played Scrabble, and Jed fell asleep right after Catherine spelled out "quintessential." He knew that neither he nor I could beat that. Catherine and I put the tiles back into the box, trying not to wake him.

She watched him sleep, her eyes filled with longing. There's a way that only a mother can revel in the beauty of her child. I recognized it, even without having a mother of my own.

"He's always been stronger than me," Catherine whispered.

"Really?" I said. "I figured he got his strength from you."

Catherine put the cardboard top back on the game and came to me. She placed both hands on my cheeks and kissed my forehead. "You, my dear, are an easy person to love." She gave me a smile, but it was a substitute for tears. "I applaud Jed's choice of you."

Thursday, August 29, 2002

Smudges on Catherine's glasses glistened in the fluorescent light. There were dark circles under her eyes and deep lines etched around her mouth. She looked old, impaired, and weak.

But when she spoke, the whole room shook with fear. "What do you mean? *Why* can't he go back on the transplant list?"

"His reflux test is still positive," said Dr. Rutland. "Even if Jed got new lungs, the same thing would happen again."

"Then what do we do?" Jed asked.

"Continue with radiation therapy," the doctor replied. "For chronic rejection, that's the best option."

Jed removed his mask to speak. "Best option for what? Will it make me better?"

Doctor Rutland's eye twitched. "It's our best option to stabilize you."

Catherine put her fingers in her hair, clenching her scalp. "But he did everything he was supposed to! Why is this happening now?"

"Sometimes, the transplanted lung quality isn't as good as we'd like."

"Because they were smoker's lungs!" Catherine cried.

"Mom," Jed rasped. "Calm down."

Dr. Rutland spoke to him. "You wouldn't have lasted much longer on the lungs you had. I'm sorry it's only been a few months rather than a few years, but hopefully it was time well spent."

So there it was: the death sentence. Now *I* couldn't breathe. The reckless, selfish side of me had half a mind to grab Jed's oxygen mask and use it myself.

Catherine, however, went still. "How long, do you think?"

Dr. Rutland gazed down at his clasped hands before looking at Catherine, his face full of regret. "With radiation . . . a couple of months."

"And without radiation?" Jed asked.

"Without radiation, a few weeks."

"I don't want radiation," said Jed. "Unless you think another transplant is possible, I don't want radiation."

"At this stage, no, another transplant is not a possibility." Dr. Rutland's voice was softer than I'd ever heard it. "I'm sorry."

We all said nothing.

"But," he continued. "Please consider radiation." For the first time, he glanced in my direction. "It will buy you time with your lovely girlfriend."

"Excuse me," I murmured, rushing to find a bathroom where Jed and Catherine wouldn't overhear me retch.

I found a toilet just in time and heaved out all the scraps of food I'd eaten over the last few days. Then, shaking like the ground in an earthquake, I washed my hands and rinsed out my mouth. The floor swayed beneath me, and my head swam, so I grabbed the edge of the sink to keep from passing out.

I didn't faint. But when I raised my eyes and saw my reflection, I couldn't recognize myself. Was Dr. Rutland being funny when he called me lovely? My face was haggard, my hair was greasy and stringy, and I was too skinny.

And I needed to get back to Jed. Only pure, unadulterated terror kept me grounded to this spot.

The bathroom door swung open, and Catherine walked in. "Oh, there you are," she said.

"Are you okay?"

It was a senseless question, so I gave a senseless answer. "Yeah, fine."

Catherine stood next to me and leaned against the sink. "Will you talk to Jed about radiation? He'll listen to you."

I nodded like I understood, but both her words and this new reality made no sense. "You want me to convince him?"

"Yes." Catherine squirted hand soap from the dispenser into her palm, turned on the sink, and scrubbed. Constant hand washing was second nature for us both so we wouldn't infect Jed. "What if his reflux tests change? Maybe there's hope. He could still get a transplant, but not if he doesn't get stabilized first."

I let go of the sink. "Okay," I told her. "I'll try."

She patted me on the back and pushed me towards the door. I walked, my feet heavy and confused, back to Jed's hospital room. He was lying in bed, his gaze fixed on the ceiling. As I entered, Jed pressed a button, raising himself into a near-sitting position. Then he took off his Bi-Pap mask, as if ready for a serious discussion.

"I'm sorry it's not better news," I said.

"Me too."

His breathing sounded strained and desperate. How could he endure it, even for a few more weeks?

"I need you to promise me something." Jed struggled to get his words out. He reached for me, so I sat down, and our legs pressed together, though the covers separated them.

"Okay, what?"

He brought my hand to his mouth and kissed it. "Never get married. Don't even date anyone, okay? And only have kids if you adopt." Pausing, he took a heavy, labored sigh. "Save yourself for me, Robin, so we can be together someday in heaven."

His blue eyes glistened like water in the sunlight. At that moment, I would have promised him anything. But Jed started laughing.

"Sorry," he wheezed. "You should have seen your face just now." He put his mask back on and took a sharp inhale. "Classic!"

I hit his knee. "That's not funny, Jed."

"Yes, it sort of is."

"Well, if I was speechless, it's because I don't think you should sign up for heaven just yet."

"Yeah. I doubt it's where I'll go." He was laughing again.

I stood and paced around the boundaries of his bed. "Why don't you do the radiation? It's your best option, and maybe they can put you on the transplant list after all."

"Did my mom tell you to say that?"

"What if she did? She's right."

Jed closed his eyes, and his body sagged. "Remember right before my surgery, when I mentioned Barry?"

"Yeah." I was almost too afraid to ask. "Who's Barry?"

"He was our cat." Jed kicked his covers away as if he was suddenly hot. "He got cancer, and treatment was super-expensive, and it wouldn't have worked for long. I wanted my mom to pay for it anyway. But after my medical bills, she couldn't afford it. So we put him to sleep."

"You're not a cat, Jed. And Catherine's insurance should cover another transplant."

Jed shook his head and attempted another inhale. "I cried for Barry, but my mom said he'd had a good life. That he wasn't afraid of death, because animals know something humans don't." Another raspy breath, in and out. "They understand when their time has come."

He looked at me, and I looked back.

"This is my time, Robin."

Tears streamed down my cheeks, and my response was toddler-like. "But I don't want it to be!"

And like a toddler during a tantrum, I longed to throw objects around the room. The ugly cornflower blue water pitcher and the unopened Mayo Clinic info packet that sat on the end table. Then I imagined lashing out, jumping onto Jed's bed, and shaking him until he promised to fight and stay with me.

Or, there was escape—running through the halls and out into the world until the pain was far behind.

But none of that was an option. I was out of options, and so was Jed.

"I'm sorry," said Jed. "I know I'm being a shitty boyfriend right now."

"Don't be sorry, and stop making jokes. Why aren't you angry? You should be furious."

Jed's hand rose and fell as if in defeat. "I know, and I would be, if I wasn't so, so tired." He motioned for me again. "Please sit with me."

I sniffed back my tears and sat with him on the bed. He had

lost all his steroid weight, and then some. His limbs were like spaghetti noodles.

Jed reached out and stroked my hair. "Listen. I need to finish my play. If I die before I can do that, then I *will* be mad. But if I'm on radiation, I'll be too tired." He forced himself through another inhale and exhale. "I'd rather have a few weeks of cognizance. So, will you bring me my laptop?"

I nodded because I was crying too hard to speak.

"For what it's worth, I am sorry, Robin. I wouldn't leave you if there was any other way."

"I know," I whispered. Then I curled up and put my face in the crook of his shoulder. I stayed like that as he fell asleep.

It was too late to transform my heart into something that didn't beat for Jed. And I couldn't become someone who didn't care, who didn't want him every day, for the rest of my life.

All I had were a few more days, when I needed thousands of them.

Thursday, September 3, 2002

I waded through my first day of classes like I was drowning in bathwater. Yet halfway through Ancient Arts and Humanities, the drain opened, and I came up for air. The professor showed us a slide of an Egyptian mask. Half of an eye and one of her ears had fallen off. There was a stain on her chin, another on her nose, and a fissure all the way down her left cheek.

Yet she was still golden and refined. I could swear that behind her empty eyes lurked a soul.

Around me, students chatted in whispers, took notes, or stared at the clock, waiting for class to end and for their next thing to start. They all seemed complete, while I felt full of cracks, fissures, and missing parts. Was my relief at being somewhere other than the hospital wrong? To think, even for a moment, about someone other than Jed, about something other than death?

Maybe it wasn't wrong, but it was selfish. Because that mask gave me hope that despite permanent damage, survival is still possible. I'm ashamed to admit that I was thinking about my own survival and not Jed's.

After class, I drove Jed's car back to the Mayo Clinic. He had already bequeathed his Volkswagen to me, along with the lava lamp I'd given him and all the files on his computer.

When I got to his room, he was awake and happy.

"I finished *The Next Breath*," he said, holding up a flash drive. "Wait to read it, though. I'd rather not know what you think."

"Okay." I sat next to him in bed, and he pressed the flash drive into the palm of my hand.

"But one day, after you've read it, and if it isn't a load of crap, maybe you can find someone to produce it? And maybe you can play Georgie."

"Sure." I nodded. It seemed like an easy promise to make.

"Don't tell them that I was dying when I finished it. I don't want that to be a selling point, like it was with my dad and *Simplicity*, okay?"

"Okay." I kissed his temple and snuggled up to him. He barely had the strength to put his arms around me.

"Robin?" Jed asked.

"Hmmm?"

"Don't get mad, but can you repeat back everything you just promised?"

"Huh?"

"I just want to make sure you'll remember. Because I won't have many more chances to remind you. Most of the world will never know about me, and the ones who did will forget. But not you, okay?"

I gulped down the lump that threatened to choke me. "I love you, Jed. And I won't forget, not ever." I kissed him all over his face, though that was hard to do with his BiPap mask on. Then I repeated everything I'd just promised him.

We sat, arms around each other, for several minutes. I thought he had fallen asleep, until he spoke. "Robin?" His voice was little more than a breath.

"Yeah?" I sat up so I could see his face.

"I love you. You're the best thing that ever happened to me, and if I don't remember to tell you again, I'm telling you now." He bit his lower lip, the only part of him that was still a little plump. "And thank you for staying. I know it hasn't been easy."

I lifted his mask and kissed him, soft and deep, on the mouth. It was the last real kiss we would ever share.

"I love you too," I said after we pulled apart. "And you're the best thing that's ever happened to me."

He smiled. "Oh yeah? Then I need you to promise me one more thing."

"What?"

"Let other 'best things' happen. I want you to have a lifetime *full* of the 'best things' that have ever happened. Promise me, and that will be the last thing I ask for."

I blinked back my tears. "I promise."

Friday, September 13, 2002

I wasn't superstitious, but I had a terrible feeling that Jed would die on the thirteenth. He was sleeping more and more and breathing less and less. When awake, he seemed on the verge of passing out. Like a two-hundred-pound weight pressed down on his lungs, suffocating him.

I still went to class because everyone, including Jed, insisted that I do. But I didn't audition for the fall play, so my late afternoons and evenings were always the same. Catherine and I held hands as we sat with Jed, listening to his destroyed lungs, wondering if his next breath would be his last.

That night, I was sure Jed would drift off and leave me behind. I studied his face as he slept, memorizing it. There was a tentative knock at the door, and I looked up, expecting to see a doctor.

But it was my dad.

"Robin?" he said, as if he couldn't believe it was me.

"Daddy?" I hadn't called him that in years, but I wanted to be a little kid with little problems that he could fix. "What are you doing here?"

He came over to me, and I stood up and hugged him.

"I was driving home from work," he said. "When I saw the freeway exit for Rochester, I didn't even think about it. I just turned off, and here I am." He held me tight. "How are you doing? How's Jed?"

Catherine was asleep in her chair, but our talking woke her up. When she noticed my dad, she straightened her hair and tucked it behind her ears. "Oh, hello," she said.

My father let go of me, leaned down, and gave Catherine an awkward embrace, the type that strangers give to one another in extreme circumstances. "It's good to see you, Catherine. I hope it's okay that I came."

Catherine stood, and her delicate features softened. "Of course." She let out an anxious chuckle, as if it caused her pain. "I wish Jed's father was here. He came on Monday, but he had to fly back right away." She rubbed the skin along her throat. "He's doing some show."

Dad nodded; it was clear he had no idea how to respond. "Sure." He looked over at Jed. "How's he doing?"

Catherine blinked, and her eyes grew watery from behind her glasses. "I worry that he's in pain. The doctors say he isn't, but I don't know." She sniffed. "I want his passing to be peaceful."

My father shifted and rocked in place. "Of course you do. We always want the best for our children." He tightened his arm around me as if to prove his point.

Catherine smiled, and this time her eyes smiled too. "Yes, we do, don't we?"

Later, while Catherine continued to watch over Jed, my dad and I went to the hospital cafeteria. I picked at the apple pie he bought me.

"How are you holding up, sweetheart?"

I shrugged. "Okay."

"Really?"

My father's eyes were so kind that I had to look away. "Dad, I don't think I'm doing this right."

"What do you mean?"

I twisted my napkin up into a shredded ball. "I keep wanting to run. And when I'm at class, away from the hospital, I feel relieved. Sometimes, I catch myself"—I pause, unsure if I should admit to thinking something so awful—"I catch myself hoping that he'll die soon so it will all be over."

My father reached across the table, grabbed my hand, and held it.

"Oh, Robin," he said with a shake of his head. "You're too young for this."

"Too young for what?"

Dad pushed his own plate of apple pie off to the side. "For the pain that comes with losing the person you love. It's soul-crushing, but it changes you into a different, stronger version of yourself."

I examined my father—his receding hairline, his sagging jaw, and the circles under his eyes. Who had he been before he'd lost my mom? I would never know.

"Honestly, Dad, I'd rather be my same weak self and keep Jed alive."

His voice was soft, like he was telling me a bedtime story. "That's not a choice you get to make."

Thursday, September 20, 2002

It had been exactly a year since Jed said he needed me. When we'd made love for the first time in that corn field. But there was no anniversary celebration.

Instead, Jed opened his eyes one last time. In the space of a moment, we connected for what should have been forever. Then his body relaxed as he finally stopped fighting to breathe. As he stopped fighting altogether. Peace spread across his face, and the lines on his heart monitor went flat.

Catherine never left his side. "Oh, Jed. Oh, my baby," she whispered. "My sweet, beautiful boy."

Tears streamed down her face. She held him and kissed him, but I stepped away, dry-eyed and stone-like.

For weeks, icebergs built inside me as I waited for Jed to die. He'd struggle to breathe, and I knew. His looming death was a boat floating in icy water. A crash was always inevitable. But then he'd regain his breath, his ship would pass, and the ocean stayed a bottomless, empty shade of blue.

Not this time. This time, his boat just sank, swallowed by the deep, infinite sea. He fell into nothingness. I wanted to be like Catherine. I wished for the strength to sob and to hold him. Instead, there was more ice inside, more bracing for disaster.

I didn't know how there could ever be a thaw.

Because one thing was clear: Starting with that moment, and with every moment that followed, he would sink further and further into the depths. And once I reached land, every step I took was another step away from Jed.

Friday, September 28, 2002

Both my dad and Isobel drove up for the funeral. A bunch of people from the Hoyt theater department also came, the same ones who were in the hospital waiting room during Jed's transplant. And there were some friends of Jed's I barely knew. Maybe we had met once or twice before, during the year that Jed was healthy, or they had come by the hospital when it was time for last goodbyes.

I don't remember much of what they said about Jed at his service. I sat there, like a young widow, in the front row pew that had been reserved for Catherine and me. And afterwards, I moved around the reception, going through the motions of eating, talking, and nodding my head. I was numb, then quite suddenly, sorrow would punch me and leave me winded. As soon as I caught my breath, I'd look around, scared for the next assault. Grief was a dark shadow lurking in the corners of the room, with the power not just to injure me but to rip me apart.

Isobel stayed for the entire weekend, so after the reception, she came back to Catherine's house. She and I went to the spare bedroom and sat cross-legged on the bed. I clasped the flash drive Jed gave me.

"How are you holding up?" asked Isobel. She leaned against the dresser, arms crossed, covering the black wool dress she'd borrowed from her mom.

I shrugged. "I don't even know what that means."

"Have you cried yet?" Isobel asked gently.

"There's plenty of time for that later." Reaching back to run my fingers through my hair, I realized it was in a bun. I didn't recall having pinned it up.

"What's with the flash drive?" she asked. I had been carrying it around like it was a good luck charm.

"Jed finished his play right before he died." I traced the outline of the small device with my thumb, the cold plastic a stark reminder of his absence. "His last wish was to finish his play. He wanted me to produce and star in it one day."

Isobel raised her narrow, arched eyebrows. "That's wonderful!"

"It is?"

"Aren't you happy to have something left of him?"

I nodded and stared down at the flash drive as if I could see his face if I looked hard enough. "I'm too scared to read it, though." I rolled my head around, stretching my neck. "What if it's not any good? He was pretty loopy when he finished it." I pressed down, massaging one of the knots in my neck. "And once I read it, that's it. Right now, I have something of him left, but once I read this, it's over."

Isobel sat down and put her arm around me. I rested against her shoulder, wishing to capture her warmth. "What if I read it?"

she asked. "I could tell you what I think. Then you could wait to read it until you're ready."

"You'd do that?"

"I'd be honored."

I gave Isobel the flash drive and brought her my laptop. Then I went downstairs while Isobel read Jed's play. My dad and Catherine talked in her living room.

"Zeke could never deal with it; I'm not surprised he took off right after the funeral," Catherine said. "I believe Zeke was Jed's biggest disappointment. He could handle the CF, but his father leaving? And when Zeke tried to produce *Simplicity* without Jed's consent, it broke his heart."

My father leaned forward in what was supposed to be a reclining chair. "That must have been hard for you, being both parents to Jed."

Catherine nodded and sipped her tea. "I'm sure you can identify."

Dad started to speak, but he looked up and saw me. "Oh, hi. I thought you were upstairs with Isobel."

"She has some work to do. I'll go back up in a while."

"Well, you're welcome to sit with us." Catherine patted a space on the couch. I sat down next to her, close enough to press our shoulders, arms, and hips together. She spoke to my dad. "Have I mentioned how much I love this girl? And how much Jed loved her?" She squeezed my knee. "He did, you know. With his whole heart."

"He loved you, too." I told Catherine. "I've never known anyone who was so close to his mom."

Catherine grew misty-eyed. She started telling this story about when Jed was twelve and wanted to go to sleep-away camp, and Dad and I listened. Her words were like raindrops against the window, comforting as long as I didn't get too close.

After a while, Isobel came to the foot of the stairs and motioned to me. I stood, and we climbed back up to the guest room.

"Well?" I asked once the door was closed behind us.

Isobel answered with a sharp intake of air. "Oh, Robin," she said. Her face was wet with tears. "It's beautiful."

Sunday, October 6, 2002

The sewing machine's whirring sound comforted me. I also liked the feel of the fabric in my hands. Best of all was putting together scraps and spare buttons and transforming them into something complete.

I caught Catherine's reflection in one of the many costume shop mirrors before she saw me. Her beautiful, long hair was pulled back into a sloppy ponytail, and her clothes didn't quite match. But when she turned the corner, she smiled. "I thought I'd find you here," she said. "What are you working on?"

"Just a shirt." I held it up. It was blue cotton with floral trim and green buttons at the collar.

"Lovely," she said. "Are you just about done? I was thinking of ordering a pizza tonight. And maybe watching another video?"

Catherine and I spent most of our evenings together watching TV. I appreciated the relief of staring at a screen and not interacting with anyone. "Sure," I told her. "That sounds great."

"Okay, so I'll see you at home?"

"Yeah."

Catherine started out, but I called after her. "Wait!"

She turned back. "What is it?"

My stomach clenched. "Catherine, I've been meaning to say something. I feel stupid, but I never checked into student housing. I sort of forgot, and the housing office gave my room to someone else."

Catherine stood there, her head cocked and her expression quizzical, until she broke into a laugh. The sound was so unfamiliar that I had to remind myself what it was.

"Why are you laughing?" I asked.

"You 'forgot' to check into student housing? Who does that? It's like one of those dreams where you forget to wear clothes or don't realize that you've signed up for a class until the day of the final."

"Yeah . . . I guess," I stammered.

"I mean, come on." Laughter bubbled out of her. "Was your boyfriend dying or something?"

My mouth fell open. Catherine put her hand against her lips, and her chuckles morphed into tears. "Oh my God," she cried. "I can't believe I just said that! I . . ." She shook her head. "I laugh at the weirdest things, and my jokes are terrible now. Just awful."

I gripped the hem of my shirt, twisting and scrunching it up. But there was no use. My own laughter escaped. "Come on, Catherine. That's no excuse. Unless . . . did your son just die or something?"

"Oh!" Catherine's jaw dropped. Her shock was cartoonish, and she realized it at the same moment as me. Then, the corners of her eyes crinkled, just like how Jed's eyes used to. She giggled and it was contagious. Soon we were both doubled over, hysterical, with tears coursing down our cheeks.

A couple of minutes later, the mood fizzled, like how soda goes flat after you pour it. We wiped our eyes and stood up straight.

Catherine found her voice first. "Robin, please stay with me for as long as you'd like. But also promise that as soon as you're ready, you'll move out and start having fun with people your own age."

"You sound like Jed. He made me promise him something like that, too."

She nodded and brushed away a tear. "He wanted us to look out for each other. That's perfect for me because I've never had a daughter. You're the closest I'll get."

The thickness in my heart made it difficult to speak. "Well, you're the closest thing I'll ever have to a mom, so we're a good fit."

"Oh, honey." She took me in her arms. I started to shake.

"I just miss him so much." My voice trembled along with the rest of me.

"I know," she said. "Me too."

She hugged me hard. Then my latent tears for Jed finally burst. I sobbed into Catherine's shoulder, and she soothed me in a way that only a mother could.

Thursday, March 20, 2003

I lived with Catherine for the rest of my junior year. On Jed's birthday, I was at rehearsal for *The Glass Menagerie*, reciting lines about fragile beauty, while Catherine went out for dinner with well-meaning friends. We both got home after ten, and Catherine pulled out a Sara Lee chocolate cake from the freezer.

"One year, I was super busy. I thought I was the worst mother in the world because I bought him a frozen birthday cake." She put it on the counter and took two forks from the silverware drawer. "But he loved it. He insisted on the same cake for every birthday after that." She stabbed her fork into the cold, brown block and pried off a little wedge. "Now Sara Lee chocolate cake will always make me think of Jed." She put her fork in her mouth and swallowed down the cake. "But then again, everything makes me think of Jed."

"Do you think he'd be out right now, hitting the bars with all his friends?"

Catherine took another bite. "Maybe. But I expect he'd have been happier spending time with you."

I ate a few bites of cake, which was pretty tasty. We each talked about our day, and we talked about Jed. Then Catherine yawned and called it a night. I went upstairs too, but my plans didn't include sleep.

Opening the drawer of my bedside table, I took out Jed's flash drive. "Okay, Jed," I whispered. "Happy birthday. You'll finally find out what I think."

The Next Breath
By Jed Reardon

Characters:
Grayson—Mid-twenties. Writer. In love with Georgie
Georgie—Early twenties. Painter/daycare worker.
Lea—Mid-twenties. Arts administrator. Grayson's ex-girlfriend. Can't get over him.

Setting: *Fall, present day, in the apartment Georgie and Grayson share. Finished paintings hang on the walls. An easel in the middle of a room holds an unfinished painting. There is also a desk with a computer and lots of clutter. Over the desk, a bulletin board holds index cards with Grayson's notes for his play.*

Act 1

(Grayson speaks to the audience.)

Grayson: *Human beings aren't so complex. We're not snowflakes, and even if we look different, underneath, our blueprints are the same. We all want love and a sense of purpose. We all want to be heard. We spend our lives figuring out our message. We're terrified of death. We talk a lot, but mostly, we just make noise. Sometimes it's better to listen.*

As a writer, I must remember that. I've written a lot of crap—words that are just me babbling to myself. But if I'm ever lucky enough to write something worthwhile, it will come from listening first.

There's too much sound and not enough substance. If I'm confused by my own message, how will anyone understand?

(Grayson sits at his computer and types his play. He's hunched over, drinking coffee. Occasionally, he gets up and moves the index cards around on his bulletin board. Fingers through his hair, lots of snort-type breaths, general air of frustration. The buzzer rings. Grayson gets up to answer. It's Lea.)

Lea: *Hi, baby! (She walks in uninvited and plops her briefcase down.) You wouldn't believe the day I've had. The spring season is all fucked up, we're in a budget crisis, and Flynn's in a tizzy. Thank God we're doing your show. It's the one bright spot in a shit season. (She looks at her leg.) Oh no. (Lea leans over, and her cleavage shows. As she checks for a run in her pantyhose, Grayson stares.)*

Lea *(standing up)*: *What?*

Grayson: *You don't live here anymore. You know that, right?*

Lea: *Oh, but I do live here, baby. I rented the apartment next door.*

Grayson *(disturbed)*: *You're joking, right?*

(Lea shrugs.)

Lea: *Maybe. (She holds up her wrist, showing a bracelet.) Look what I found in my jewelry box this morning. Remember how long you saved up just to buy this, Grayson? It means so much to me.*

Grayson: *Yeah, I remember. You threatened to leave me if I didn't get you that stupid bracelet. Well, I got it for you, and you still left me, so why would you move here now?*

Lea *(smiling, coy): Calm down. I happen to like the location.*

Grayson: *In this low-rent district? What's to like?*

Lea: *The low rent!*

Grayson: *And with all the cheap, craphole apartments available, you chose one in my building?*

Lea *(letting her sexiness show): I'm still not over you, Grayson. I can't move on.*

Grayson: *People don't "move on" from each other; they just move away. You need to move away too.*

Lea: *You're such an asshole.*

Grayson *(suddenly intense and angry): Why are you here? What do you want?*

Lea: *Guess.*

Grayson: *If I guess right, will you leave?*

Lea: *Sure.*

Grayson *(calmer): Then I'll give it my best shot. (Rubs his forehead.) You want to get back together.*

Lea: *Well, yeah. But that's not the reason for my visit.*

Grayson: *Right. You want to torment me, then.*

Lea: *No.*

Grayson: *You're here to pressure me about my play.*

(She sighs and nods.)

Grayson *(Cont'd): You could have just called.*

Lea: *But I live next door now. It's easier to stop by.*

(He stares at her for a moment, still unsure if she's telling him the truth.)

Grayson: *You know what, Lea? You're a lot like that bracelet I gave you—so shiny and beautiful, but you serve no purpose. Even you don't understand why you're here or what you want.*

Lea: *We're the same that way, Grayson. You don't know what you want either. You haven't moved on from me.*

Grayson: (He takes a broad step back.) But I have moved away.

(Lea approaches him and runs her finger down his chest.)

Lea: I'm back now, and you still need me.

Grayson: No, I need to overcome you—the way people overcome poverty or a disability.

Lea (Angry): Okay. Let's talk about your play. The scenes you sent are dreadful, and you know it. If you don't deliver something good soon, we're breaking your contract. Is that what you want?

Grayson (Contrite): No.

Lea (Getting close to him again): It will be okay, baby. You just need your muse back. (Runs her fingers through his hair.) I know you miss us. We used to be so good together.

Grayson (Takes her shoulders): Lea . . .

(Their eyes meet.)

Lea: What, baby?

(He gently but firmly pushes her away.)

Grayson: I guessed right. You need to leave now.

(She quickly recovers and grabs her briefcase.)

Lea: You have twenty-four hours, Grayson. And don't send me junk. (She exits.)

(Grayson addresses the audience.)

Grayson: I fell in love with Lea because she's broken. I believed I could fix her. That I could ease the sadness living underneath that tough, shiny shell. I didn't realize that cracks in the center of your soul are beyond repair. Kindness isn't superglue. The more I tried to mend her, the more she came apart.

I put my computer down and stood to stretch, rolling down my spine one vertebrae at a time.

Jed's opening scenes could have been written by anyone, and that thought pained me. I didn't know if it was worse for the play to scream Jed or to be lost among countless others. The responsibility to honor his goodbye weighed on me, and I couldn't hide from it forever. So, I straightened up and continued reading.

(*Georgie comes home. She moves around the apartment while Grayson addresses the audience. She is in the kitchen, scrounging for food in an empty refrigerator, tending to a sink full of dirty dishes, and sorting a stack of unpaid bills.*)

Grayson (Cont'd): *Then there's Georgie. I fell in love with her because she's whole. She's one of those people who seems to never have real problems or ugly moments. And when she does, it's endearing.*

(*Georgie approaches Grayson, and he breaks out his monologue.*)

Georgie: *We need to move out of this hell hole, Grayson.*

Grayson: *Let's talk about it later.*

Georgie (*shaking her head*): *No. You always want to talk about difficult stuff later, but I want out of here now. I'm tired of falling asleep to the sound of gunshots.*

Grayson: *We can't afford to move.*

Georgie: *You can't afford to move because you don't have a job.*

Grayson: *Georgie, do you think you'll find an Upper-East-Side apartment on a daycare worker's salary? At least I have money coming in.*

(*She glares at him.*)

Georgie: *Wait. What money do you have coming in?*

Grayson (*mumbling*): *Nothing. We'll talk about this later.*

Georgie: *Grayson! You took Lea's deal!*

(*Grayson gets up and crosses the stage, away from her.*)

Grayson: *I had to, Georgie. It has nothing to do with Lea.*

(*Georgie grabs her suitcase and shoves clothes, books, and art supplies into it.*)

Georgie: *Lea will never let you go. I'm an idiot for thinking things could work between you and me.*

Grayson: *Don't say that, Georgie. This deal will be good for us both.*

Georgie: *No. Not if you're connected to Lea.*

Grayson: *Me taking the deal doesn't connect me to her. You're the only person I'm connected to.*

(*Grayson takes her bag and drops it to the floor. She grudgingly lets him drag her to the bed. He sits on the edge, yet she still stands, and he buries his head in her stomach.*)

Grayson (*cont'd*): *George, I'm sorry. I shouldn't have told Lea yes without talking to you first. But please don't leave me. Without you, I'll float away.*

(Their eyes lock.)

Georgie (with affection): You're so full of crap.

Grayson: No. If I was full of crap, I'd have gravity; the crap would weigh me down.

Georgie: Oh, please.

Grayson: I just need you more than you need me, Georgie. (He gets up and kisses her.) Show me your painting.

Georgie: I haven't done much to it.

Grayson: I still want to see.

(Georgie gives in and leads Grayson to her easel.)

Georgie: Last night, I added some color, but I can't get the face right. (She moves Grayson so he stands side by side with her painting.) I don't have the dimensions or the shadows. (She traces the contours of his face with her fingers.)

Grayson: You can feel my shadow?

Georgie: Of course.

That line made my stomach grow heavy, like I'd eaten too much. *Keep reading*, I told myself.

There was love, betrayal, and murder. My eyes were torn between wanting to read more and crying so hard that my cheeks stung.

"Death hasn't made me stop loving you."

I spoke to an empty room. "It hasn't made me stop loving you either, Jed."

I couldn't finish reading it that night. So I put my computer away and hugged my pillow as I tried to fall asleep.

ELEVEN

I fold my hands in my lap as I finish my story. Nick listened the whole time, never once interrupting. And yet, he kept his gaze focused on anything but me. Now he uses his index finger to trace the rim of his coffee cup, still avoiding my eyes.

"How long did it take you," he asks, "to finally finish reading the play?"

I shift in my seat. We've sat in this restaurant for so long that my legs are sticking to the vinyl booth, and the morning rush has morphed into the lunchtime crowd.

"Several months. Senior year, I got an apartment with some friends, and I started going out more. After a while, it wasn't quite so painful to think about Jed."

I meet his eyes, but Nick looks towards the window.

"What about Catherine?" he asks.

"I spent a lot of time with her, up until I graduated." I press my fingers against the table edge. "Afterwards, we kept in touch . . . you know, weekly phone calls and emails, stuff like that. On Mother's Day, I always send flowers and a card because I hate the idea of her not getting anything."

Nick nods. "And because you have that bond." He finally meets my gaze. His eyes are soft—compassionate. "A bond that not many people understand. The bond of shared loss."

I nod, swallowing past the lump in my throat. "Yeah." There's

208

a moment of silence between us as I struggle to maintain my composure.

"How did you keep her from me?" Nick's voice is gentle as he scratches his chin. "I mean, logistically . . . she's still a big part of your life. I don't get how you managed that."

"I wasn't hiding her from you, Nick. Catherine just got back from a year-long teacher exchange in Northern Wales." I rub my palms against my thighs. "Anyway, it's not like you tell me everything. It's clear you've been hiding something."

Nick's face says I've hit a nerve. I expect him to grow defensive while he spews out hot-air explanations. Instead, his tan cheeks turn pink. "You've always been perceptive."

I want to arch my neck and hurl. "Are you cheating on me?"

"What?" Nick jolts back and frowns. "No!"

"Then what is it?"

His chocolate eyes roll to the ceiling while his hands go limp. "I'm going back to school."

It takes me a moment to realize I heard him right. "I'm confused. Why would you keep that a secret?"

"Because it's for music education, and I have to drive all the way to Ames, which is inconvenient and expensive. But I love it, and I need to be something other than a real estate agent." Nick's voice is all hoarse and scratchy, and I'm not sure if that's from coffee or emotion.

"Wait, so when you're done, you'll be, like, a high school music teacher?" I picture him wearing a tie and jeans, practicing scales on the tuba with some chubby-cheeked kid. He'll be handsome Mr. Davies. All the marching band girls will have crushes on him.

"Yeah. It's not some huge, lofty goal, but it's what I want to do."

"But that's great!" He doesn't return my smile, so I let my face fade to neutral. "I still don't understand why you didn't tell me."

"I was waiting for the right time. But it seems like you're always either busy, distracted, or exhausted." With a sigh, Nick slumps against the padded booth, and his shirt puckers a little around his chest. "And . . . I was scared. My biggest regret was dropping out of college. But Robin, you're years beyond dating a college student who wants to teach music. It's impractical."

The urge to reach for him, to soothe him, is powerful. But his "don't touch me vibe" is even stronger. So I hold back, aching to cross the chasm that's opened between us.

"And you're nothing if not practical. Right, Nick?" My voice is light, trying to lighten the mood.

He just scowls.

"Okay," I say, "why did you bring up buying a house when you should be worried about student loans?"

Nick fiddles with his watch like it's his security blanket. "The house was a stupid idea. Forget it."

Several days ago, I would have loved for him to say that, but now my heart sinks. "Nick, come on."

"No." He shakes his head and leans forward. "I'm all over the place, and so are you. And let's be honest. You don't want to buy a house together because you're still in love with Jed."

Tears of shame gather behind my eyes. I can't deny what he said, and that's the worst part.

"Nick, I just need to work through some things. And I was worried that if I told you about Jed, you'd be threatened by his memory."

Nick crooks his jaw, and I want to gulp back my words.

"Right," he mumbles. "Because I could never do something so romantic like writing you a play."

"It wasn't *exactly* for me."

"Whatever." Nick rubs his face, and when he lowers his hands, he looks exhausted. "Here's my problem. I can't compete, and if I try, I'll feel petty and small. And meanwhile, you'll just continue to pull away from me and—"

"Whoa!" Heat gathers under my cheeks. "I don't 'pull away' from you."

"Yes, you do! All the time!" Nick counts off on his fingers. "You don't need me to have kids. You don't need me at your dad's birth-day or at your play. You don't even need my umbrella in the rain!"

"That's unfair. You're taking all that out of context, and when you look at our entire relationship . . ." I pause, realizing that I don't know how to finish. "I'm doing my best, okay? After Jed, I stuck to dating guys who didn't care about me so I wouldn't have to care about them either. You're the first guy to offer me something real, the first one I'm willing to risk . . ." My hands wave up and down in defeat as my voice trails off. "Risk everything for."

Nick looks at me for a moment, his eyes searching mine. I can see the battle raging behind them—hurt and anger wrestling with longing and love.

"That's just it, Robin," he murmurs, his voice barely above a whisper. "I don't want you to risk anything. I want . . . I need to be more than just the safe choice after Jed."

"You're not! I wasn't saying that, and I am sorry—"

Nick presses two fingers against the bridge of his nose and winces. "Don't be sorry. *I'm* sorry, okay? I'm sorry you were sad, and I'm sorry you were going through all this, and I'm sorry you couldn't tell me. But . . ." He looks off in the distance, and his chest heaves. "I need some time alone."

He may as well have stabbed my heart with his coffee spoon. "You want to break up?"

"I think we should take a break. We've both been hiding from each other, and we need to think about why and how to fix it." He pauses, weighing his next words. "Or if we even ought to try."

"Don't say that," I mumble.

"Why not?" Nick stretches his thick fingers out, and my mind jumps to an image of him playing the piano. "You need something I can't give you, Robin, and I need . . ." His voice cracks. "I need to focus on myself. I've spent the last few months trying to be the perfect guy for you. But I can't, because I'm not Jed, and that's a problem."

It's like I've been punched in the stomach. "Alright," I manage to say, though the word is unrecognizable to my ears. My heart pounds so hard, I'm afraid it will shatter my rib cage from the inside out.

Nick moves his hand across the table in an attempt to hold mine, but I pull away. He recovers and speaks with a gentle edge. "If you ever need anything, you can still call me."

"What if I need you?"

He doesn't answer right away, and then I realize his eyes are watery. "You don't need me, Rocky."

"But—"

Nick holds up his hand to stop me. "No, please don't. You don't need *me*, and you've made that clear." He gets up to go, but first he comes to my side of the booth and kisses the top of my head. "I understand why you still love Jed, so please try to understand how I feel too, okay?"

Before I can answer, he walks away. As I stare into the vacant space where Nick sat, the diner's hum grows oppressive.

I've never been so alone.

Tuesday, July 2, 2013
6:00 a.m.

Jed is in the passenger seat. No matter how many times I turn my key in the ignition, the car won't start. His lungs are flooding faster than the engine, and I must get him to a hospital.

I need help, and when I need help, my first thought is to call Nick. So I do.

"The number you have dialed has been disconnected. Please hang up and try again."

"I'm sorry, Jed." But he's wheezing too loudly to hear me.

When my eyes shoot open, I don't try to go back to sleep, and I don't try to analyze my dream. Instead, I pop out of bed, pee, brush my teeth, and hurriedly change into my running gear.

I get to Flashdance Girl's house earlier than usual. She's

stretching, her back is to me, and she doesn't hear me approach. Perfect.

"Hey!" I shout, and she turns around. "How old are you?"

She narrows her eyes and extends one leg. "Sixteen."

These are the first words we've ever exchanged. "Why are you up so early? Teenagers are supposed to sleep late."

"Not me. I'm a morning person." Her voice carries weight, like her words could vacuum up dust particles. "And I'm not a normal teenager."

That's clear. Her 1980s-style running gear is proof enough. Maybe there's more to her story. Maybe, like me, she's encountered circumstances that both stunted and forced her to grow up fast.

"Old people like to get up early, don't they?" she asks.

I shrug. "I suppose."

She gives me an evil smile. "Then try to keep up, old lady." Flashdance Girl sprints off down the sidewalk, leaving me far behind.

Or maybe she's just a punk.

3:30 p.m.

I have a very productive day at my studio, and the tips of my fingers sting from all the pin pricks. After finishing four garments, I package them, head to the post office, and send them off. I pass a car wash as I drive back, and I turn in. "I'll take the full package," I tell the lady at the desk. Then I wait while they vacuum, polish, and shine my 2001 Volkswagen.

Jed's car held up quite well over the past twelve years. Much better than his lungs did anyway, though now it's giving me problems.

Nick doesn't know it was Jed's car, so he can't accuse me of holding onto it for sentimental reasons. Yet, given the chance, that's what he would do. And he'd be right.

I pull into the first used car lot I can find.

Two hours and a $2,500 down payment later, I'm the proud owner of a 2004 Kia Spectra. It's red, has 48,000 miles on it, and the used car salesman promised it was an excellent deal. Whatever. It's a grown-up's vehicle. More importantly, I only cried a little when I said goodbye to Jed's Volkswagen.

A car's a car. At least this one will be mine.

7:00 p.m.

When I drive into the theater parking lot, Isobel's there. She seems confused as I climb out of my Kia.

"Hey!" I say. "I'm revved up for rehearsal tonight. You can expect my 'A' game all the way."

Isobel squints like she doesn't recognize me. "Great." Her gaze goes past my shoulder, toward my new car. "Where's your Volkswagen?"

"You mean Jed's car? I traded it in." I hitch up my shoulder bag and pick up my pace. The sooner we get started, the better.

"Just like that?" Isobel asks.

"Yup. It was time to make a change."

Isobel unlocks the theater door and pushes it open. "Why? Because of Nick?"

"No." I bristle. "Nick didn't know that car was Jed's. My decision has nothing to do with him."

"Okay." Isobel turns on the lights, illuminating the dark rehearsal space. "But if it *did* have something to do with Nick, that's understandable. You've been putting on a brave face, and I want to make sure you're okay."

"Fine!" I chirp. Looking around, I take in the empty room. "Where is everyone?"

Isobel looks at her cell phone. "We're early. And you're *really* early."

"Huh?"

"Remember? We're running Miranda and Andrew's scene first?"

"Oh." And I rushed through buying my car just to get here on time. "No problem. I'll watch. That will help me get into character."

"Actually, since you're here, let's do the second half of Act One."

"Sure! Wonderful!" I rub my hands together. Isobel smiles like she might say more, but she keeps her mouth shut as she sets out the props. A moment later, Lucas shows up.

"Sorry, Isobel," he says, rushing in. "You're totally doing my job." He pushes his Elvis Costello glasses up his nose as he nudges her out of the way.

"That's okay," Isobel tells him. "Was Jonah gassy again?"

"We think it's colic."

"That's tough," I say, and Lucas startles. He must not have realized I was here.

Miranda and Andrew walk in, sharing some joke. Miranda's knotting her mermaid hair into a bun when she sees me. "Hey! You're here early."

"Yeah." My eyes pass between her and Andrew; they're both still laughing. "What's so funny?"

Andrew waves a dismissive hand and smirks. "Man troubles. I got dumped. AGAIN. No guy I've been with has ever cared about me. At least you don't have that problem, Robin."

Andrew's words don't compute. "What do you mean?" I ask.

"Jed wrote you a play," Andrew answers. "Now that's devotion."

I force out a smile. "Yeah, he wrote me a play, but then he died, which was rather thoughtless of him. Now Nick, who is alive, healthy, and capable of devotion, is over me." I square my shoulders. "I understand man troubles just fine."

Andrew's face grows pink and fish-like. "Sorry," he mumbles.

"No worries!" I jump from my chair. "Are we ready to get going? I'm in the mood to work!" I turn towards Isobel. "Can we get started?"

Isobel goes toward her director's chair in the first row. "Sure, of course. Let's do this."

We take our places. The stage lights go up, and we're all in character. As Georgie, I grab the collar of Andrew/Grayson's T-shirt and kiss him on the mouth.

Georgie: Sorry I didn't listen to you, Grayson. (Kisses him again) You were right. We're linked, and we'll change our destiny together.

Grayson: We will? I thought you were angry with me.

Georgie: Nope. Your dreams are my dreams, and my fate is your fate. Except right now, I have to go to work. (Kisses him passionately) I will miss you every moment we're apart. (Exits)

Grayson (Stunned, he runs back to his computer and mumbles as he reads his writing.): We're linked, and we'll change our destiny together. (He looks up from his computer.) How the hell did that happen?

She said all the lines I gave her, word for word. (He runs his finger along the lava lamp sitting on his desk.) What was I thinking? You can't change destiny, and it has nothing to do with love. It's about dust and pain. Destiny is a doctor's waiting room or getting lost on the highway.

Grayson's monologue continues, and he plots more ways to write the perfect relationship between him and Georgie.

Miranda stands behind me and whispers in my ear. "How are you?" she asks.

"Fine," I shrug.

"I think Jed would be happy with how the play's coming together."

"Oh yeah. *Why?*"

I probably sound angry because Miranda's expression goes blank. She silently stutters.

"Never mind," I whisper. "It's your cue." I push her onto stage, and she becomes Lea again.

Lea comes over to seduce Grayson. She takes off her blouse, sticks her tongue in his mouth, and promises to do all the things she used to do. Plus, she'll make his play a success. Grayson's tempted until his gaze falls on Georgie's painting. That reminds him not to succumb.

Grayson: It's over. Don't come back. (Stands by open door)
Lea (Weepy): Don't do this to me, babe. I'm nothing without you.
Grayson: You've never been anything with me, Lea. I don't care if the deal is off. You have to go.
(He turns away. Lea drops her bracelet in Georgie's paint tray while he isn't looking.)
Lea: Goodbye, then. (She walks to the door. Then she leans in and kisses him one last time. He doesn't return the embrace.) We'll love each other again. (Exits.)

The lights dim, and it's my cue. Coming home from work, I enter and begin painting. Of course, I find the bracelet Lea left behind. I let the realization harden over my face like plaster. Then I wipe the paint off the bracelet with water from my jar and place it on Grayson's keyboard.

When Grayson enters, he finds the bracelet, and we fight again. Grayson's pleading and groveling can't convince me he's over Lea or that he isn't tempted by everything she offers. I repack my suitcase and put on my sweater. The sound of rain hitting the windows fills the room.

Grayson: It's pouring outside. (He stands in front of the door, blocking it.)
Georgie: Rain won't keep me here, Grayson. Nothing you'll say or do will stop me from leaving.
Grayson (Defeated): Fine, go if you have to. But promise you'll come back.
Georgie: I don't make promises I can't keep. (She moves past him and out into the night.)
Grayson (Speaking to the audience): I was a fool not to write more. As soon as my words ran out, we started fighting again, and now Georgie is gone. (Moves to computer) I need a revision. I need a new scene. There has to be an Act Two.

Left alone on stage, Grayson writes another scene with Georgie, hoping it will come true. Sure enough, I come home the next day, wet and cold, saying I couldn't stand to be away from Grayson. He takes me in his arms as the lights dim.

"Perfect!" yells Isobel. "Let's take a five-minute break before we run scene three."

I jump off stage, grab my cell phone, and go outside for some fresh air. My chest deflates when there are no texts or voicemails from Nick. I shouldn't have let myself hope, but even a simple hello would stop my world from spinning. Instead, I send a text of my own. To Catherine.

Do you have plans for the Fourth? Want to come to my brother's barbecue?

Once our break is over, Isobel orders us into place, and I think for the zillionth time that bossy people make great directors. "Let's do this," she says. "Like last night, only upped a few notches, okay?"

"Yes!" I cry. Everybody looks at me like I'm on something. "What?" I ask. "I'm feeling it tonight."

"Good," says Isobel, "but you've been talking really loud."

My whole body flushes. "Oh." I keep my voice soft. "Sorry."

"It's fine." Isobel pats me on the shoulder. "Okay, let's go."

We get into place, and Lucas brings the lights down. I stand backstage, listening for my cue. Once Georgie returns home, Graysons resumes writing their relationship. But it's a power he doesn't understand, and it's dangerous when Georgie strays from the script. Andrew/Grayson sits at his desk when the scene begins. He speaks to the audience.

Grayson: *When Georgie left me, my heart bottomed out. My ears are ringing, I'm kind of dizzy, and I have this dull, throbbing head-ache that began in my chest. But now that she's back, I'll ignore the spinning sensation and make her the center of my world. I'll create our life together, one word at a time.*

When I enter, I use my burst of energy to add passion to my lines.

218

Georgie: You're so profound, Grayson. I will never leave you again, and I promise to devote my entire life to loving you.

I leap into his arms, and Andrew/Grayson knows to catch me. But he acts surprised.

Grayson: Really? You want to devote your entire life to loving me? What about art?

Georgie: Forget about art, Grayson. The only true art form is love, and I'm in love with you.

I kiss him again and again.

Grayson: Wow. Well, that's good.

He carries me towards the bed, but his mind works faster than his body. Grayson puts me down. His face scrunches with tension.

Grayson (Cont'd): Wait a second. Are you happy? This won't work if you're unhappy.

Georgie: I'm only happy when I'm in your arms!

Grayson: No, no, no. That's not right.

Georgie (Upset): I need your approval, Grayson. You make me complete and fulfilled.

Grayson places both hands on my shoulders and speaks in a calm, low voice.

Grayson: Georgie, that's not how you are.

Georgie: Oh. How do you want me to be?

Grayson: L . . . like you've always been, but willing to fight for me.

Georgie (Kisses him.): I'll fight for you, Grayson. I'll do anything you want, but as a self-actualized, strong individual with a life of my own. It's all to the good.

Grayson (soft laugh): It's all to the good.

Grayson holds me tight and kisses me. I return the kiss hungrily. At first, it was weird having to make out with Andrew, but

I'm past it now. The lights fade.

When they come back up, Grayson is gone and I'm painting. The buzzer rings. I put down my brush, square my shoulders, and open the door to find Lea.

Georgie: *Ah, just who I was hoping for.*

Lea: *Oh yeah? Why?*

Georgie: *So I can tell you to screw off. Grayson has moved on.*

Lea (laughing): *Grayson says people don't move on from each other; they just move away. Besides, he'll change his mind once the baby is born.*

(Moment of shocked silence)

Georgie: *You're pregnant?*

Lea: *Oh, yes.*

Georgie: *Liar.*

Lea: *Hmm. In a few months, you'll know for sure. (Looks Georgie up and down.) It must be refreshing to wear sweats to work.*

Georgie: *Stay away from us.*

Lea: *Not going to happen.*

Georgie: *Why? What do you want?*

Lea: *I want Grayson.*

Georgie: *But you don't love him.*

Lea (controlled but becoming unhinged.): *True. In fact, I sort of hate him, but I'm trying to love him. Love is more comfortable than hate, you know?*

Georgie: *I'm starting to.*

Lea (jumpy, impatient): *So, can I have my bracelet?*

Georgie: *Sure. If you promise to leave and never come back.*

Lea (false laughter): *Not worth it. I can go to Tiffany's and buy another one.*

Georgie: *It won't be the bracelet that Grayson bought you.*

Lea (shrugging, but tense): *A bracelet is a bracelet.*

Georgie: *I disagree. You think that Grayson still loves you, and you're clinging to that.*

I drop the bracelet on the floor and pretend to crush it with my foot. This is the final straw for Lea, and she snaps.

Lea: You bitch!

She lunges for me, and we're in a hair-pulling, nail-scratching girl fight. But Georgie is no match for Lea. Soon, she has me in a death grip.

Georgie (struggling to escape Lea's grasp): You know what, Lea? Grayson NEVER loved you; he was just lonely and horny. And now he's using you to sell his play.

Lea tightens her grip around my throat.

Lea: That's a lie!

I struggle and flail, but Lea is in a trance-like rage. She squeezes my throat until I gasp and wilt to the ground. Lea looks at my dead body, stunned, and kicks me with the tip of her shoe.

Lea: Shit!

She makes a quick exit, and the lights go out.

When the lights come back up, I raise myself to my feet and brush the stage dust out of my hair. "How was that?" I ask Isobel. "Any more convincing? I've been working on my gasping and gagging."

Isobel runs her fingers through her ebony hair and gives me a quiet smile. "It was great, Robin. Spot-on. But let's save notes for after Act Two."

"No problem!" I say.

I go prepare. It's time for me to come back from the dead.

Thursday, July 4, 2013
6:00 a.m.

"I told you to not talk on your cell phone while driving!"

Jed gapes at me from his hospital bed. "What are you talking about?"

221

"Please! Stay off your phone and out of your car. That's how I'll keep you here."

Jed puts on his BiPap mask and takes a deep breath. "Nothing will keep me here, Robin. You know that."

I bolt up and reach for Nick. But there's just a pillow and some cold sheets. The sun peeks through my shades. It's time to run. It's time to face Flashdance Girl again.

Just five more minutes, I tell myself. And I drift back to sleep.

9:30 a.m.

When I discover how late it is, I roll over and shield my eyes with my arm, cursing my empty bed and my empty stomach. It's too late to catch Flashdance Girl. I decide to skip my morning run and eat cinnamon rolls instead.

I get dressed and go to the mall. There's a Cinnabon in the food court. After stuffing my face with gooey, buttery dough and frosting, I window-shop and enjoy being anonymous in the echo. When I pass a hair salon, I turn and go inside.

"Can I help you?" the girl behind the desk asks.

"I can't believe you're open today!"

"Yeah . . ." She sucks on her bottom lip. "So did you need something?"

"A haircut?"

The receptionist sighs and shouts back to one of the stylists. "Hey, Judi? Do you have time for a haircut?"

A large, middle-aged woman looks up from her magazine. "Sure," she says. "Send her back."

I sit in Judi's chair. She drapes a smock over me and sweeps my hair off my shoulders.

"What can I do for you today?"

"Cut it all off." Speaking to her reflection, I keep my eyes off myself. "I want it gone."

"All this beautiful blond hair? No way." Judi scowls. Her hair is short, highlighted, and spiky.

"Give me a cut like you have."

"I have this cut because nothing else works with my hair. You don't have that problem."

My frustration builds, and I squeeze my fingernails into my palms. "Look, Judi. I need a change. Please, will you help me?"

Our eyes meet in the mirror. She must sense my desperation.

"Maybe we can figure something out," Judi tells me. "Let's start with a shampoo."

1:00 p.m.

Catherine arrives at my apartment right when she said she would. Her hair is pulled back into a ponytail, and she has on a pair of cropped yoga pants and a faded black T-shirt. I give her a hug.

"I'm so glad you're here."

"Me too." She pulls away and strokes my short hair. "What's this? When did you get it cut?"

Self-consciously, I tuck a lock behind my ear. "Just today. What do you think?"

"It suits you. Brings out your cheek bones."

"Thanks." Her presence is like a healing balm. Then something occurs to me.

"What is it?" Catherine asks. She must have seen my face fall.

"Nothing." I look away. "How about we take your car to Ian's?"

Catherine and I get to the barbecue, and right away we run into my dad. He's in Ian's immaculate kitchen, wrapping an ace bandage around his knee.

"Peter!" Catherine says. "It's been a very long time. How are you?"

My dad smiles in pleasure, and his eyes brighten. "I'm good, except for my knee." He chuckles and stammers a little. "Robin didn't tell me you'd be here. How was Wales?"

"Oh, fabulous!" She reaches into her purse and pulls out her phone. "Do you want to see pictures?"

"Please."

I've seen the pictures already, so I leave them to themselves and walk out to the poolside. Isobel sits by Jack on a reclining porch chair. When she sees me, her face melts into a stunned slant.

"What did you do?!"

"It's just a haircut." I tilt my chin. "Georgie could have short hair."

"Yeah, but she's always had long hair." Isobel circles me, taking in every angle. "I mean, it's cute, but couldn't you have waited until after the play?"

"I acted on impulse."

"You've been doing that a lot, haven't you?"

I start to defend myself, but Ian approaches. "Whoa! Robbie! What's with the breakup hair?"

"Huh?"

He takes a swig of beer. "You know the old cliché: getting dumped and chopping off all your hair. It's a rite of passage."

I reel back. "Breakup hair is a thing? I had no idea."

"I like it," says Jack. "It's Peter Pan-ish."

"You mean it's a pixie cut," corrects Isobel, smiling.

"It is sort of androgynous," Ian adds. "Like Leonardo DiCaprio."

I bite my trembling lower lip. "You're not funny."

Ian's laugh is a self-satisfied yap. "Come on." He slaps my back. "Have a beer. We need you intoxicated before water polo. You're on my team this year."

I walk to the keg, thinking intoxication sounds good. But my mission is intercepted by Lucy. She has on huge Jackie O sunglasses, a plain blue T-shirt, and a pair of khaki draw-string shorts.

"Wow!" she says, gesturing to my hair. "I love it!"

"Really?"

She nods. "It's super chic." Then she tugs on my arm and pulls me aside. We stand in the shade of the patio, and she speaks in a hushed tone. "Hey, Monty feels bad for upsetting you at your dad's birthday by bringing up Nick. Is everything okay?"

"Sure!"

It comes out louder than I intended. Lucy steps back, so I turn down the volume. "I mean, you know, we broke up. But it's fine. I'm fine. That's how these things go sometimes."

Concern lurks behind her dark shades. "I'm so sorry. Is there any chance of talking things through?"

"He doesn't want to see me." Looking past her, I try not to let my words register. Ian and Eddie have a huge yard, and people are using the space for a rousing Frisbee game.

"Maybe he'll change his mind."

I look back at Lucy. "Doubtful. Don't worry, though. I'll let him know you're looking for a house. He's happy to help you find something."

"That's not what I'm worried about."

"Aren't you guys moving here?"

"Yeah, probably, but . . ." She pauses and pushes her sunglasses up so they're like a headband. Our eyes meet. "Let me know if there's anything I can do, okay?"

I'm not sure what she means, but whatever. "Sure." I squeeze her arm, trying to express affection. "Thanks."

Then I block everything out by drinking beer and kicking ass at Frisbee and water polo.

Sunday, July 7, 2013
6:00 a.m.

I'm at rehearsal. Isobel is angry, but I'm not sure why. "We'll run it again, and we'll keep running it until you get it right!" she yells.

"What am I doing wrong?" I ask.

She throws her script down in frustration. "I thought you knew Jed, Robin! You shouldn't have to ask!"

"But—"

"Take the carrot out of the notebook and divide the sugar in half!" she cries.

"What?"

Andrew and Miranda come on stage and perform a complex song and dance routine.

"When was that added in?" I ask.

Andrew laughs. "Guess Jed wasn't so devoted after all. He wrote you a play, but he never told you it's a musical!"

Emotional residue from my dream weighs me down as I run this morning, so I save my energy for a final sprint at the end. Yet when I get to Flashdance Girl's house, she's not there.

"Seriously?" I ask myself. "Come on!" I say that part out loud, and a neighbor's dog starts howling. Flashdance Girl's windows remain dark.

Maybe her family went out of town. Maybe there was a family emergency. Maybe Flashdance Girl realizes she can't keep beating me, and she's retired out of fear.

Maybe I am losing my mind. When they lock me away, I'll sing "Cuz she's a maniac, maniac."

I run home at full speed, like I have something to prove and someone is watching me prove it.

10:00 a.m.

Once I've showered, eaten breakfast, and cleaned out my closet (a three-hour task), I open the Sunday paper. Sitting alone on my couch, I try to be content while reading the news. I even sip my coffee like I'm at a Parisian café. But I'm my only audience member, and I remain unconvinced.

When I search for the Sunday magazine, the real estate section falls out. My wretched little heart yelps because Nick's picture is a tiny square in the middle of the front page. It's his real estate agent headshot. He chose the one with the glint in his eye.

After staring at his photo for several minutes, I read the accompanying listing.

Better than new. Fabulous 3-bedroom, 4-bath home with a

finished basement located in Ankeny. You'll fall in love with the hardwood floors, beautiful woodwork in the kitchen, and modern appliances. Upstairs are 3 large bedrooms, and the master has its own bath, twin closets, and a patio to enjoy your morning cup of coffee. The outside has a fenced yard, a handcrafted deck, beautiful land-scaping, and a storage shed. Don't miss out on this gem!

There's an open house today, from 12 to 4 p.m.

I pick up my phone.

"Lucy!" I say, as soon as she answers. "You said to let you know if there's anything you can do? Well, there is."

12:15 p.m.

I drive my new car through the streets of Ankeny. Lucy's in the passenger seat.

She twirls a lock of hair around her finger and stares out the window. "Why is every house either beige or gray? If I got a head injury, I'd forget which one's mine."

"Please don't get a head injury." I hang a left down a curvy road. "Is it definite? You're moving here?"

Lucy rubs her forehead. "I think so. Everything's happened so fast. I have a job interview next week. Monty all but accepted a new position. He'll be in DC part-time, but it should work."

"That's great." I smile. "Really."

"Yeah. I was surprised Monty was willing to compromise." Lucy gives me a light, gentle tap on the shoulder. "Sometimes people surprise you, you know?"

"Sure." I turn again at the bottom of a hill. A huge piece of undeveloped land is to our left. "I wonder if they get a lot of deer out here."

"Probably. I think West Des Moines is more our speed, but it's nice to see our options."

At the open house sign, I pull up to the curb and turn off the ignition. I inhale to keep my hands from shaking.

"What's the game plan?" Lucy asks.

"I tell Nick you looked in the paper for open houses, saw this one, and called me. I'm just here to introduce you."

She nods. "Got it. Then should I disappear to take a look around so you two can talk?"

I swallow back my nerves and realize my throat is dry. "That would be great."

"Let's go, then." Lucy smiles and opens the door. We both climb out of the car. Walking towards the house, I smooth wrinkles from my sailor blouse, the one Nick said he liked. I also smooth my hair, scared he'll hate the new cut.

Lucy links her arm through mine. "You look great. Don't worry. This will be fine."

When we get to the door, part of me wants to bolt, but I force myself to enter.

"Hello! Are you here for the open house?" A woman in a pink cotton blouse and tailored gray pants greets us. Her hair is pulled back, and so is her smile.

"I, uh, um . . ."

"Yes, we are," Lucy states.

"Great! Please sign in." She hands Lucy a pen, and Lucy signs our names while the lady reads them.

"Lucy and Robin Bricker? Wonderful!" The woman shuffles some papers. "That's so great. I love that Iowa has marriage equality."

"Oh, me too!" Lucy says as she gives me a broad smile and a wink.

She hands Lucy the papers. "My name's Gloria. Here is information about the house, and this is my card." Her grin is as polished as her acrylic fingernails. "Please let me know if you have any questions. Feel free to explore."

"Thanks," Lucy says. "Come on," she tells me.

We start up the stairs, but Gloria calls after us. "Oh, wait. Just to warn you, one of the rooms upstairs might be a little shocking."

Gloria looks us up and down and beams. "But I'm sure you can handle it. Enjoy!"

When we get upstairs, Lucy leads me into a bedroom. "I figured we should take a look around, since we're here." She knocks on one of the walls. "Thin." She crosses the room and looks out the window. "But that's a huge backyard. In Seattle, this house would be a million, at least."

Queasiness rolls through me like an undigested hotdog. "I wonder why Nick's not here."

"Yeah, that's disappointing. Maybe he's on his way?"

"Maybe."

I must look miserable because Lucy comes over and hugs me. "Don't worry. Now you have a reason to call him, right? To introduce us."

"Yeah." I rub my hands over my stomach. "I'll ask Gloria if Nick is coming."

"Okay." Lucy goes out into the hall. She enters the master bedroom while I approach the stairs. Just as I'm about to descend, the front door opens. Nick's unmistakable brown loafers scuffle through the entryway.

I panic.

Bolting out of view, I press myself against a wall.

"Hey, Gloria. How's it going?" I hear Nick say.

She sighs. "It's been slow. But there's a lovely lesbian couple looking around upstairs. I warned them about that room."

My hand wanders to my hair. Was Ian right about me looking androgynous?

"Well, thanks," says Nick. "I owe you one."

"Oh, it's no big deal. How did the brunch go?"

Brunch? Nick doesn't like brunch. Even when he makes me chocolate chip pancakes, he almost never eats before noon.

"Great. They asked us back for next week."

"Congratulations!" Gloria squeals. "Pretty soon I'll say I knew you when."

"Thank you," Nick says, chuckling in that warm way I love so much. I'll flatter him over anything, even his sock choice, just to hear it. My heart pangs. I'm not special; Gloria can elicit his laugh too.

"I'll say hello to those women," Nick says, and he walks in my direction.

Shit! This is not how it's supposed to happen. Looking around, I see a door ajar. I scurry over and enter. Lucy's in here too, and she's the only normal thing in the room.

Every inch of the walls and most of the ceiling are covered with mirrors. The middle of the ceiling holds two huge, industrial-strength hooks. On the floor is a large mound of something, covered by a blanket. The rest of the room is bare.

"Robin," Lucy gasps. "This is a sex room! I mean, what else could it be?" She points up to the hooks. "Those have got to be for a swing." Bouncing up and down on the balls of her feet, she mimics the hypothetical swing's motion. "I've never used a swing before, you know, for sex. Have you? I wonder how people balance."

Lucy travels over to the blanket-enclosed mound and uncovers it. Underneath is a saddle. "Robin, it's bolted to the floor!" Her laugh is breathy. "This is so weird!"

"Hello?" Nick calls from out in the hall.

At the sound of his voice, Lucy stands up straight. "Is that Nick? Is he here?"

I nod, stunned and mortified, wishing I could hide in this funhouse room. But Nick's about to be confronted with my image at every single angle.

"So you two found 'the room' huh?" Nick is laughing, but when he realizes it's me, his face falls. "Robin? I thought . . ." His confusion comes out in a squeak. "What are you doing here?"

Nick's handsome gaze makes me woozy. His hair is combed and gelled, as neat as I've ever seen it. He's all tucked in and wearing a tie, but his green shirt sleeves are rolled up. I look at his hands and wish they would touch me. My hands hurt from not touching him.

Lucy steps up. "Hi, I'm Lucy, Robin's cousin."

Nick shakes hands with her while keeping his eyes on me. "Nice to meet you."

"So," Lucy says, sounding rehearsed, "I asked Robin to come with me today and formally introduce us. My husband and I are relocating. We're hoping you'll find us a house."

Nick creases his brow, and his eyes dart back and forth between us. "Oh. Um, sure."

I shift my weight under his stare.

"You cut your hair," he states.

"Yeah." I rub my bare neck.

"It looks nice."

"Thank you."

Lucy clears her throat. "Okay!" Her voice is still loud and stiff. "I'll look at that deck off the master bedroom now."

Nick shakes his head like he's trying to wake up. "Do you want me to show you around?"

"No, no! I'm fine." She laughs. "But *this* is quite the room. A saddle mounted to the floor! Wow! The sellers must be very creative." When she gets to the door, she looks over at me and mouths, "He's CUTE!"

Of course Nick sees, because everywhere he looks, he's assaulted with our reflection.

When she's gone, my shoulders droop. "Sorry. That was awkward."

"Yeah, you think?" Nick tugs on his collar, loosening his tie. "Gloria said the only people here were a lesbian couple. I had no idea I'd see you—hey, why isn't your car out front?"

"I traded it in."

Nick just gapes at me, his jaw crooked. "Is there anything else you've changed?"

"Nick, I—"

He holds up his hand. "No, wait." He turns away, but I catch his earnest expression in one of the mirrors. After a moment, he faces me again and lets out a deep breath. "I've been thinking a lot. When we first met, I thought, 'Wow. She's the perfect woman.' And when you agreed to go out with me, I couldn't believe it, because you're so out of my league."

"Nick, come on. I'm not out of your league, and I'm not the perfect woman."

"Uh huh." He paces the empty room and gives the saddle a half-hearted kick. "But you're charming and beautiful. Then there's Jed, who was so special and talented and tragic." Nick examines the saddle with his foot as his voice trails off. Then he pivots and stares right at me. "I should have said this before. I'm sorry Jed died and broke your heart. Of course, if he hadn't died, you'd still be with him. So in a way, I'm *not* sorry, but then I'm like, wow, I'm an ass for even thinking that way." He rolls his eyes toward the ceiling. "This isn't coming out like I rehearsed in my head."

I sniff and wipe my nose. "That's okay. I took you by surprise, and I wasn't expecting a big speech. Just say we can figure things out together."

"Why?" He waves his arms around. "So we can settle down, start a family, and live somewhere like this?"

"Why not?" My laugh is choppy from the turbulence inside me. "Living in a house with a sex room is every woman's dream."

"I'm serious." Nick crosses his arms over his chest. "You want more than I can give. I'm not talented, and I could never write you a play."

I literally hear something snap, maybe a synapse inside my brain. "I don't care if you write me a play! I don't want a play! I never wanted a play, and I never *asked* for a fucking play!"

The silence that follows is restless and ready to explode. Nick speaks in a voice several decimals below mine. "Robin, I'm not trying to be mean, but I'm working, okay? More people will come, and I have to focus. Can we talk some other time?"

"Yeah, sure, of course." I can't look at him, and I can't look at myself, so I stare at the saddle in the middle of the floor.

"Rocky, are you okay?"

Hearing him use my nickname takes the wind out of me.

"Fine!" I plaster on a smile. "I came to introduce you to Lucy. Do you have a business card handy? I'll give it to her."

Nick's eyes grow big and dark, like mud puddles. He reaches into his pocket and hands me a card, which I take.

"Thanks," I say. "Hey, why were you at brunch?"

Nick momentarily screws his face up in confusion. "Oh. I was playing piano, and Dave was playing guitar. We're doing contemporary classical for the Sunday morning crowd."

For a second, I forget we're in a fight. Pride and excitement bubble inside me. "That's great! Where? Maybe I can come listen next week?"

Nick bites the inside of his lip and frowns.

"Or not," I say, hiding the burn of rejection.

"I think we should talk first, and I'd like to wait until after your play is over."

My stomach is going for the gold in gymnastics. "Sure. So . . . are you coming to my play?"

"You mean Jed's play?"

I flinch, and he continues in a softer voice. "I don't know, Robin. It might make me crazy." His cheeks flush, and I marvel at his honesty.

God, I wish I could kiss him.

"Well, I don't want to make you crazy." I smile one more time. "I should find Lucy and get going. Good luck with your open house."

"It's nice seeing you," he says so softly that I pretend not to hear.

Thursday, July 11, 2013
6:15 a.m.

I peer down from a cliff's edge at an ocean that looks like a discolored mirror. Icebergs bob and bump into each other, and the refracted light sparkles into bursts of color. My body tilts forward so I can plunge, headfirst, into the icy depths.

Then Nick bellows at me.

"Robin!"

He is at my side in an instant, gripping and pulling me to safer ground. "Don't dive in. Stay here with me."

I yank my arm from his grasp. "Why? You left me!" I hustle back to my jagged diving board.

"Oh, good God!" Nick follows, shaking his head.

"Go away, Nick."

"No!" He steps in front of me.

"You are so annoying!" I yell.

"So are you!"

My cell phone rings.

"Hello?"

"Robin? Where the hell are you?"

"Jed?"

"You promised. You promised you'd do my play. Why aren't you here?"

I realize it's curtain time. I put my phone down, ready to offer Nick a million explanations and apologies.

But he's gone. And the cliff beneath my feet is about to collapse.

I wake up unsurprised. It's clear what that dream was about. Tonight is opening night.

I get dressed and go for my run.

It's been days since I've seen Flashdance Girl, but when I turn the corner, she's doing squats by the big tree in her yard.

"Hey!" I yell. She pivots toward me. "Where have you been?"

Raising her chest, her teenage-girl attitude sings at full volume. "Not that it's any of your business, but there was a family emergency. We had to leave town."

My stomach plunges. "Is everything okay?"

"Oh, sure," she says with an eye roll. "My brother is a selfish dick face, but otherwise, everything's great."

"Alright." I shift my weight from one leg to the other. "Do you want to race?"

She squints and smirks simultaneously. "Why? Are you in the mood to be humiliated?"

I jut out my chin. "I'm in the mood to settle this once and for all."

"Fine." Flashdance Girl walks over to the sidewalk and puts her feet over one of the cracks. "We start here, and we go until the end of the next block."

I line up next to her. "We'll both count to three," I say, "and then we go."

She arches her body forward, and the sun bounces off her dark curls, held back today by a red headband.

"Are you ready?" I ask.

"Of course. You?"

"Yes."

We count together, "One, two, three!" and then we're off, just two beasts set free in suburbia.

And I'm faster than I've ever been.

I channel my inner tornado and imagine each of my demons chasing me down. The hospital corridors I've wandered, the lies I've told, the painful truths I've avoided, the fears of self and loss, and the false hope of finding a lasting love. These monsters chase me. If I reach the end of the block before Flashdance Girl, I'll conquer them all.

They'll never terrorize me again.

At first, I'm winning. My feet shoot forward and steer me toward victory, toward relief. My chest constricts, but my breath is even and healthy, and so, so, so strong. It's a strength I never asked for, a strength I don't deserve. But it's mine, and I'll use it. This strength is the only thing I have that's real.

Flashdance Girl is a blur, but she's gaining on me. The houses, trees, sidewalk, and sky are also just blurs. The one thing that's clear is my destination—the end of the block—and I'm almost there.

Then I run my left eye straight into a tree branch.

I bet that branch woke up this morning, hoping for some

sucker's eye to come along and complete it. Like chocolate thrust into peanut butter. But the result is neither salty nor sweet. It's blinding tears and searing pain. As I stagger back, my ankle turns. Then I fall to the ground.

"Son of a bitch!" I yell, covering my eye with one hand and grasping my injured ankle with the other.

Flashdance Girl is by my side. "What happened?" she cries. "Are you okay?"

"Hell no, I'm not okay!" Tears stream from my eye, and it hurts to keep it open. It also hurts to keep it shut. Meanwhile, my ankle swells up like a grapefruit, a tender lump of throbbing pain. My breathing hitches, and my mind reels to make sense of the burning sensations raking my body. "My ankle and my eye!"

"We should get you home," Flashdance Girl says. "Come on, I'll help."

She hoists one of my arms around her shoulders and pulls me to my feet. "Don't worry about it," I say. "My apartment is just across the street, so I can take it from here."

"No. Let me help you."

Her arms tighten around me. I can tell she means business. So I limp home while Flashdance Girl holds me up. It's just several hundred feet, but it may as well be a trek up Mount Everest. I need a distraction from the throbbing, twisted pain, so I make conversation.

"What's wrong with your brother?" I ask.

"He keeps trying to kill himself."

I almost say *I'm sorry,* but I bite my tongue. I hate it when people say that. "God, how awful! That must be very hard for you."

"Oh no, no, not at all."

I turn my head toward her. "I get your sarcasm. But I was trying to express genuine sympathy."

She bends her knees, heaving me up a little higher, struggling under the burden of my weight. "Sorry, but you seem like a person who's never had a real problem in her entire life."

"So I've been told."

She sighs. "You know this about yourself? Then your life *must* be super easy. That's why I enjoy kicking your ass every morning. It makes my day."

I stumble as I accidentally put some weight on my ankle. "My life has not been super easy, okay?"

"How do you know?"

"Huh?"

We've crossed the street, and as we stagger up my drive, she talks like a teacher, slow and methodical. "If you've never had a real problem, you'd think a hangnail is an emergency. Maybe you don't realize your life is easy. Maybe you only think that it's difficult."

Huh. Was I this arrogant at sixteen? I don't remember.

"My apartment is right there." We falter down the final stretch of pavement.

"Do you have someone to drive you to the emergency room? You should get that eye looked at."

"Yeah, I'll be fine." As I breathe out those words, I realize how much I want them to be true.

Flashdance Girl stands to the side as I bang on Isobel's door. "Isobel!" I yell. "Are you there? Sorry to wake you, but it's an emergency."

The door opens, but it's Jack who answers, wearing a T-shirt and boxers, his thinning hair sticking straight up. His mouth forms a shocked little O when he sees me. "Robin! What happened?"

There's a flurry of talk and action, and soon both Isobel and Jack are wide awake, dressed, and driving me to the ER.

8:45 a.m.

There's a long wait at the emergency room, and my condition is not life-threatening.

"You'd better not go blind, because they took too long to see you." Jack keeps shifting in his seat, unable to find a comfortable position. "How will you design clothes with only one eye? I say you sue for lost wages." He leans forward, the skin of his forehead crinkly with stress.

Isobel sits between us and rubs his back with one hand. "Since when are you so litigious?"

He grips his knees. "We're talking about Robin losing an eye!"

"And it's all fun and games until someone loses an eye."

They both glare at me, refusing to smile at my joke.

"What?" I ask.

"You should be more worried about this." Jack waves an incriminating finger at me. "If you won't complain, at least let me say something."

"No," I state flatly. "I'm not cutting in line. There are people here with real problems."

"Losing an eye is a real problem!"

"I'm not going to lose my eye!" But I still feel the rip from that vicious tree branch, and bloody tears gather around my cornea.

Isobel looks at her watch. "I should call Catherine and reschedule."

"No, no," Jack tells her. "You go ahead. Take my car and come back when you're done. I bet we'll still be here, in the waiting room."

"You think?" Isobel asks.

"Wait," I say. "You're meeting Catherine? My Catherine? Why?"

Isobel's ears turn pink. "I knew her first, you know. Catherine was my mentor at Hoyt."

"Okay." I try to sound neutral and not like a whiny bitch. "But why are you guys meeting?"

"We talked about my theater company at the barbecue, and she wants to continue the conversation." Isobel knots her fingers together. "Since she's in town for opening night, it's a good time."

"Oh." Makes sense, but why couldn't they invite me?

"I'm going to call her." Isobel takes out her phone, scrolls through her list of contacts, and presses the right buttons.

"Hi Catherine!" She pauses. "Yeah, no, me too, but can we delay an hour? Robin ran her eye into a tree branch. We've been waiting forever in the emergency room, and she refuses to complain—what? Oh. Sure. See you soon." Isobel hangs up and speaks to me. "Catherine says she's on her way."

"What? Why?"

Isobel shrugs. "I don't know. Maybe she likes hanging out with you in hospitals."

"Is that supposed to be funny?"

"Sorry." She squeezes my shoulder. "I'm a little stressed. I wasn't going to say anything until afterwards, but Lucas got his Guthrie connection to come tonight. They might workshop *The Next Breath* as part of their black-box season this winter."

"Really? That's great."

"Not if you can't perform!"

I hang my head. "I'll perform. I promise."

Fifteen minutes later, Catherine enters the emergency room dressed like Joan Collins in a power suit. She walks over and examines my face. With her hand still on my cheek, she asks Isobel, "How long has she been waiting?"

"Almost two hours," says Isobel.

"Have they offered her anything at all?" She touches the lukewarm, soggy ice pack discarded on the table next to me.

"Nope, nothing," Isobel replies. "It's like she's invisible."

"I haven't lost my power of speech, you know." I glare at them both with my good eye.

"Heaven forbid," says Catherine, and she strides up to the admittance desk. Then she does what she trained for years to do: make a fuss in a hospital.

"Excuse me!" I can hear her from many feet away. "My daughter needs medical attention. She has done *serious* damage to her eye. Unless you want to be responsible for her going blind, find a doctor to see her immediately."

The nurse mumbles something, and Catherine cuts her off.

"No, you don't understand. She needs to be seen. Not in twenty minutes, and not in ten. NOW. And I will stand here, hovering over you, until she is sent to an exam room. Are we clear?"

The nurse nods, and I'm ready to shout an apology, not just to her but to all the people in the waiting room. But I stay silent, and lo and behold, moments later I'm called back.

Catherine returns to my side and speaks to Isobel and Jack. "I'll go with her. I'm good at making sure doctors do their job."

"Okay," says Isobel. "Call me when you're done?"

"Of course." Catherine escorts me, her maternal hands around my waist.

The doctor checks me out and declares I have a sprained ankle and (not in so many words) a big-ass corneal abrasion. "I need to clean it out," the doctor says. "But don't worry; I'll give you local anesthesia so you won't feel a thing."

"Does the anesthesia involve sticking a needle in my eye?" My palms sweat.

"It's not that bad," the doctor says. He leaves to get his mad scientist tray.

Catherine takes my hand and squeezes. "I'm sorry this happened. But the doctor is right. You'll get through it."

I pull my hand away and wipe it against my thigh. "I don't have a choice."

Catherine sighs. "Not unless you want a glass eye."

"Of course I don't," I huff. "But it wasn't quite on that level. Catherine, while I appreciate your concern, was it necessary to yell at the nurse?"

Catherine stares at me, refusing to cower. "Perhaps not. I like to err on the side of caution."

"Obviously."

She gets up, as if to read the informational poster about STDs. But then she turns, and her intensity shakes me. "Robin, I couldn't love you more if you were my flesh and blood. But you can be so frustrating. You have to speak up if you're suffering."

"Other people were suffering more."

She throws her hands out, delicate fingers splayed. "How do you know? Even if they were, they'll be taken care of. Who's taking care of you?"

"I can take care of myself."

"No, you can't. Not all the time." She comes close and grasps my shoulders. "Nobody can. It's okay to ask for help, and it's even better to demand it. Sometimes, demanding help is necessary."

"I know." I give her a defeated smile.

She reads my expression and, satisfied that I'm sincere, sits back down next to me. I slouch and rest my head against her shoulder. "I just hope I haven't ruined opening night. How will I perform with one eye and a limp? Georgie isn't a pirate."

"Maybe you should delay the opening."

"No. Isobel has important people coming. She's banking on this show. I can't let her down. I can't let Jed down either."

"Honey, nobody wants to honor Jed's memory more than me. But are you sure about this? I don't want you sacrificing your happiness to do right by Jed. He wouldn't want that either."

"I know, but—"

Catherine holds up her hand, cutting me off. "As for Isobel, don't worry about her financial difficulties. I've come up with a way to help."

Huh? What financial difficulties? "I don't know what you mean."

"All the stuff with her ex-husband, who's been threatening her theater company? Isobel didn't tell you?"

"She mentioned it, but she didn't go into detail." Guilt overwhelms me. All this time, Isobel's had her own problems, and I've been too self-involved to notice.

"Well, anyway, I've decided to retire." Catherine's smile is serene. "Being away last year made me realize I need a change. So I'm moving down here. Isobel and I will pool our resources and work together on Mirror Image Productions. It's perfect, really."

She strokes my cheek. "I'll have more opportunities to see you, and well, to see your dad."

"You want to see my dad?" I scrutinize her. "You mean, as in date him?"

Catherine fiddles with her beaded bracelet. "Yes. After Jed died, he understood me in a way none of my other friends could. We talked on the phone a lot, and it was very unexpected, developing such strong feelings for someone in the middle of all my grief."

"Oh. I had no idea. What happened? I mean, why didn't you . . . ?"

She tilts her head to the side. "Because you needed us both. We couldn't risk starting something. If it didn't work out, that would have been unfair to you."

Regret washes over me like a wave. How could I have been so oblivious? "Catherine, if you had told me, I would have understood. And the thought of you and my dad making each other happy . . ." My voice breaks as I trip over words. "I would have welcomed it."

Catherine takes my hand and intertwines our fingers. "Thank you. But, to be honest, there were other factors. For a long time, I was stuck. Jed was gone. How could I allow myself to be happy?"

I let out a strangled laugh. "Jed knew, though. He saw how well you and my dad got along at our 4th of July barbecue, and he approved."

Catherine gives me a small smile. "That doesn't surprise me. And I am grateful for his approval. But, to be honest, Jed's feelings from all those years ago don't matter now."

"What do you mean?"

"Just that I must choose happiness because it's what I truly want. Not because it's what Jed would have wanted for me. And darling girl, it's time for you to make the same choice."

"Huh?"

"Robin." Catherine heaves a sigh. "You've spent so much time running away from happiness. It's time to slow down. To let life's messiness catch up with you. Not because it's what Jed would have wanted, but because it's what you want for yourself."

I'm desperate to give her a worthy response, but no words materialize.

And then the doctor re-enters the room carrying his tray, complete with a huge needle. He sits down on the other side of me. "Okay, relax, and try not to blink."

He jabs an elephantine piece of metal toward my cornea, and for the second time today, my eye becomes intimate with a foreign object.

5:30 p.m.

The doctor gave me a spoon-type thing to wear over my eye, which is not quite a black patch. I still look like a pirate. All I need is a peg leg. Instead, I have a swollen ankle, which I was instructed to elevate and ice for as long as possible. I told Isobel the show would go on, even if it meant hobbling around like Richard the Third.

"Okay," she said, the doubt on her face nearly overpowering the relief.

Now, I'm resting. Yet I can't quiet my mind. After hours of staring at the television, I pick up my phone.

I get his voicemail. Maybe Nick's in his car, honoring my wishes by not answering. So, remembering what Catherine said, I leave a message.

"Hey Nick, it's me. I know you want to wait until after the play to talk, but, well . . . what I didn't say before is, um . . ." Shit. The doctor said to keep my eye dry, and I'm tearing up. I tilt my head towards the ceiling and push my anxiety down. "There's so much I haven't said. First, living with a high school music teacher in a suburban home with a sex room sounds awesome— if that high school music teacher is you. Second, I loved your protractor speech. You're my protractor too; you help me make sense of things. I realize we can't always be each other's protractors. That we must take turns. And, um, can I have my turn tonight?"

Pausing, I brace myself for the next risky plunge. "You were wrong about one thing. I do need you, Nick. I tried not to, and I'm sorry I was scared. But I'm more scared of losing you, and if you're not at my play tonight, well . . ."

Well, what?

"Nick, please come to the play." I inhale sharply. "I need you to understand how loving and losing Jed turned me into this person who's now madly in love with you." I release a long, wistful breath of air. "It's an unfair request, and I'm rambling, but will you come tonight?" I pull the phone away, staring at it and hating myself for groveling. Then I put it back to my ear. "If you can't make it, it's okay, but . . . no, I take that back. It's not okay. I need you, and I love you, and I'm desperate. Desperate for you to find a way of loving me back, even the part of me that still loves Jed."

8:40 p.m.

It was a 7:30 p.m. curtain, and we have a full house. Before the show, I went outside for some air, scanning the parking lot and up and down the street. Nick's dented silver Honda was nowhere in sight.

I forced him out of my mind. Just like I'm ignoring the pirate jokes.

Arrr! Avast, me matey.

Ian said that when he came early to help with last-minute set repair. Now I'm backstage, waiting for Act Two to begin.

Andrew approaches and squeezes my shoulders. "Are you hanging in there?" he asks.

"I'm fine."

"Really? Your ankle and your eye don't hurt too bad?"

"Nah."

What's the point of complaining? Andrew can't do anything. So I give him a smile. "Have a great Act Two."

"Yeah, you as well."

He prepares for his entrance, the house lights dim, and the audience's murmurs subside. When the stage lights come up, Grayson's at his computer.

Grayson (Speaking to the audience): Georgie is dead. Lea disappeared. And every morning, an earthquake wakes me up. (Sighs) It always takes a minute to realize that the earthquake is from inside me. Once the shaking subsides, I straighten the furniture and replace everything that fell from our shelves. I create order from chaos. Then I sit down to write Georgie, my world, back into existence.
Since Georgie's murder, our relationship has been bumpy. But death is easier to overcome than love. I keep writing her as if she was alive. Often, dead Georgie appears, speaking the lines I wrote for her. Other times, it's like I don't know her at all. Death changed Georgie in ways I can't comprehend. (Softly laughs) I don't think about it too hard. The real world doesn't make sense, so there's no reason my fictional world should make sense either.

That's my cue. I walk onto stage like my ankle isn't a hot ball of complaint.

The Fresnel lights are blinding. Looking into them would for sure irritate my corneal abrasion, so I'm grateful for my stupid eye patch. However, it's a problem—not being able to cry. Forget how I look and how I limp. How will I survive Act Two without shedding a tear?

I thrust that worry away. I have to be Georgie now.

Georgie: I love you, Grayson. I could exist forever like this, just a breath away from where you are.
Grayson: I love you too, Georgie. So much. (Puts on jacket) I wish I didn't have to go out.
Georgie: Don't go. I hate being alone.
Grayson: But you love your alone time, Georgie! You get to paint.
Georgie: Not anymore. Everything's changed now that I'm dead. I can't paint anymore. When I'm by myself, I go crazy. (Grabs his sleeve) Stay here, Grayson. Please!

Grayson: I wish I could. (Kisses her) I'll see you tonight. (Grayson exits through the door, stands at the edge of the stage, and speaks to the audience.) I can't send Georgie to work; a dead daycare worker seems wrong. But my deal with Lea is off. Since I can't write myself a paycheck, I must find a job.
That means leaving Georgie alone in our apartment.

I paint at my easel, but I throw my brush down and move to the window.

Georgie (Shouting out the window): Grayson! Hey Grayson! Grayson, get up here! I'm lonely, Grayson. You can't just leave me here! If you don't come back right now, I'll float away and never come back! Or I'll haunt the entire building and get you evicted!

I scream. The lights flash. A door swings open and slams shut.

Georgie (Cont'd): See, Grayson, I mean it! That's just the beginning of what I'll do. Get up here, NOW!
Grayson (Moves from side of the stage and into their living room): I decide we'll never leave the apartment. It's easier than letting her go. I can watch over her. I'll write our lives so they exist between these walls.

I hear Grayson's speech for the umpteenth time, but the words resonate like they are new. The audience, the lights, the fulfillment of Jed's dream—the combination makes me, Robin, swallow a huge, hot lump of pure emotion.

But Georgie? She sits on the couch, indifferent and reading a magazine.

Georgie: Grayson, I'm bored. Let's go out.
Grayson (Approaching the couch): No. We're staying here, Georgie.

I stand and limp towards a window that, in reality, stares into a black wall. But looking out, I imagine the evening sky.

Georgie: Grayson, the moon is full.

Grayson (From the couch): That's great. Beautiful.
Georgie: You're not looking at it.
Grayson: I've seen the moon before.
Georgie: Not this one. Wow, it's incredible. (Dreamily, still staring out the window) You know how when you're little, you think the moon follows you? I thought I could reach it.
Grayson: Huh?
Georgie: Like if the moon's close enough to follow me, then I could touch it. I just needed to reach high enough.

I open the window and reach out, trying to touch the moon. Grayson ignores me, and I lose my balance and "fall." In the script, we're several stories up. In real life, the window is three feet off the floor, and a mattress catches me. Still, I land with my bad eye smooshed against my shoulder. I bite my lip to keep from gasping in pain.

Grayson rushes to the window.

Grayson: Georgie! Georgie! (To the audience) I should have seen that coming. Every time I stop writing, something terrible happens. Then she's gone. I can't continue like this. If I'm always scripting out our lives, we never get to live. And not living is even worse than dying.

Grayson crosses the room to my canvas. He picks up a brush, tentatively making strokes, but he curses after a mistake. He knocks over the dirty glass of water meant for my brushes and grabs a towel to wipe the spill. Frustrated, Grayson speaks to the audience again.

Grayson: Georgie will leave me, no matter how I revise the script. Sure, I can write her back into existence again. But each time I do, the real Georgie fades. She changes in little ways: Her laugh sounds different. Her hair is combed wrong. She doesn't understand what she used to know. She's a reflection in a distorted mirror, and I don't recognize her.
Georgie made me a better person. When she's gone, I can't write. I

247

can barely breathe. But I can't give up, not when, at any moment, Georgie could walk through these doors, ready to argue and ready to make up.

Grayson sits at his computer, staring at the screen. With his hair combed that way, and in his jeans and T-shirt, he looks so much like Jed. He places his fingers on the keyboard, just like Jed used to. It's my moment to re-enter the stage. So I hobble out, take a deep breath, and say my line.

Georgie: Grayson, we can start again. All we have to do is . . . we only have to . . . we just need to figure out how.

Still at his computer, Grayson shakes his head and presses the delete button. I do a backwards gimp-walk to the same spot where I began.

Georgie: Grayson, I belong to you, so you can do anything you want with me. You just need to understand that. I mean, you need to understand how to . . . no, no. I need to understand how to be a fully developed dead person who belongs to someone else. And that's easy! I just need to—

I keep acting out Grayson's various "rewrites." It's a challenge because my peripheral vision and balance are screwed up. I travel all over the stage, attempting different tactics composed by Grayson to make me alive and happy. Nothing works.

Grayson slams his head on the keyboard. The lights go out. When they come back up, I am gone, and Grayson sleeps at his desk. Then, I enter and wake Grayson by blowing on his cheek.

Grayson: Huh?
Georgie: Wake up, hon.
Grayson: Georgie?

He stands to hug me, but I move away. Now that Georgie's a ghost, we can no longer touch. I'm air-like, floating around without impact. Throughout the scene, Grayson keeps reaching for me, but I always slip away.

But tonight, my slipping is less like that of a ghost and more like that of a goblin.

Not how Jed wanted it to be.

Grayson: What are you doing here? How did you return when I didn't write a new script?

Georgie: It's easy. As long as you're here in the apartment, I'm here too. As soon as you go, so will I.

Grayson: But why?

Georgie (Pointing to Grayson's computer): Once you leave to live your real life, rather than the one you made up, I'll disappear.

Grayson: No problem. I prefer my make-believe world to reality. Especially if I can be with you.

Georgie: You're forgetting one important detail.

Grayson: What?

Georgie: At some point, I must leave you behind.

Grayson stares at me, betrayed. He walks towards me, wanting to take me in his arms. I back up and stumble over a chair leg. I catch myself before I fall. Even still, there are audible gasps from the audience.

Grayson: Why won't you let me hold you?

Georgie: No one who's alive can touch me. Only other dead people, and God.

Grayson: I don't believe in God.

Georgie: What do you believe in?

Grayson: Nothing.

Georgie: Liar. We all believe in something.

Grayson: Fine. I believe in sweat and tears.

Georgie: What? Why?

Grayson: Simple. Everything worth living for makes you sweat. Everything worth dying for makes you cry.

Georgie: Haven't got that mixed up?

Grayson and I move around the stage, reciting punch lines about the meaning of life. My goal is to stay in character, thinking only Georgie's thoughts. Yet, I glow when the audience laughs.

Jed would be so proud, but he'd pretend that he didn't care.

Grayson approaches. He holds out his hands. He pulls them away. He shoves them into his pockets.

Grayson: Now that you're dead, what do you believe in?

Georgie: It's the same as when I was alive. Art and beauty. And you... you made me believe in words and concepts. Freedom. Bravery. True love. Themes of all the great stories.

Grayson: So, you believe in fiction?

Georgie: Whatever exists in fiction exists in reality. It just gets twisted up.

Grayson (Pausing, thoughtful): Is death painful?

Georgie: What do you think? Your bitchy ex-girlfriend strangled me to death. I couldn't breathe! Yeah, it hurt. Also, I was pissed. I always thought I'd do better in a fight. (Shrugs) Guess I was wrong.

Grayson: What about afterwards? Does it hurt—the physical act of being dead?

Georgie (Laughs): That's an oxymoron. There is no physical act of being dead. (Crosses to the lava lamp and looks at the glow.) But needing people? That doesn't go away. Who'd have thought that death wouldn't cure loneliness?

I do my best to float across the stage, lyrically, the way Jed envisioned Georgie would. And I wonder, Is Jed floating around now, observing me? Is he laughing at the absurdity of Georgie with an eye patch and a limp?

Does he wish he could touch me? Heal me? I walk to the set window and point out.

Georgie (Cont'd): Grayson, can you see the light from the streetlamps? They're bouncing off the sidewalks, wet from the rain. It used to be my favorite sight—the city after a storm. But I can't feel the rain anymore. Light and dark are the same to me now. I don't know what the world holds for me out there.

Grayson: Then stay here.
Georgie: I can't. I have to leave soon.
Grayson: Well, maybe I could come with you.
Georgie: Where?
Grayson: Wherever you have to go.

Where did Jed go? He joked about heaven before he died, but he never said what he believed.

I was so stupid to have never asked.

Georgie: If you leave with me, you can't return. Not to this spot, not
*   to this life. And there's no guarantee we'll stay together. I could*
*   still lose you.*
Grayson (Nervous): How do you know? Is there a chance you're wrong?
Georgie: It's doubtful. Do you want to take that chance?
Grayson: I guess not. Maybe it's better to play it safe. I'll stay where
*   you can find me.*

We keep talking. Reaching for each other without touching. After a while, the lights dim. As I walk off, my ankle turns and a shot of pain sears through my entire leg. I'm hobbling, and Lucas grabs my arm once I'm backstage.

"Are you okay?"

"Fine," I say through gritted teeth. No way am I quitting now. "Really." Lucas is trying to be nice. "Don't worry. I'll get through this."

Lucas steps away and whispers into his headphones, giving the light cue. When they rise, Grayson does his inner monologue.

Grayson: I can't concentrate. All my thoughts are brief notions of her.
*   I look at one of her paintings and notice something new. I catch*
*   a whiff of her perfume as I pass our closet. I close my eyes, ready*
*   to sleep, and hear her voice, like she's in the room with me.*
Then she's not really gone. The edges of my memories don't bleed into
*   something unrecognizable. My memories will be made of paint,*
*   paper, and twisted bed sheets. They'll form the truth.*

The truth. Heartache changes the truth. Heartache becomes the truth. It threatens you, upsetting your routine and your stomach.

I take a deep breath and ignore the ache as I walk on stage. Grayson reaches for me, but I step away.

Georgie: You have to let me go, Grayson.
Grayson (With an inhale): Hey. Remember that time we visited the Cloisters? We had so much fun! Wanna go again?
Georgie: You're ready to leave the apartment?
Grayson: I stayed here for you. The more I think about it, the more I realize it's time to take a chance. We can't stay here forever. So I'll leave, but you'll come. It will work out. Right?
Georgie: Maybe.

It's harder and harder to glide around the stage, but I do it anyway. I owe it to Isobel. I owe it to Catherine.

I owe it to Jed.

I pick up Georgie's stuff—things Grayson couldn't part with. My books. The lipstick on my dresser. A pair of sandals thrown by the door.

Georgie (Cont'd): Hey. Last week, I met this guy who died on his motorcycle. Okay if he comes too?
Grayson (Hiding despair): You want to bring a dead guy along on our date?
Georgie: Don't say "dead guy" like it's a bad thing. I'm dead too, remember? Anyway, you should meet him. I've talked you up. He knows how much I loved you.
Grayson: Oh. Thanks, I guess. But why'd you use "love" in the past tense?
Georgie (Dismissive hand gesture): Don't worry about it. You and Adam will get along great. He's smart and funny. That's hard to find with dead people. It's like their sense of humor died too, y'know? (Laughs)
Grayson (Trying to get the joke): Sure. Can't wait to meet him.

Georgie: Like yesterday, after Adam and I made love, he starts talking about God. Adam's met God, and he gave me all the details. Out of the blue, Adam tells the funniest joke: Why did God drop ground beef from the sky?

Grayson: Dead people make love?

Georgie: What? Yeah. Of course. Anyway, try and guess. Why did God drop ground beef from the sky?

Grayson: I . . . I don't know.

Georgie: He wanted a meatier shower!

I laugh. Some audience members laugh too. But not Grayson. Jed wouldn't laugh either. Not if I broke his heart by sleeping with someone. It's my least favorite part. Where I must hurt him. Where I must move on.

Georgie (Cont'd): Don't you get it? Meatier and me-te-or—

Grayson: I get it, but it's stupid. And if God wanted a meteor shower, why didn't he just—boom!—create one?

Georgie (Sort of angry): God isn't as powerful as everyone thinks.

Grayson (Explosive): Whatever! Why do you sleep with someone who tells such bad jokes?

Georgie: That's what you care about? I tell you God exists, and you're worried about my sex life.

Grayson: Screw God!

Georgie: I can't screw God!

Grayson (Sarcastic): Oh, just other dead people? Well, good. God is one entity I can cross off the list.

Grayson gets up and looks around, like he wants to throw things. Instead, he straightens up the apartment. He can't look at me, so he looks at my things, trying to create order.

Georgie: Grayson, we're both in the same place. Don't you see that? But for me, the laws of nature have changed. One day, you'll understand.

Grayson: What about the rules of love? Have they changed too?

Georgie: Hon, when it comes to love, there are no rules. And that's all to the good. When we lose someone, we also lose part of ourselves—the part that can't admit how scared we are. Once you die, the fear is gone. That's the difference between you and me, Grayson. I'm not scared anymore.

He tells me that he needs me. That he wants me back. He runs to his computer and types a scene where I've come back to life. But I won't recite the lines. I start to leave and ask him to come with me, but Grayson stays put.

As I clumsily glide out the door, the lights fade again.

Limping off stage, I wish to ice and elevate my leg. But I can't, not until the play is over.

Tonight, speaking them to a crowded house, each syllable Jed wrote hits me in the gullet. How did he know so much? How could he have foreseen what losing him would be like?

When the lights rise, Grayson speaks to the audience yet again.

Grayson: I can't go on this way. My heart is empty from losing her. Eventually, my body will shut down. Things will fade to black. Sleep is my best escape, but I always wake up again and remember she's gone. I'm still here, between these walls, wanting to evaporate but clinging to survival. Trying to throw away my survival instinct like it's a pair of worn-out shoes with broken laces.

I walk back onto the stage, attempting to put equal weight on both feet. Perhaps pure adrenaline will carry me through these next few minutes.

Georgie: I have to go now, Grayson. This is the last time you'll see me. I won't come back.

Grayson chokes up. Real tears fall down his cheeks. But I can't let my own tears fall.

Grayson: Why? Why do you have to leave?
Georgie: It's because I'm already gone.

Grayson hangs his head in his hands and cries. The urge to comfort him is overpowering. Like my urge to change what's coming. To switch the ending and make it all okay.

Georgie (Cont'd): Oh, hon. You knew this was temporary. Nothing in life is permanent. Permanent doesn't exist. That's how the world works.
Grayson: The world needs an overhaul. It needs new management.
Georgie: The world tries to accommodate us as best it can. That's no simple task.
Grayson: It ought to be!

He reaches for me. I want to collapse into his arms. But that's not what I'm supposed to do. Not yet. Not ever. I can't reverse what's happened; it's never been in my subtext.

Grayson (Cont'd): Please, can't I just hold you one more time?
Georgie: I've already broken the rules just being here. (Slow, sensuous music plays.) Stand up, Grayson.

I force myself into a happy place. Grayson looks at me, responding to the laughter in my voice. We slow dance, not touching but feeling each other nonetheless. It's supposed to be lyrical, so I close my eye and imagine I'm weightless. That Jed's here, lifting me somewhere higher than earth.

Grayson: Death hasn't made me stop loving you.
Georgie: No, it won't. You'll still look for me. You'll still need to tell me things. Maybe I'll hear you; maybe I won't. Either way, I can't respond.
But Grayson, death didn't make me stop loving you either. Death imposes rules that can't be broken, but there are no rules when it comes to love. You're doing nothing wrong deciding to be happy again.

There's a weight on my chest, and my breath catches.

You won't let me go just by going outside. I'm already gone. Yet, part of me exists. In here (Pointing to his head) and here (Pointing to his heart). That will be enough for both of us.

Grayson: You're lying!
Georgie: No, I'm not. It's a version of the truth.
Grayson: You're leaving me.
*Georgie: Then be angry! (The music changes to Ben Folds Five's
   "Song for the Dumped.") Blame me. Remember all my flaws. All
   the blemishes on my heart.*
Grayson: They only made me love you more.
Georgie: But they didn't mean anything.
*Grayson: Then nothing means anything! I'll stop looking for meaning.
   I'll go mad if I try.*
Georgie: You'll go mad if you don't try.

I trip over that last line, and it stings like never before. I look
at Andrew, who's actually Grayson, who really is Jed—or is he
me? Maybe I'm Grayson, and Jed and Andrew are me—Robin and
Georgie. Or maybe the logistics will make me lose my mind.

I throw away the nonexistent rules. I go to him and very, very
slowly place a hand on his shoulder.

Because I've always wanted to touch Jed one last time.

When I feel his soft shirt and the warm, breathing human
underneath, there's a bolt of electricity powerful enough to thaw an
iceberg. But I can't melt. This drainage can't happen through tears.
It must be released through breath. Through air. Through reality.

I sigh, remembering everything. His beautiful face, his tender-
ness, and his glorious laugh.

I've held onto them for so long. How can I let them go?

That's what he's telling me to do.

*Georgie (Cont'd): For you to live, you must let me die. So I release
   you, Grayson. I'm releasing you.*

Then I chuck the rules and give him a ghost-like kiss on the
mouth.

When I pull away, Jed stares back. But I also see myself. So
much roils inside me, and I stop for a second. Jed needs me to keep

going. He needs me to mean what I'm about to say. My heart's been flattened, but I speak up loud and clear.

Georgie (Cont'd): The next breath you take will heal you and make you whole.

I fill my lungs with energy and air. And I realize it all at once. Recovery doesn't come from running, but from standing still. When I exhale, the weight on my chest evaporates.

I exit.

Backstage, I collapse into the first chair I find. Grayson still has a monologue, so I rest for the last few minutes of the show. Lucas has an icepack waiting for me, and I sit, pressing the cold compress against my ankle, struggling for breath and to keep my tears from falling.

Did I just release Jed for real this time? It's like our pretend game of Marco Polo—me blindly calling for him, him moving through the arctic water and away—has ceased. I'm lighter now. My iceberg melted into the swirling sea, and somehow that frees us both.

Is that okay, Jed? Have you been trying to release me this whole time?

Grayson's voice fades, as do the lights. The audience starts to clap. I struggle to get on the stage for the curtain call. Vaguely, I take in the standing ovation and the wet-cheeked, beaming faces of the audience members; some are friends and family, some are strangers. None of them are Nick.

After our last bow, I struggle to go backstage and into the dressing room. I claim a chair amidst the clutter of Aqua Net cans, stage makeup, and discarded costumes. Isobel finds me right away.

"You were amazing!" she cries. "I've never been so proud!"

My lips tremble, and though I need to swallow, I can't. Isobel looks at my face. "Are you okay?" she asks.

I start to say *yes, fine, never been better.* But the words stick in my mouth like gum plastered to my teeth. "I . . . I just need a minute, okay?"

"Yeah, of course." Isobel squeezes my knee. "Take all the time you want. Everyone will understand."

I nod, unsure if she's right. My whole family came tonight, and they're waiting for me. Plus, Catherine's out there. Above everyone else, I must find her.

Isobel starts to leave. "Wait!" I cry, and she turns back.

I look her in the eye. It's the first time we've really seen each other in weeks. "Thank you," I say. "Jed was scared of being forgotten. But he won't be. Not now."

She comes back over, leans down, and hugs me. "Not now, not ever." Isobel smiles through her tears. "I won't lie—I love his play, and I wanted to be the first to direct it. But I also wanted to give you the chance to keep your promise to him and say goodbye." She pauses, letting the sentiment in the air settle. "You're my best friend, Robin."

"You're my best friend too." I take a huge sniff. "And I'll always be grateful."

She shakes her head. "Don't give it another thought." With a kiss on my cheek, she gets up. "I'll tell everyone you'll be out soon but that you need a moment to rest your ankle, okay?"

I nod. As she goes, I stare at my lap, trying to reconcile myself to this weird, de-thawed sensation. Frozen emotions are now fluid, and I gulp back breaths, telling myself not to cry.

Whatever I do, I can't cry.

There's a knock. "I'll be out in a minute," I say, loud enough for whoever it is to hear. But the door opens anyway, and I look up, expecting to see Andrew, Lucas, or Miranda. Or Catherine. But it's none of them.

It's Nick.

One of his hands is shoved into his front jean pocket, and the collar of his blue jersey is unbuttoned. The humidity causes his short, dark hair to stick up a little, but that's a detail only I would notice. I take in all of him: the watch that hangs at the bottom of his wrist, his parted lips, raised eyebrows, and tender gaze. The combination makes my heart hum with relief.

"You came," I say.

"Yeah," he replies, his voice soft. "I was late, so I sat in the back. But I couldn't stay away." He looks around nervously. "That message you left meant a lot."

Everything I should tell him is congested in my throat. I cough, trying to find my voice. He comes and kneels by my side. He holds a small paper bag, which he places in my lap.

"For you," he says.

I stare at it, too mystified to understand what to do.

"Open it," Nick tells me. "Please."

I look into his eyes, which are as warm as hot cocoa. I take the bag and pull out a protractor, just like what I used in middle school geometry. A laugh flees from my throat, but it morphs into a smothered sob.

"I thought it would be good for us to have an extra, just in case we're both falling apart at the same time." Nick uses a low, movie theater voice.

"But what about . . . everything?"

With a ragged breath, he takes my hand. "I'm sitting there tonight, watching you say these lines that he wrote, so you could say goodbye, and . . ." Tears well up in his eyes. "And I had this moment where I understood how much you loved each other. What you must have gone through while you were losing him. I always thought you were beautiful, Robin, both inside and out. But tonight? You were like the Mona Lisa of strength and beauty. I was just in awe."

"Nick . . ."

He squeezes my hand. "You asked me to love the part of you that still loves him?" I nod and he stares right into me. "I can do that. It's the easiest thing I'll ever have to do. But maybe one day, if you could love me like that—"

"Oh, Nick, I already do." My chin trembles, and tears drip from my eyes. "Damn. I'm not supposed to cry." I lift the edge of my eye patch, trying to release the gush of tears underneath.

He reaches for it. "Why don't you just take it all the way off?"

I tilt myself back. "I can't. I'm supposed to wear it for a couple more days."

"What? You mean the eye patch wasn't part of your costume?"

I don't hide my exasperation. "No. Of course not. Why would Georgie wear an eye patch?"

He shrugs and speaks at normal volume. "I don't know. I'm not the one with a theater degree. I figured it was symbolic."

"Symbolic for what?"

Nick's mouth twists into a sarcastic smile. "You were blinded by love?"

"What about my limp?" I demand. "Was that also symbolic? I was crippled by love?"

"The limp is real?

With a frustrated sigh, I nod my head in agreement.

Nick places a cautious hand right above my ankle. "You hurt yourself?"

"Yeah."

"Rocky, I'm so sorry." His hand travels up my leg and caresses my thigh, which sort of makes me forget the pain. But I see the wheels turning in Nick's brain. "Did Flashdance Girl have anything to do with it?" he asks.

Shrugging, I mumble a "maybe" and lean down for a kiss, hoping to distract him. But he's too quick for me.

"She did, didn't she?" He laughs, and I push his shoulder—hard.

"It's not funny. I almost lost my eye."

"And it's all fun and games until someone loses an eye." He smirks.

"That's what I said!"

Nick forces a serious expression back onto his face. "Are you okay?"

For the first time in forever, I'm not compelled to lie. "I'm getting there. I'd feel a lot better if you'd kiss me already."

Nick's sly smile makes my body grow flush, and I'm impressed with the deft way he leans in, lifts me, and takes my seat while transferring me into his lap. "I'll kiss you," he says, his tone deep and dusty.

He tightens his arms around me, and I'm wrapped in such delicious warmth, I forget ever being cold. Our lips meet. His kiss is urgent yet gentle. The energy between us satisfies me, yet it makes me desperate for more.

My face is in his hands, and a low groan rumbles from the bottom of his throat. "Can we get out of here?" he asks. "I'll carry you home if I have to."

"Umm . . ."

He kisses me again, and I hate to pull away, but it's necessary. "I should say hi to my family. And I want to introduce you to Catherine."

Nick puts my arm around his shoulders, circles my waist, and supports me as we get up. "I'd love that," he says.

We make our way out to the theater lobby. The whole time, Nick helps me walk and stand. It's better than if I could do it all on my own.

Friday, July 12, 2013
8:15 a.m.

Our boat rocks gently in the harbor. Nick lifts the anchor right as there's a balmy gush of wind. The sail blossoms, and we're off, riding the ocean, surrounded by a blue sky and a friendly sea. I lean over the edge of the boat and brush my fingers along the crest of a wave.

"The water is so warm," I tell him.

He sits next to me and places an arm around my shoulders. "We're too far south for icebergs." Then he plants a kiss on my forehead.

I hear laughter in the distance. I cup my hands over my eyes and spot a boat far away on the horizon. "I think that's Jed's boat. It sounds like his laugh."

261

"Do you want to try and catch up?" Nick asks.

I consider this. I remember what Jed and I told each other. Boats longing for the sea yet afraid. When I look out again, I see his boat facing the elements with strength. He braves the wind and waves without sinking.

"Maybe later," I tell Nick. "It's enough for now, knowing he's happy."

Nick relaxes in his seat, and I curl into him.

Then I wake up.

We're in bed, and Nick's arm is around me. I turn over so I'm facing him and trace a finger along the contours of his face. His eyes flutter open.

"Guess what," I say.

"Hmm?"

"I slept in." I laugh. He smiles as he glances at the clock.

"Eight fifteen is not sleeping in." He kisses my neck. "I'll show you what a morning in bed should be like."

His head is still nuzzled in the curve of my shoulder. I run my fingers through his hair. "Will you now?"

"That's right. And when we get up, I'll make chocolate chip pancakes. Then I'll play you that song I wrote."

"Really?" I hiccup. "That sounds great."

He kisses me. "I wrote it for you, by the way. Every song I write is for you. Even the crappy ones."

"Oh no," I respond. "I haven't even started on your corduroy suit."

Nick plunges his fingers into my hair. "Then you'll have to make it up to me."

So I do.

Saturday, September 21, 2013
6:40 a.m.

Nick shifts in his sleep and rolls onto his side, no longer spooning me. I turn towards him and press my front against his back. He nestles into my arms, and I drift off for around twenty minutes.

Until my alarm goes off.

Quickly, I turn it off. If I want to run before my day starts, I need to do it now.

Outside, the air is dry and cool. I always love when summer morphs into autumn, and I look around, trying to memorize this phase of my life before it ends. In a couple of days, Nick and I will move in together.

The neighborhood I run through will change. I'll confront a new set of peaks and valleys. Nick's in school, we're negotiating when to have kids, and our new house won't have a sex room. But it has a beautiful backyard, where we'll sit and watch the sun go down. Where we'll talk about our dreams and all the days to come.

Yet for now, I enjoy my jog and let my mind drift—not to the future but to the past.

I tend to think about Jed when I'm running. That's when I focus on my breathing and the rhythm of my heart. I'll always love him, but now that love isn't crammed into a corner. Now, my love for him can coexist with other emotions and with other loves.

As the sun rises, shadows appear on the sidewalk, mostly from houses and trees. I see my shadow as I run. Sometimes, when I'm lucky, I feel Jed's shadow behind me.

When I turn the corner, there's Flashdance Girl. She ties her shoes in her front yard and stands up straight as I approach. Today her hair is pulled back in a simple ponytail, and she's wearing a black tank top and blue running shorts. She looks like a present-day teenager. I'm pinched by disappointment.

"Where have you been?" she asks.

I slow to a stop. "My ankle needed to heal. Then my insomnia let up. Now, I don't go running until after 7:00 a.m."

"Oh." She turns away and stretches her calves.

"Hey," I say. "What's your name?"

She turns back, her face dancing with skepticism. "Tina." Her tone is flat. I realize she won't ask for my name in return.

"Well, Tina, it's been nice knowing you."

She squints. There's more I could say, but I won't ramble about my life or give her advice about hers. Except for one thing.

"I hope you keep running. But remember to slow down sometimes. To let the world catch up. And if you ever need help, ask for it."

"S-u-r-e," she says, drawing out the one-syllable word into four.

"Take care of yourself, Flashdance Girl."

I turn away and tell her goodbye inside my head. As I run down the block, I feel her shadow descend upon me, yet I don't speed up. I stay even. My next breath will be deep and strong.

My journey has only just begun.

Author's Note

I did not know much about cystic fibrosis when I began writing *The Next Breath*, and I am extremely grateful for the information so generously shared by people who live with this illness. In particular, Eva Markvoort and Laura Rothenberg gave amazing detail about what it's like to struggle with cystic fibrosis. Both Eva and Laura wrote about their lives with humor, bravery, sadness, and strength, and it's clear that both young women will be remembered for their remarkable contributions to this world. And I will always admire them.

Also, special thanks to Brett Carter, Matt Corey, Cate Hogan, Lynn Osterkamp, Allan Press, Shauna Slade, and Heather Spencer for all the help and amazing insight they gave while I was writing this book. It was invaluable!

I hope you enjoyed *The Next Breath*. If you did, please check out my other books, and please consider writing a review on Amazon. And THANK YOU so much for giving my books a try!

My other books include:
Beautiful Little Furies
Favorite Daughters
Just Like the Bronte Sisters
The Holdout
The Standout
Starring in the Movie of My Life
Following My Toes